Amazons
and
Angels

IAN SALMON

Copyright Ian Salmon 2011
Design by Weber and Partners Pty Ltd
ISBN 978 0 9585852 2 4
Printed by CreateSpace

BY THE SAME AUTHOR

Practical Forms & Precedents

Water (NSW) A to Z

Some Andalucians

French Honour Lost

Fun Tennis for Old Farts

For Lexie

1

In early 1939 three young men were starting on a voyage to France that was to save them from terror in Spain. The boat was small and old. The men had different backgrounds, but some very important things in common. One was a Spaniard, or maybe he would say Catalonian; one a French Jew originally from Germany; the third a half-breed, having an English father and a French mother. The best educated was the half-breed, Neil, and as his manliness was at least the equal of the others, he was accorded a little extra status among the group, but not much, for the others weren't shrinking violets, nor dull. The Jewish one they called Manny, and really was Manfred Mayer. He had proved himself as a natural leader as Neil had, in the war they had left behind. And it must be said, on the score of fighting qualities at least, that Diego, the chunky and muscular fisher, was at least the equal of the others. Each had accounted for more than his fair share of General Franco's soldiers during the war, a fact that neither pleased nor displeased them, since it had been simply their frontline soldier's work, just as the enemy soldiers had done their best to kill the men now in the boat. In fact, they had come close to succeeding with both the fisher and the half-breed, for fascist bullets had hit them hard, and might have wiped them out but for the Jew's quick thinking and selfless bravery.

It was Diego's boat. Until a few weeks earlier it had been an old wreck, careened on the beach of the tiny fishing pueblo of Móntago, and its owner, who was Diego's uncle, had given it to him when talk of sailing to France came up. It was not much of a gift, given its condition, yet was like gold for the three men, facing a collectively disastrous future, unless they got out of Spain quickly. The pressure to do so came along two paths. For Neil and Manny it was to get to France without being intercepted by Franco's Nationalists. They had been headed for the border on foot, but looked like being beaten by Franco's soldiers who were also on their way, intending to close the frontier escape points. If they lost they risked the firing squad because they had been fighters in the leftist International Brigade, and had succumbed to ideological passion and stayed on fighting after its members were supposed to have gone home. Any way they looked at it, capture meant probable death, or gruesome death were they to be tortured first, as was not unusual. The trouble was, with Neil wounded, their progress was too slow. It was made worse by the presence of the hundreds of thousands of desperate republicans, soldiers and civilians, of all ages, slowly streaming north for France along the same inadequate roads. The two had taken stock when at Figueres, twenty or so kilometres from the border, so close, yet so far that getting there would take more time than they had. Rumour had it that an advance party of fascists had already arrived.

The pressure on Diego was that he, having been a republican frontline infantryman – although an unwilling one, a conscript – would be taken by the victorious Nationalists to have killed some of their men. There would be no actual evidence, for only Diego held that. The likelihood and suspicion remained, and were soon proving to be sufficient reason to deal out, to those caught, prison terms of up to 30 years; or a firing squad. That was enough, even too much, for most men. For Diego the problem was worse. He identified with the sea more than the land. His mother used to say: "That Diego, if he had had the choice he would have been born a fish instead of a person." He denied it, yet he had seen more than enough of inland Spain in his two years as a soldier. To be imprisoned in it for something like a lifetime, ordered about by fascist guards all the while, was to him a prospect worse than death. Certainly, you would have to be caught first, but that seemed to him an event more probable than not, because unless he were on the run he would be like a fish waiting to be caught: the catching would be assured, and only the date uncertain. Like fishers, a roundup squad would come one day, and they could only catch what was there in the fishing ground. So he had been wondering about what to do when his comrades had come out of the blue, found Móntago, found him, and asked his advice about escaping to France by sea.

After deciding in Figueres they had little chance of getting to the border in time by road, and trains no longer ran, Neil and Manny had had few options. They talked about taking a remote inland route over the high Pyrénées into France, but with little enthusiasm, because it was mid-winter, and they had neither the strength nor the clothes for such a journey. Manny found a doctor to look at Neil.

He prescribed minimal movement and much rest. He also gave the wound a fresh dressing. The healing so far was satisfactory. He warned Neil not to attempt the hills. So their thoughts turned seaward. A fit person could walk to the coast within a few hours, so that getting there was not as much the problem as leaving it might be.

The fugitives knew some refugees had left Spain by water, and here they were quite close. They knew nothing about it other than it was said to be a wild and rugged coastline which, they guessed, would also be free from enemy soldiers for the time being, and not as coldly forbidding as the hills. They supposed the area to be more peaceful, quieter, and cleaner, than what they had known for many months past. They sat on the kerbside, opposite the hospital, smoking and thinking. They looked no different from many other men, and a few women, untidy and armed, sitting alone or in clusters nearby, gathering strength for the next step north. But Manny and Neil were starting to think differently, and kept on about the sea. After a while Neil's face lit up. He exclaimed: "Why don't we find Diego? He might know how to do it."

"Brilliant! That's right. He's just the one. But where does he live?"

They thought, their faces creased with the strain of recalling anything that Diego had ever said that would provide a clue. Nothing came to them. At last Manny spoke. "We need a map of the coast. Something there might ring a bell. Let's try the town hall, or the library. You stay here. When I find one I'll come and get you." When he had tracked down a map, Manny had fetched Neil, and they soon agreed that La Escala was a port near Diego's village, which they thought of as being close by on the south, and east of Gerona, so it had to be Móntago, although the name was not one they knew. They studied how to get there, thanked the librarian, and left. It was about twenty five kilometres distant, which they expected to cover faster than a journey of similar length to the French border, and with no greater danger. They learned a delivery van went to La Escala each day, at midday. Manny found the driver, a small, stooped, elderly man, with twinkling grey eyes and no visible teeth, with a cigarette hanging out of the right corner of his mouth, so that his words, few and grudging, came from the other side. Manny approached him by the vehicle, and asked: "Excuse me, are you Pepe?"

3

Softly, hoarsely, the reply: "Yes."

"Can you take me and a friend to the coast tomorrow?"

Pepe saw the speaker was a dirty and bedraggled young man, sturdy, in clothes that at one time had been a uniform, with a rifle slung from his shoulder, and large green eyes lighting up a friendly face. Turning away, he muttered: "No passengers."

"Wait. I have lots of money."

Hopefully, Manny produced a bundle of notes. Pepe glanced at them and said: "They're no good now. They're shit. Is that all you have?"

"Yes. It's our pay. You mean it's worthless?"

"Yes. They say so. Bad luck."

Pepe knew he was dealing with a republican soldier trying to escape. He asked: "Did you say you'd shoot me if I don't take you?"

Manny digested this. To say he had might be their fare to the coast. But admitting to a threat might not be smart. He said: "That's not some sort of trap, is it? You know we're in enough trouble as it is."

Pepe smiled: "No, my friend, I heard you and you frightened me and I'm going to take you." He reached out and patted the younger man's arm.

Manny was greatly relieved, and showed it with a grin, and a hug of the old man, who said: "Be under the bridge next to the school on the La Escala road tomorrow morning at 10 o'clock. You and one other." He turned away.

While waiting the fugitives went shopping for some civilian clothes, and by the time they were picked up were dressed as Catalonian peasants, and had shaved. To get clothes they had bartered away as much of their gear as they could spare. They had entered Figueres slowly, on foot, looking no different from tens of thousands of other ragged and haggard soldiers fleeing northward. When they emerged from under the bridge to get in the back of Pepe's van, they were greatly pleased to feel they were starting to put war behind them.

They left the van on arriving at the outskirts of La Escala mid-afternoon. The map had indicated only one place that fitted the hazy understanding they had of where their friend lived. To find it they had to keep close to the coast, bearing south, and the high walking

4

track they found seemed correct. As they went the few people they met, just walking, or with animals or carts, gave them a wide berth at the sight of their rifles, which lost them any chance of a ride.

The spacious countryside exuded space and peace and quiet, free from conflict, and contrasted strongly with the anguish and density and fear of the refugee masses they had left behind. It was though a magic carpet had whisked them into a different world. True, there was occasional bomb damage, but this was an entirely different Catalonia, and also a different Spain. It was all silence, with glimpses of a startlingly blue sea on which sunlight danced daintily. The fears and tensions that had gripped their souls for long, and not least on the refugee road, seeped away. They walked quietly, each in his own relaxed cocoon, until the village appeared. There was no name, but they knew. They paused for the view from the point where the track turned from the escarpment down toward the secluded pueblo of white buildings and thatched roofs. Beyond lay a white beach and then a small, enclosed bay of calm and shimmering water, and small boats at moorings. Rock outcrops, like upright aquatic sentinels, stood in the bay, cousins of the hillside rocks above. Rugged cliffs and high bushland formed the other sides of the panorama, so that the pueblo was a nest in nature's wilderness.

The inaccessibility pleased the soldiers. They concentrated on the important plan of how to enter the village below, now becoming shaded, as the sinking sun dropped below the coastal hills. Manny went on alone and unarmed. He knew enough Spanish words to ask about his friend, but his efforts produced only blank stares. So he went down the small main street asking in the shops and bistro if anybody could speak French. In the chandlery he was fortunate, and met the wife of a fisher. He had to run any risk and tell her who he was and who he wanted. He gave her enough detail for Diego to identify himself and also Neil. He would wait outside the chandlery. She listened politely, looking him over all the time, and did not say she knew Diego, but only: "I'll think about it." She left and with her went his best chance of contacting Diego. He sat and waited. He sensed eyes on him. Dusk was gathering when he was exhilarated to see the woman returning with an older woman who looked like Diego's mother. The younger woman asked Manny some questions on behalf of her companion, and translated the replies for her, until the point came where the mother accepted Manny by throwing her arms around him, laughing and kissing him, while her companion stood by clapping.

Diego appeared soon after. He greeted Manny warmly, and went up the hill with a hand cart to fetch Neil. He took them to his parent's home, where they were plied with bread and wine, and talk. He asked them: "Why are you here?"

Manny replied: "The roads to the border are blocked with traffic. We can't move fast. The fascists are going to beat us to the border. Neil and I being French won't help if they find out first that we served in the Brigade. We heard boats have taken some people. We don't know where, but suppose France."

Neil added: "We came here hoping you would get us a boat ride to France. We know nobody else. We're really leaning on you, because we have no other cards to play."

Diego mulled over this unexpected scenario. 'What a coincidence', he mused. 'They come just as I'm thinking France.' To them he said: "I'll help. My parents will help. You can stay here for a while. I'll get you to France. Don't ask me how just for a while. I'll probably stay away as I'm worried about the fascists shooting up their enemies. I think they're playing it hard, but there's not much true news about."

Manny continued: "You mean you might come too?"

"Yes. That's right. Y'see, the stories going around make me think they'll come for me one day, and I don't want to be here then. I reckon I should be away until things settle down, and I know where I stand. The sea's my place, and will give me a chance."

Neil spoke: "So you think we can sort of help each other. Now that's just wonderful." Looking at Manny: "Isn't it?"

"Bloody marvellous, I say. What about your parents though? What do they think?"

"Well, actually, that's the next step. I have to work out something and talk with them. They know I don't want to go to prison, and they don't want me to die, so they have to be on side, and as I don't have a boat of my own, I have to find out what's possible from Papá. I'll think about it and talk to him tomorrow. But we'll do it."

In the morning Diego took his father aside and said: "Those guys are in a hole, and I'm in it too. What do you think of this? I get a boat, I take them and me to France, and then I fish there, say from a port on the Golfe du Lion. Only until things quieten down here."

Eduardo cried: "Oh, it's so easy to say, yet to do what you say sounds a very big project. I've never heard of anything like it, so I'll need to think about it. I'll talk with your mother, and if we think it could work, we can go down to the beach and see what's sitting there."

Diego knew some abandoned boats were careened, and he had in mind as his father spoke, and he felt sure his father was of the same mind, that one that belonged to his father's brother, also Diego Gómez, was to be preferred. He said: "That's great. Tell me if you want to know anything. I'll tell the boys what I'm thinking, and they know it's not me who decides things. But if we go to see a boat I'd like Manny to come, because he's really good with his hands. He's a cabinet maker y'know."

"I'll keep that in mind. Actually he could be just the man to make this work, but let's not get ahead of ourselves, and wait until I've talked it over with your mother, then we can all join in."

The parents could not think of anything better, so sadly cooperated. The last thing they wanted was to see their son punished for simply doing what the then legitimate government had ordered him to do. They agreed that Diego's idea should be followed through. They would keep the escapees under cover, but it could not be for long as the house was small, and the guests would quickly become restive. A boat would have to be procured, and any preparatory work needed for a longer voyage would have to be carried out in a secluded cove, of which there were at least two options nearby. The two fugitives could live there while working on the boat. But would this plan suit the visitors? It would take longer to get to France than they had expected. They had realised that by turning off to the coast they were taking a path of no return. Should they go back they would find the refugee road north already under fascist control, preventing them from crossing the border. But the prospect of substantial delay in a sea passage had not entered their minds, and they were a taken aback by the news. Yet, they also saw that by helping them here Diego was drawing attention to himself so he, too, needed to escape, more than ever. Therefore they must not be impatient, but go along

7

at his pace. They accepted the prospect of fixing a boat and escaping by sea, and that decided, the time it would take to get going mattered less and less. They had jointly confronted peril in the war, and were content to do so again. As always, the challenge brought them closer together, and kept their spirits high.

Alicia nursed Neil and placed restrictions on his movements. As there was not enough room for more than herself, and Eduardo, and her mother who lived with them, she set up a makeshift bed for Neil and Manny in the annexe which housed the animals, creating a mattress from old sails stuffed with dried seaweed. Since coming home Diego has always slept on board his father's boat, in keeping with custom where a small house was overflowing with people. The whole family and the visitors knew that the two visitors should be kept out of sight as much as possible, and those who found out should keep the secret as well as they could. But harbouring soldiers was not something to do for long, as one day Franco's men might search the coast. That Móntago might have low priority when it came to official searches, would not help if in fact a search was made.

During the civil war two conditions combined to reduce the number of seagoing boats out of Móntago. The first was a reduction of manpower, as several fishers were either conscripted into, or voluntarily joined the fighting forces of the Republic. The other was the extreme shortage of parts for boat repairs. This led to boat cannibalisation, one victim being a boat of uncle Diego, and which would now have to be reincarnated. He decided to give it to his nephew, hoping it would help him to survive, as his own son, for whom it had been intended, had died in Málaga when the Italian allies of Franco had attacked the republicans there. Diego decided to leave the registration intact, so as not to draw attention to himself through transfer. That could wait. His uncle cleared himself by handing over a signed transfer, and left its registration for Diego when he chose. Or if he chose, as their names were identical.

They went to work on the boat at once. The first thing was to make it seaworthy for the short voyage to the cove selected for its refitting. At the northern end of this cove were two large caves, dry enough for storage and residence. Its seclusion, and location, were admirable for their purposes.

2

The Mayers, cabinet-makers, had long been resident in Offenburg, between the Black Forest and the Rhine River, when one day in early 1938 Abraham said to his wife Klara: "I'm concerned that the way the country going we need to save what we can of our assets before they're all taken. It was bad enough to be forced out of business after the Nazis came in 1933, but since then their work restrictions have stopped us even getting jobs, except with other Jews, who can't afford to employ anybody now. "

Klara responded: "How true. But at least we have some assets secure in Switzerland in my name, and Herr Shutt will pay off his purchase of the business into my account there. For the rest of it, we have time to help our brothers and sisters who are even worse off than us, so maybe it's all part of a grand design for us."

"I can't deny that possibility, and surely we are kept busy trying to help our brethren, and even though our successes don't amount to much, they mean a lot to them. But isn't it getting harder? Isn't the constant anti-Jewish propaganda causing ordinary Germans to think less of us, and undeserving?"

"It is so. It would be hard for someone who is proud of Germany's successes in creating jobs and fine roads and buildings, and which I daresay is most of us, not to believe the Nazis when they say any troubles in Germany past or present are the fault of Jews."

"And so the Nazis are encouraged to go further against us, and who is there now to stop them? Through being clever, and ruthless, they're right on top, and they know it. How else could those discriminatory Nuremberg Laws have come about? One evil effect has been to allow the State to take Jewish assets without compensation, since last year; or was it 1935? Anyway we were lucky to have you as a French woman to save something. Pity the other poor Jews."

"Yes, pity is the word. Yes, we must count our blessings, few though may seem."

"In fact they're many compared with some of our friends."

"Yes, one must not get into self-pity."

"I looked further into emigrating, as you wanted me too. You know I would much rather believe this present wave of discrimination is a passing phase, and not the true Germany, but it's getting harsher than softer, so to be business-like we must take notice. You'll remember the publicity about the international conference on refugees held recently at Évian-le-Bains showed that the very great majority of nations would take in only a handful of Jewish refugees. The exceptions were difficult for people like us: Dominican Republic, and Shanghai. I guess most us felt something more to our understanding would turn up, but not so. Ironically Palestine, which we thought was to be a homeland for Jews, alongside Arabs, is also largely closed to us, just when the need is greatest. And anyway emigrating is an awkward business. Passport validation and exit visas take great amounts of time, even when accompanied by bribes and influence; then documents run out of time and have to be updated; and when it's all done the host country can change its rules."

"Not to mention ships that change their schedules."

"Indeed. It's so hard to understand, and even harder to work through. Besides, there's the cost of leaving. Unless one is really rich, the effect of low prices when assets are sold in a hurry, plus the high exit taxes recently brought in, is to prohibit emigration through regular channels." Ab hung his head, saying softly: "I'm sorry I can't do better."

"So Jews can stay here and be persecuted beyond belief, or be robbed in leaving. No wonder we hear of Jews committing suicide, even knowing it's a sin."

"Some leave illegally. It's quite understandable."

Ab and Klara were not of that mind. Patriotism, and disbelief that the country that had succoured his immigrant father, and for which Ab himself had fought in the Great War, and been wounded and gassed into partial permanent invalidity, would continue on its recent cruel and callous path, kept them loyal. Klara, originally French as much as he was German, was not as sanguine as Ab though. She had resolved when they married that her Frenchness would never, as far as she could control any relevant situation, ever be a problem in the marriage, and Ab had been of like mind, and being people of strong principles, they had made a good fist of the situation. But Klara was starting to feel there had to be a limit to acceptance of discrimination, which she knew to be immoral and ungodly, and once it was reached a new path would open for them, and taking it would be their fate. But those ideas were more in her mind, than stated in their discussions, and she felt that if they were reasonable ideas the time would come when Ab would see everything as clearly as she did, and so there was no need for her to make any fuss in advance.

So they kept on, until the time came. It came in the form of a pogrom across Germany on the night of 9 November 1938, called der Kristallnacht, or Night of Broken Glass, an event that violently damaged the private and communal property of the Jews, alongside many arbitrary imprisonments and assaults, and some murders. And afterwards they were required to pay for the damage and so save insurance companies that expense. It was clear to even the most patriotic Jew that life for his kind in Germany would be more, rather than less hazardous, in the future.

Ab and Klara had heard that Jews with energy and initiative, or small or compact families, had been known to cross the Rhine River into France without papers. If that were late in the 1930s, they became stateless Jews there, for Germany by then regarded Jews as non-citizens, and in France naturalisation applications were no longer being considered, and in fact the State later revoked some recent ones, as if citizenship were a government toy. They fled to Lyon, abandoning their few remaining belongings, to join Ab's brother and family, reuniting the close family group whose members had long sustained each other in family and business in Offenburg. When, a year and a little later, in mid-1940, control of France passed from the wobbly but democratic French government of the Third Republic to the collective of the dictatorship of Marshall (Maréchal) Philippe Pétain and the German and Italian conquerors, they knew that dangers still lay ahead of them, and there was nothing much they could do to avoid them.

3

The *alcalde*, the mayor of Móntago, having been appointed by the defeated government, knew he would be replaced shortly. He was anxious to avoid complaint from the new regime, or from the guardia civil, the paramilitary police, which could come if he failed in duty, such as reporting the presence of the two soldiers. He did so secretly, so as to avoid criticism from the villagers. There was no immediate response, which did not surprise him, as many republican soldiers were on the loose in Catalonia at that time, and the police posts were disorganised and undermanned. Many guards had followed their officers and fought for the fascists, and being hated because of their tradition of cruelty to and repression of the lower classes, they were prime targets in the fighting, and successfully so because of their unique uniforms. Those who had stayed loyal to the Republic were making themselves scarce, as they had no future under Franco. So the district office could not act promptly on the mayor's report, which was one of many of the same kind anyway.

But it did act, and one morning an army troop consisting of a sergeant, a corporal, and four soldiers arrived at Móntago in a truck. Or, rather, nearby, for they had to walk down the track through the communal olive grove, and were observed, as all visitors were, by many eyes, and word was passed around at once. The soldiers sought out the mayor, the priest, and two senior fishers. They explained they were obliged to look for republican soldiers so as to remove danger to civilians, and had heard there was, or had been some, thereabouts.

The remoteness of the village, the obsession of its inhabitants with the sea and fishing, and grinding poverty, meant that the cultural and physical boundaries separating the villagers from the rest of the world were rarely crossed. Beyond a few essentials, it was not needed. Selling the catch was one necessity. This they packed in ice and straw into carts drawn by the two mules owned by the pueblo's cooperative, and headed for La Escala, for the daily fish auction. Handcarts too might be used. Fish was also sold to those villagers who were not fishers, and traded for other foods with residents of nearby inland pueblos. The few shopkeepers saw rather more of the outside world, because their business affairs sometimes took them there, but they generally kept news from outside to themselves, because the others were little interested. Those few villagers who moved to other places found, if they were ever to return, the same apathy. But few left. The outside world was a grim, unfriendly, and dangerous place. The village was safe and supportive, if poor; and nobody went without food or work, or some sort of help in times of difficulty. It was not just that the village was remote. It was also almost part of the sea. The soul of the village was there, and in fishing. Activities on land were of secondary importance.

The sergeant did not expect the villagers to tell him much. He knew where their sympathies lay. Those to be interviewed knew not to talk too much, and none wanted to give more information than would seem reasonable. But what was that? There was nothing to go by; yet they knew they would be questioned from all angles after the soldiers left, until everybody had a good idea of what went on. Then opinions would start to emerge as to whether or not the interviewees had crossed the line and talked too much. The more they thought about their dilemma the more rapidly ebbed the prospects of the soldiers drawing out useful information. So without any discussion each intended interviewee set up a mental barrier between questions and answers. Hence some did not understand the questions, for their main language was a patois unknown to the soldiers. In using it in reply they were speaking a foreign language to the sergeant, a Castilian. Those who understood could rarely think of anything useful to say anyway. None could recall exactly what he had heard, or from whom or when, and certainly none had never actually seen anything. And this was so even after much scratching of heads and anguished expressions, as they strove to recall that which they had already irretrievably sent from their memories. The meeting frustrated the sergeant, but he ended it with warm thanks, and in turn was assured by each they were only too glad to be of service. He headed to the bar with his troops for food and drink. They had more success there, for the barman was a ready talker, and could understand the sergeant. "Yes," he said, "I believe there were some republican soldiers here some time ago, but I can't say when, or how many. Let me keep thinking about it."

The sergeant asked: "Did you meet any, or anyone who did, so we could get a description."

The informant thought for a few seconds, and responded: "No, I don't believe so. I didn't meet any. Actually I don't remember how I came by the information because, as I hope you understand, in this job I meet ever so many people that the past is often little more than a blur. But villagers you could ask and who often knew of comings and goings, are the mayor, the priest and the senior fishers."

"Well, we've been in touch with some of them. They said you

would be a likely contact for us. Where could fugitives hide?"

He scratched his head before slowly answering: "Y'know, that's a big question, but I think I can help. There are many places in the bush, and in the rocky cliffs we can see from here. Then there are caves in the cliffs facing the sea, though they're hard to get to. In fact, come to think of it, the whole of the surrounding area is a hiding place, if not a comfortable one. Funny, but I'd never thought of that before. Then there are the houses. Who knows who is, or was, in them? I don't. It's a more difficult question than I thought it would be. Really I wouldn't know where to start looking among the houses." He laughed as he added, "You can start with my room if you like." The sergeant did not laugh as he said: "Thank you sir. We'll leave it at that for the present." The troop then went to the beach and found a quiet stretch of sand which would do well for siesta. Afterward the sergeant led them in discussion of the problem. If anybody had any other ideas he should speak up, for they were pretty well at a dead end. Should they search? And if so, where to start? From what the barman had said, and the look of the place, they could still be searching in a month's time, but they only had this day. Everybody digested those views. The others had to be careful. It was not right to say anything that might imply the sergeant was not clever, so they confined themselves to grunts of agreement to his views. The question of whether refugees could hide at sea on fishing boats was not mentioned by any who thought of it, for sea searching was not their work. The sergeant looked along the beach at an old couple who had just taken up position for repairing fishing nets. They showed no interest in the soldiers. He thought of interviewing them until he reflected on the polite nonsense he had been offered already, and did not. The sooner he was away the better for his self confidence, so he gave the order, and the troop walked off, up the hill to their truck, the sergeant first dropping by the mayor's office to report the end of the mission. Their departure was carefully observed by many, but not by the three republican soldiers who were out on the sea, out of sight of the harbour, fishing. They returned on a prearranged signal. They were not then concerned about the soldiers coming back in the dark, because the village dogs could be relied on to bark out loud and untiring complaints about nocturnal visitors invading their territory.

Back in barracks the sergeant wrote a discouraging report on his visit, and the poor prospects of locating enemy at that pueblo. It was adopted by the captain of the civil guard for the district, and he issued an instruction that there was no need to search for fugitives in that area until further notice. This accounted for a long period in which there were no visits to the village by guards or troops of any kind, so that Diego and his guests were able to go about their business in peace and quiet.

As sardines, an important catch, were running, Diego left Manny to work alone, and as he became stronger Neil was allowed to help him. The boat activity brought them into contact with the life of the village, and in the process eroded their secrecy. They knew they should move along quickly, as another search party could come one day, but in the meantime they enjoyed the peaceful fraternisation. Drinking, talking, and fishing were pleasant ways of spending the little spare time they had. Another was visiting Dolores, an attractive young woman from Valencia who ran two small businesses in the village, one openly as seamstress, the other, more discreetly, as a whore. She was not a problem in the village. If she were she would have been expelled; not by any formal, enforceable edict, but by exclusion from the society of the other villagers. In a way she was the holder of a public office, which provided a social service to some of the men of the village, including some of the married men, for control of births was economically essential for the villagers in their poverty, and one of the forms of control was abstention from impromptu sex. The wives of her customers were not informed of such visits, nor did they want to know, recognising that arguably they were the cause of them. Dolores had taken over both businesses a couple of years before from one Carmen, who herself had followed another. Dolores would, in time, transfer her position to another newcomer. She knew she must then leave the village, as there was not enough room for two, and there would be a risk of disruptive gossip if she remained.

4

Whenever Diego tried to form a plan for his future after delivering his comrades to France, other than that he would fish, he became confused, and gave up. His parents could not help, as they knew very little more about France, and fishing there, than he did. Neil and Manny were concerned for him, and assured him they would work out something together, but that left a lot of unknowns. After a while he became relaxed and fatalistic, and ceased to worry, and that was pleasing to those around him. His main concern was to keep out of the clutches of the Nationalists. Death or long imprisonment would follow, as he understood the sketchy reports that swirled around, not as much those in the official media as on the grapevine. Not death, nor trouble in France, worried him as much as imprisonment. He drew comfort from there being ever so many refugees in France, so he would not stand out. He liked to think, as his parents also did, that a fisher with his own boat would not be seen to be a refugee. It didn't matter that he could be wrong, or that he never really went into the risks before actually leaving, because there had been an inevitably about his future once his brothers in arms came to him for help.

The *Santa Maria* had got its name from its first Christian owners upon their purchase of it many years before from a Tunisian who had fallen on hard times, and it was a near wreck when Diego took possession. Bits were missing, so that the refitting was daunting, even for driven young men. Eduardo and his brother Diego surveyed it from stem to stern to find what parts needed repair or replacement, and then made a priority list. Tools were borrowed from other fishers, and timber and parts acquired from both decommissioned boats and from the village chandlery. Some original parts were reclaimed from borrowers. Shortages of materials produced fine feats of improvisation, largely through Manny's woodworking skills. It was a steam sailing boat, the power sources being the small steam engine, and the single large, triangular, or lateen, sail, which indicated the north African origin of the vessel, all of which were quite readily brought back into working order. Coal was hard to get, but there was no shortage of the alternative of anthracite from mines in the local hills. There was no limit to Diego's enthusiasm and determination to make it and its gear seaworthy and fishing ready. He enthused everyone around him. From the village slipway, where the hull was made watertight and painted, the boat steamed to the secluded cove where it, and the workers, would be practically out of sight from sea or land.

The cove was like that at Móntago, but smaller and less accessible. The solitude was ideal. From the boat anchored close inshore, the men could go ashore by wading, or swimming, or in the boat's tiny dinghy, and there had shelter in a cave, where they kept a fire going to help them through the cold spring nights. Water oozed from the cliffs into several shallow channels through the beach. Seaweed, sea grasses and many-hued fish, crustaceans and molluscs were clearly visible in the pristine sea water, proving the aquatic food-chain in operation, and meals for the workers. Diving for crayfish two metres or so down became an occasional pastime for them, only limited by the coldness of the water a little below the surface. They also fished with set lines, especially before their occasional visits to Móntago, when they could barter the catch for necessities, such as tobacco, wine, olive oil, bread and vegetables.

They knew not to spare any effort in making the old vessel seaworthy. There would be longer sailing distances, and less chance of taking cover in rough weather, than for the average Móntagon who, unless crewing a longliner, would rarely be out of sight of land, or stay at sea for more than a day at a time. Besides, there would be the hazards of navigating the currents of wind and water in the new seas. Eduardo, who had sailed them, warned of *la tramontana* and *le mistral*, both cold and tempestuous offshore winds from the Pyrénées and the Rhône River valley respectively, and their warmer counterpart, *el siroco*, strong offshore southerlies from Africa. The water currents too, would have to be understood, for which purpose charts were obtained from the chandlery. But for all that they could expect to sail in relatively calm waters most of the time, such was the reputation of the western Mediterranean, whose surrounding lands had the effect of limiting the frequency and severity of storms and waves as compared with the great open oceans. Moreover, its tidal range was relatively very low, because there was simply less water for the gravitational pull of sun and moon to work on.

The boat was 11 metres long, with a beam of just over 3 metres, and a draught of 1.2 metres when loaded. The shaft drive from the engine turned a four-bladed propeller. The engine and boiler and furnace were housed immediately aft of the cabin cum wheelhouse, itself set forward, leaving an uncluttered deck for working, and for the ice and fish holds, and for the winch for bringing in the setlines

17

and raising pots. The single mast rose through the cabin. The deck supported a large shade frame whose tattered canvas cover had been replaced by Diego's mother with one of woven esparto grass. Fishing gear was stored out of the way wherever space was available, including over the sides, and in a cane rack overhanging the transom, just above the rudder. Amidships, and in the cabin, short ladders enabled full usage of the vertical space around the mast, close to which navigation equipment, the bunks, toilet, cooking and eating space were located. There was no means of communicating with shore, and no sextant. Like the local coastal fishers visual landmarks would be heavily relied upon, and Diego intended to keep close to land. Eduardo gave him lessons in setting a course, and adhering to it by dead reckoning, and in correcting compass deviation caused by disturbances in the magnetic field, and in countering the effects of wind and currents on a chosen course, always including the other two fugitives in the lessons as they had a common interest in safe passage. Six weeks of hard work passed before Eduardo declared the boat ready for sea trials. Soon, fishing gear would be stowed: 40 lobster pots, a set line with a range of hooks for different fish species, a bait net, and a gill net. But they would not fish the waters of the Costa Brava with the Móntagon fleet, as they wanted to leave for France.

Diego raised with his father and his uncle his concerns about possible trouble for their helping him with the boat. They put him at ease with their opinion there was little risk, as it seemed a normal enough thing that Diego should acquire a boat, and if he delayed registration of the transfer that was his affair and not theirs. Any assistance given to him was in the ordinary course of family affairs, and the extent of it could only be known to family. Besides, the fishers had seen many small boats headed north with refugees over recent months, so the *Santa Maria* had companions in adventure.

When the time for sailing came, the crew loaded the boat with provisions, ice in the hold for keeping fish fresh until they made port, and after some doubts decided to take their rifles also, without knowing exactly why, but aware they were not wanted in the village, and could be jettisoned at sea. With its crew all dressed as Spanish fishers, the vessel motored away from the Móntagon shore early on a misty Monday morning in April. They had been there long enough to learn that Spanish republican refugees were being harshly treated by the French in internment, while the sifting for punishment of those who had stayed home had commenced, with execution by firing squad or long imprisonment being common penalties. The news from France was not good, but it was far worse in Spain.

They fished as they sailed, keeping close to the coast in the manner of other fishing boats in the vicinity, but not so close as to attract attention from shore. They were all fascinated by the passing scene of rugged cliffs, sandy and rocky coves, mist, sunlight, gradations of blue in sky and the sparkling sea, the whole enlivened by swooping seabirds. The slight breezes were enough to drive the boat forward for a few hours each day without using the engine, at the same time giving the crew, and Neil and Manny in particular, the chance to settle into boat routine and fishing. When passing ports, large and small, they withstood all temptations to make land, because if the French were on the lookout for Spanish refugees, it could be more intense near the border than away.

Neil offered the others advice on the art of pretending, in the interests of their survival. He explained he had done some amateur acting in his time and had a feeling for pretending to be something or someone he was not. He raised the matter now because he wanted them Manny and Diego to get used to pretence, so far absent from their natures, but which could help them should dangerous situations arise. The idea was novel, nor was it something they readily took to, but by recurring discussion and examples they came to see the sense of it, and had fun practising. Though Diego was to be the most vulnerable in France, all joined in.

Eventually they took the boat closer inshore to find a suitable port, and on the morning of the third day made for the tiny harbour of the French fishing village of Valras-Plage, up the coast from Perpignan. As the boat stood offshore Diego said: "We make land here because the ice is running out and the fish won't last. We might have trouble selling the catch, as the locals mightn't like outsiders. We'll wait until a boat is going in, and talk with them. They might even buy our fish, and if they get a good deal we might have some friends."

They stowed the fishing gear and waited for a boat making port. One slowed down in passing and Diego beckoned it to stop. Manny called out to them: "We're Spanish. My skipper can't speak French. We're running out of ice and can't make it back to Spain in time. Móntago is our port but it's too far away. Can we sell our catch here? It's not much. Mostly mackerel."

Bruno, the other skipper, replied: "It depends. If all catches are light, like ours, you should be able to sell yours. But if there's a lot of fish you might find it hard. Sorry I can't do better."

"Thanks. Can you show us where to tie up?"

"Sure. By the way, if you get stuck with your catch I might be interested. We can talk inside. Follow me."

"Right. See you there."

Neil said, as their boat chugged slowly inshore: "We must get our story tight. Try this. We met Diego for the first time at Móntago when we got lost on our way out of Spain. He wanted to go fishing but his crew was sick. He asked if we had any experience. We didn't, but we got talking. He said it was the off season so there weren't many fish for him to catch anyway. We asked him if he'd like to take us to France, as we wanted to get home. That suited him because he'd never been out of Spanish waters or to France, and we'd be paying him. For us it was to be a bit of fun, and keep us away from possible hassles at the land border. We would've pulled in farther south but our catch was disappointing so we just kept on. Diego will return to Spain as soon as he drops us off, probably at Marseille where he wants to inspect a boat. Now if we all keep to the same story nobody will know better, and will think Diego is off home soon, and nobody will think of him as a refugee hanging around France." He added: "We must also avoid anybody who speaks Spanish, as they might get the idea of dobbing him in to the police. So you'd better keep your mouth shut my friend, otherwise you may as well wear a badge saying you're a Spanish soldier. Can you do that?" Diego replied by nodding, and pointing to his throat.

Inside, Bruno indicated a place to berth at the wharf, and they waited there. Soon he came and spoke with Manny, saying: "It's hard to make a sale from a foreign fishing boat just at present, but if you're stuck I'd consider taking the catch off your hands at a price."

Manny sensed at once they would be taken advantage of, but then the fish were only a small part of their overall game. He said: "Thanks. I'll talk with the boss, and let you know."

Diego smiled wryly about the offer, saying: "As I expected. They want to protect their own market, and also take advantage of us. We'll find the same thing at any other port so we may as well go along with the sale. We can put the fish in crates on the wharf for him to see, and you can sell them for what you can get. Expect him to start with an offer half of what he has in mind, but still let him walk away feeling he has made a good deal, because we're in no position to be tough."

After the catch was crated Bruno came, showing little enthusiasm for an excellent display before saying: "Look, I don't really want these fish, but to help you I will offer you three francs per kilogram, take it or leave it."

"Cash now?" Bruno nodded. Tongue in cheek, Manny continued: "Actually that's not a bad offer, and thank you for it. I'd take it but I know my boss would like more, and I have to sail home with him. Could you possibly go a little higher?"

Bruno thought, then said, grudgingly: "At three francs there's not much in it for me, but I'll go another half and no more."

"Thanks," said Manny. "We have a deal. Will we take them to the weighbridge now, together?"

Bruno nodded and they started. After weighing the catch the cash was handed over, and Manny went back to the boat with the empty crates to report to the others. Then he found the chandlery to get information, including where to sleep.

5

In the morning, while Manny was away shopping, and Diego was working on the boat, Neil went looking for information. He introduced himself to a middle aged man sitting on the wharf and repairing a net. Georges noticed the care with which Neil lowered himself and asked: "Are you OK? You look as though you might have been in an accident sometime." Then: "Not in Spain? I only ask because I've seen a few like that lately. I don't mean to be personal."

Neil was taken aback. He cursed himself for not being prepared. How should he answer? He decided he had nothing to lose by being open about himself, so nodded assent.

Georges put down his net and needle, swore, moved his pipe, and growled: "Pity France wasn't there with you. The trouble is our government is frightened both of Hitler and his threats, and of losing England as an ally, so they give in to both all the time. They felt that going against Franco in Spain would make Hitler mad. But Germany's going its own way anyway, taking no notice of France or anybody else. It's all a big worry."

Neil was not displeased by this, showing both political aware-ness and sympathy. But Georges might be a man who liked to know, so he had better take care. "Well," he said, "We surely could have done with French help. I mean, besides the volunteers. The fas-cists had the best of the help department, yet France ends with all those refugees. It seems we weren't ready for them. And they come on top of the Jews running from the Nazis. It's a hard world." Neil paused. He looked away while thinking how to wind it up, and find-ing it, continued: "Speaking of Spaniards, are there refugees loose around here? I thought the police had put them all in prison camps down south."

Georges secured his pipe in his mouth, thought a moment, and muttered: "Yes. I think most are. Then I think some got home-sick and went back. Others have been helped to disappear; you know there are Spaniards all over the south? They've been coming here for jobs for many years, and a lot have stayed. Some refugees are al-lowed out to work on farms, where labour is short. Then there must be some just drifting. You see somebody, or hear them talk, and you think they must be Spanish, but you can't tell what category they be-long to. Certainly the police are on the look out, but it must be hard to keep up, as so many have come. I heard half a million. Could that be right?"

"I can't say. I saw so many on the way I wouldn't be surprised." And he thought it was time to turn the conversation in case it led to Diego. He added: "You're pretty switched on if I may say so. But just thinking of those refugees makes me sad. They were my people while I was there. "

Georges understood. And as Neil had thought, he was busy putting two and two together in his mind, but not with any malice. He just liked to know. He understood a wounded soldier feeling sad about this subject. "That's quite OK," he said. "I guess you've had a

22

tough time. I'm just sorry it wasn't more successful."

"Thank you, friend. Now I wonder if you know about getting registered as a French boat. For example, say I bought a Spanish boat and made this my home port, what would I do to register it, and also get a fishing licence?"

"You'd better check this with somebody else, but as far as I know you must have a commercial fisher's licence, and register the boat; at the sub-prefect's office in Sète, I think. Then there are annual fees to keep up. You're supposed to have the papers on board all the time. I think the boat number should be displayed too, but you can see from looking around that some don't bother."

"Thanks. You know a lot. Do you happen to know what the registration fee is?"

"No, but it varies with the size of the boat. I think an inspector comes to measure it. But you'd better check everything I say."

"Fine, fine. I bet you're spot on. Thanks again." He changed the subject to navigation hazards the coast, and the best fish and crustaceans for the local market, and in leaving he also asked about ice, and was directed toward a shed with an aged sign *La Glace* outside. With a smile and a wave he thanked Georges and departed.

It was almost dark when Manny returned from shopping. He agreed with Neil how good it was to be back among French people and talk in French. They all discussed the events of the day and the next day's repair program. He and Neil went off to make telephone calls to their respective homes, Manny to Lyon, Neil to his mother in Paris. They were then ready for a night ashore with a meal and a few drinks. Before leaving the boat they pledged themselves to maintain their guard, and say or do nothing to endanger Diego. The semi-silence he had been sworn to earlier was re-imposed. They found a corner table in a café. Neil sat facing out so as to keep an eye on movements in the room. Diego sat facing the corner. Alone and relaxed, they saluted each other with great smiles and hand clasping. Later, Neil said: "Today I got the idea that the French government is concerned about national security because of the presence of our soldiers, as there are so many, they're so experienced in battle, and many are communists or the like. I would have thought Germany is the big devil for France, not communists: maybe both are. Then there's the expense. So the government wants the refugees to go home, or emigrate, and in the meantime they'll keep them together in misery, where they can be watched, and won't become happy. The camps sound like places to keep out of, so Diego, we must take care. But there's a lot of sympathy for the Republic. We have lots of friends among the French. And Diego, I get the idea that fishers are a sort of brotherhood, whose members come from all over the world, and are just as likely to be socialists and the like as anything else. I think you'll be safe among them."

Still, they decided to move further away from the border, to a larger port, Sète being favoured, with a wide range of vessels from both the sea and inland canals in and out all the time. Their boat should be even less conspicuous there. It was also a place to test the level of acceptance of a foreign fishing boat.

The money from selling the mackerel catch was going, and more would be needed soon for provisions. Drawing money from the French bank accounts of either Neil or Manny would take time, or from the Spanish account of Diego, longer still, even if Diego were to trust the authorities enough to try, and so they decided to wait for Sète. They would repair the hull while in Valras-Plage, then sail on. As their need for money could surface immediately on arrival, Manny left to ring his mother again, for her to telegraphically transfer money to Sète for him.

The problem of the status of the vessel in selling fish in French ports was now more real. So far they had hoped to have cover as a foreign fishing boat, one that could fish outside French territorial waters and sell its catch in a French port. The other two discussed it while Manny was away.

Neil said: "I don't think this foreign boat idea will work. French ports and fish buyers won't give you as good a deal as for locals. That means less money for a catch, and you can't afford that. Consider this instead. Let Manny, a Frenchman, be the apparent owner of the boat, and register it in his name. Then select a home port here where he will become accepted as the skipper, and you as crew. Bingo! There's a French boat. It fishes where it pleases, and sells catch cleanly. Stay with it until it's safe to return to Móntago. When? We can't tell that, but it must happen one day. Then, Bingo! There's a Spanish boat. In the meantime you'll be safer as a deckhand on a French boat. If you act dumb, eat and dress like a local, and keep out of sight, you should be OK. And being employed by a Frenchman in the useful business of fishing, and not costing France anything, would surely help you if the police came your way." He paused while his friend digested his words.

Diego was not happy. It was his boat, and the idea of giving up control grated. Neil could tell that from his look. On the other hand both knew he had few choices. He had noted Neil did not include himself in future fishing plans.

"You talk about Manny carrying on with me, but has he been asked?"

"No. Anything we say here is subject to that. And as for me, well, I don't want to be a fisher, but having said that I will help you out if Manny won't. But let's leave it until he's here."

On his return Manny was brought up to date. He knew Neil was not suited to a fishing life. He asked himself: 'Is it for me? I'm a cabinet maker. I can be a shipwright. They live ashore, with no danger and comfortable beds. That's what I want; I think. Yet this is a challenge, and there's something about the sea. And Diego needs help to keep out of prison. He'd die there. Neil can't help more than he's said. If I agree to stick with Diego I can make it clear it's not for ever, and that I can leave when I'm ready. I don't think I would mind this life for a while. One day Diego will want the boat back. I wonder if I'll mind then. Who knows? But if so there are always others. So there are options. I could do worse than give it a go for a year or so. It's not as though I'm needed in Lyon. The family are getting along alright in their business, and don't need me. Anyway, it's not my scene." To Diego: "I won't see you stuck. Tell us what would suit you most and I'll say what I think."

"Thanks." said Diego. He showed by his expressions he understood Neil's position, and Manny's offer, and continued: "No hard feelings from me. The sea's not for everybody, and anyway the boat isn't really made for three. I'm just not sure of the best thing to do. Giving up the boat isn't good for me."

Manny thought a bit, then said to Diego: "I can't see you making it on your own at present. Until you can I'm for staying with you. I think though you should put my name on the boat to make it French, so we can fish here on the same basis as the others, like Neil said. But it's up to you. I can buy a half share from you, if you give me time.

We could be partners, with me the French registered owner and front man here."

Diego replied: "Do we need to rush that? Can we start by finding out more about French registration, and in the meantime fish down to Spain and get our catch sold through my father and cousins, or in my name, depending on how things are there."

"That misses the point," cried Neil "which is that you don't feel you can be based in Spain. Isn't it like this? The boat is registered as a Spanish boat already. We can find out about registering it as a French boat in Manny's name. Who actually owns it is for the two of you to work out. You keep both registrations. Then you have the flexibility you may need to get by. Again, the *Santa Maria* to be French in France, skippered by Manny, and Spanish in Spain, skippered by Diego." He became even more serious. "I think we're talking too loudly. We should drop the subject and all think about it. Another thing. As you know I must see a doctor again soon, then I want to go to Paris to my mother for a rest, and at some stage look into returning to university. All that means I would be ready to sign off when the deck is clear here."

They kept silent, all realising that dual nationality was closing in on the *Santa Maria,* and also that their little group, after sharing excitement and danger, was about to break up. Manny said, without enthusiasm: "Let's go to bed and think it over until tomorrow. I'm getting a bit pissed, and can do without a hangover. The others nodded agreement. Manny and Neil went to the pension near the waterfront, and Diego returned to the boat.

Early next morning they moved the boat to the slipway, and by late morning had repaired the hull and it was back in the water. After lunch they continued the discussion, and Manny said to Diego: "What do you say to this? I'll buy a half interest and will sell it back if you want that at any time. But in France I'll be the front man."

Diego thought about it. He didn't know what was missing, or if anything was. He agreed; "OK" he said. They didn't put a time limit on the deal, both accepting its success relied on their goodwill and common sense. Their mutual trust was as good as writing could be. Then they dispersed: Manny to walk around the village, Neil and Diego along the beach. They met for the evening meal at the same bistro as before, and read charts ready for sailing in the morning.

Their forward plans still engaged their attention.

Said Neil: "In Sète I can find out about how to register a boat bought from a foreigner, including selection of home port. It might be better if I do it as an inquiry for a friend."

Manny said: "Yes, the more we know the better. The *Santa Maria* with dual nationality! The more I think about it the more I see it working. So long as we're careful."

Diego said: "I hope the French fees aren't too high. Paying twice is not good. But I was thinking Manny, that you might be able to make up the registration boards showing Spanish on one side and French on the other, and if the boards are detachable they can be flipped over to suit the waters we're working in."

"Good idea. Can do."

Diego continued: "So we go to Sète first thing tomorrow and find out more. If it seems OK Manny can go ahead and register right away. Yes, in his name."

They sailed early, a strong following breeze pushing the boat along briskly. They didn't fish, for they had no market in view, so had little to do besides enjoying the quiet swishing and slopping as the vessel ploughed firmly through the moderate waves, and managing the rudder to keep on course. They stayed near the coastline, within sight of land, spotting and identifying landmarks from the charts, and plotting the course. As far as possible they kept other vessels between them and land, as a sort of buffer. By estimating their rate of travel they would know when to come inshore and look for the entrance to the port. The previous night's discussion was continued. Diego told them what he could remember from his father about territorial waters and fishing rights, adding: "So the dual registration is best if we can pull it off, although it shits me to have to give up my boat. But I'll get over it.""

Neil joked: "So the old girl is getting a split personality, and no say in it. We'd better not ask her, in case she says no!"

Manny changed the subject. "My family want me to go home, or else they'll come down." Addressing Neil, he added: "And they'd be glad if you could call in on them on your way to Paris. You could even stay there for a few days to look around and rest up. We have plenty of room, and the locality is good. And of course there are good doctors there."

Neil digested that, and said: "Sounds good. I've never seen Lyon, and I'd like to meet your family. But why don't you go home as soon as we make port, but get the money your mother is sending first. Then after a few days we can swap, you back here and me there."

"OK. We'll aim for that."

The boat pulled into the inner harbour of Sète in the early afternoon. The fugitive crew were interested in the numbers of vessels and the size of the port. They found the large fishing boat area, and a vacant berth, and asked the crew of a trawler if they could tie up there for the night. They thought so, but they had better see the harbour master in the morning, as there would be a wharfage fee to pay. The boat tied up, Manny went ashore to look around the town, while Diego looked around the waterfront and boat facilities. Neil sat in the sun on deck close to the wharf and gathered information from passers-by happy to chat. Later he formed a plan of action, the first step being to attend, alone, the office of the local department (département), and collect the transfer forms, for later return. When the inspector came to assess the boat for the fee Diego should be absent, so he could not get too interested in the Spaniard, as the media said that Spanish republican soldiers and civilians, along with other refugees, were resented by many French people. Even so, Neil supposed that a Spanish deckhand who kept a low profile was unlikely to cause much excitement. In fact, looking around, it was apparent there was diversity in the ethnic groups engaged in fishing, so that Diego, like most Catalans looking as much French as anyone, would be unlikely to rate a second glance from any self respecting racist.

Manny booked a room at a nearby pension. The three men then followed the same sleeping system as in Valras-Plage. The others told Diego that as soon as it seemed safe they could swap around, but he was not concerned, as he preferred to sleep on board.

Next day Neil and Manny continued inquiring so as to settle the Santa Maria into its French persona in Manny's name. Manny collected the money his mother sent, shared it, and made for home by the night train, leaving his address with the others.

Neil and Diego had time to fill in so it was time to explore Sète, whose size and vibrancy left them feeling insignificant. In the afternoon Diego rowed Neil around the waterfront in the boat's dinghy on a discovery tour. Later they went ashore to a café to dine, before visiting a brothel. Neil wondered why Diego took so long. It turned out the sex partners had much to talk about. She was Spanish, an Andalusian, a sometime republican soldier adrift in France.

6

Next morning Neil noticed a cheerful look about Diego. They had been working together on deck and had stopped for coffee. Sitting, both reflective, Neil could not contain himself. "Well," he asked, "How was the girl?"

Diego's eyes lighted up. He had been waiting for the question. His brown, wide, pock-marked face split with a grin. He thought a moment as though reliving something happy. Then he came out with, simply: "No, it wasn't much – she made me wear a condom, like the boss said."

Neil was unimpressed. He would not be shaken off so easily. He sensed there was more. Reticence after visits to brothels was not part of their tradition. "Thanks a lot. Thanks for nothing. Is that the best you can do?"

Diego looked down: "It was OK."

"I think you're holding out on me. Or you had a bad time. And there was me waiting, and thinking you were having a good time. You should have left sooner." Then, to draw him out: "Did you score *la fellation*?" It worked. Diego was not going to admit to something that wasn't. He must explain. And he knew the expectations they all had in that regard. It gave the talker the chance to put his image as a stud to rights through wistful allusions to the frequency of *les orgasms*, and the wild pleasure of his partner. The listeners knew to discount all claims to fit the reputation of the speaker. But they still liked, indeed insisted, on knowing. So Diego knew that once he started it would be hard for him to stop, because he would like recalling his night out anyway. He commenced, staring into space and looking a little embarrassed as if something private was being divulged. Yet the urge, and obligation, to share, drove him on. In a torrent of words he told Neil how he had no idea that sex could be like it was with Conchita. He paused. He smiled reflectively. "Jesus, it was marvellous," he mused, as his voice trailed off while his mind went back to last night.

Neil did not push for more, lest he seemed too prying. "That's great. I always reckoned you would be a champion stud and now you've proved it. Won't Manny be jealous." This because Manny had been known to talk up his sexual expertise. At another time Neil might have gone on to talk about Manny and him also spending time with Conchita, since she was so hot, but something told him to be careful. For Diego had spoken with a level of respect, so there could be more to the story than simply sex. So he asked: "Did you both being Spanish help?"

Diego seemed glad to leave the passion part. "Yes. It was good for both of us. Do you want to hear about her," he asked. When Neil nodded assent Diego continued:

"She's Andalusian. She was in the anarchist militia, and her husband too. There was trouble between them and the communists, and he was killed. The militia then became part of the republican army, like us. She was a dispatch rider, and a driver. She was in the last battle of the Ebro, like us. She couldn't go home because the fascists had taken over her village. So she left along with all the others, and was interned at the border. She was sent to Rivesaltes, by the beach, just north of Perpignan. It was bad. The camp wasn't ready and the French didn't want our people. She could see that she, and the others, were going to be locked up for a long time, or sent back to Spain, which the French kept urging them to do.

"She found out that some prisoners got work on farms, and she was given the chance. It was a vegetable farm. The work was hard. She was treated well, had a room to herself in the packing shed, and turned it on for the farmer and his goofy son, as she had learned it was part of the deal. Some sort of jealousy came between the two men, and then the mother found out what was going on, and hit the roof. Conchita saw she was the one to collect the blame, and so could be sent back to camp. As the war with Germany had just started, and there were refugees everywhere on the roads, she reckoned the prospects of being picked up by the police wouldn't be high. So she did a runner. She found help from a priest, who got her another farm job, and turned her back into being religious. Smart work, seeing she thought she was an anarchist. They taught her how to pray, a little anyway. Her job was picking carrots, until the boss said the police were sniffing around and if they came while she was there he couldn't help her, and she could stay or go, knowing. She went a few days later. A workmate suggested here, where there were people from all over, and to look for a job in a cannery. But there were no jobs and no prospects either, because there was a waiting list of local people already. So she had been lucky in getting the farm work, and put it down to the priest. But here she was on her own and nearly broke. She would have to surrender or become a whore. She left the call to God, and felt he told her not to surrender. She met Spanish women at the cannery, and after checking they weren't fascists, asked for advice. They put her onto a Spanish brothel keeper, who had no immediate vacancies, but one was likely to come up soon, if she came back in a week. Conchita said she would, but in the meantime as she had so little money and nothing to do, could the madame give her a fill-in job. That was the boss woman we met. It was Conchita's lucky day, because Marta let sleep in a storeroom for the time being in exchange for working around the house. Conchita went there, and thanked God again. Then in a few days she started work. It's a live-in job. You saw the rooms. I guess they're all the same. Marta runs the place well. A doctor comes each week to check the girls. If a girl has the pox she's not allowed to work until cured, and cleared by the doctor. That means girls lose income, which they can't afford, so they usually leave instead. The police who don't mind the two small brothels in town so long as they're run right, because they provide an outlet for all the men who pass through town. Marta says the brothels help keep the town quiet." He concluded: "Altogether it's a good setup, as brothels go. How did it look to you?"

"Yeah, the bit I saw, it was OK."

Diego's story had actually come in fits and starts. Neil had never known him to talk at such length. Clearly his interest ran deeper than would be expected from a casual sexual encounter, so he chose his next words carefully: "Very interesting. What's this Conchita like close up? I didn't get a really good look at her."

"Dark, as you'd expect with an Andalusian, short like them, with black hair and black eyes too. She's really pretty, and is very well built." His words ran out, a glazed look came over his face. Neil felt the evidence was mounting. Perhaps it was time for a circuit breaker. Would he tell Diego about his own girl? No, not today. He would be wasting his breath. "Very interesting. I expect you'll be back there soon. We'd better start catching some fish so you can afford it." And after a few moments: "Do you think there's a risk of blowing your cover? I mean she tells you all that stuff, so why wouldn't she expect to hear about you in exchange? And how could not tell her? Another thing, if she opens up with you like that on first meeting, she's a girl who likes a chat, and that's always a risk. It's good to have a friend, but take it easy."

"That's right. She likes to talk. Maybe more so with me because of who we are. And she's lonely, and doing it tough. But we're both on the run, and know to be careful. I don't think anybody heard us talking and then it was in Spanish, or that's what we call it. Actually we have trouble in understanding each other, so anybody listening in would have a hard time. I hope."

"That's so. But they could tell you were speaking Spanish, which might be enough. How long has she been on the job?"

"I didn't ask, but I guess a month or so. It makes you wonder how long she can go on before somebody gives her up."

"Well, that's right, especially if she's a good talker, and she sure told you a lot in a short time. It certainly sounds risky, but then so is everything for republicans. It's really quite unfair. But we can't change that, so we must all continue to be careful." He mused: 'Maybe Conchita is going to add a new dimension to our set up.'

Waiting for the inspector, the men filled in the time looking around the port, including the catches, and how the fishers sold them, and worked on boat maintenance. After a few days the inspector came and assessed the fee on the spot, calculating its displacement as a little under 10 tonnes which meant the fee was at the lower end of the scale. Neil took the money to the prefect's office and paid up. The certificate of registration had been prepared in anticipation of payment and was receipted and issued but was held there until Manny called, or else they would post it to the address on the application form, but could not hand it to Neil. He said to post it.

During this period Diego returned to Conchita most nights. Neil did not mind as he could use the time reading, and planning his personal affairs. He noticed that Diego, a quiet man, had been even quieter lately, as though preoccupied with matters of great weight. Neil restrained himself from prying, leaving it to Diego to advance anything he chose about the woman. Rather than embarrass anybody he kept away from the brothel.

Neil had been right. Diego went back to Conchita, driven by a mix of physical and emotional needs. She was sex, companionship, Spanishness, war memory, another outlaw, and sharing all with him. But there was another glue forming, and it would take them a little time to identify it.

The certificate being ready, Manny could now join the fishermen's association, and the *Santa Maria*, a French boat, could put to sea as part of the Sète fishing fleet. So Neil, ready to move on, rang Manny in Lyon for him to return, so as not to leave Diego on his own. Not that he was really sure Diego would notice, in his dreamy state.

Manny arrived the next day and Neil left for Lyon on the night train. The departure was a wrench for all. They promised to keep in touch, which made parting a little easier. It seemed Neil would resume his city life with intellectuals, far removed from fish and the sea. Diego would be content with fishing, hopefully back in Spain one day, and Manny would decide one day what line of work would suit him most, being in the meantime an enthusiastic fisher.

7

Neil was met by Mannys's sister Ana on his arrival in Lyon. They sat in a quiet corner of the railway refreshment room, placed their orders with the waitress, eyeing each other all the time. Manny hadn't been of much help. He had not told Ana that Neil was tall and slim, with sandy hair and a fresh complexion, and dimples and a calm demeanour, nor had he told Neil that she had beautiful and large brown eyes, with matching brown hair, and a serious look about her, which could readily turn to humour with the right stimulus. They had to learn for themselves. They were satisfied with what they saw, and both knew that Manny had taken it would be so. Ana came straight to the point. "Correct me if I'm wrong, but I somehow doubt that Manny told you about our German house guests."

Neil was unsure of how to react, in case it exposed Manny unfairly, and replied: "Just at the moment I don't remember anything. Should I?"

"No. Not at all. I bet he never said a word, but left it to me to tell you our aunt and uncle are staying with us. I must explain before you decide what to do. They're from Germany. They landed here at the beginning of the year ...."

Neil threw up his hands, and cried: "Say no more. I wouldn't dream of you putting me up now. It doesn't matter. I can find somewhere else to stay, and still meet Manny's family, if that's alright. I have a doctor's appointment here anyway."

Ana blushed. She felt she had got it wrong. She said: "As you wish. But I don't mean you wouldn't be welcome at our place, or that there's not enough room. Everyone at home is really keen to meet you, and have you stay. It's just a question of you being comfortable with so many Jews. I wanted to warn you." To herself she said: 'I'll choke that Manny. I bet he didn't tell Neil in case he went straight on to Paris.'

She sipped her tea and looked around the room. Neil thought to himself: 'Well, that's a different picture. Do I want to be in it? What will my mother, with her antisemitic attitude, say when I get home? Well, I can handle that then. If I go on I'll miss out on Ana's company. He never told me about her, only that he had a younger sister. I'll kill him when I see him. I mustn't sound condescending in accepting the invitation.' Looking Ana straight in the eye, he said: "I'll tell you my position. Your brother is my friend. His family must also be my friends. The family includes your aunt and uncle. If I won't be putting anyone out I'd like to stay at your place."

Ana's eyes shone. Neil didn't feel the full impact until later, but even right away he was almost dazzled. "Oh! I'm so glad." She cried: " So will the others be. We'll do our best to give you a good time. In fairness to Manny, I must say he only found out about our visitors when he came home the other day."

Neil responded: "There's no problem anywhere. I'm so happy to be here."

34

Ana continued: "Thanks. Abraham is Dad's brother. Klara is his wife. She's French. We all lived in Offenburg, as I suppose you know." Neil nodded. "They came to us, naturally, although it's a worry because they have no papers, and refugees from Germany and other Nazi countries aren't really welcome here, especially Jews. The government would like them to migrate away. There is also a fear that if there's a war, some refugees might become spies or something for the Nazis. So France has a policy of interning foreign Jews, who are mainly those who have come lately. Many are stateless because under Nazi rule in Germany and Austria, y'know, Jews lost citizenship. No citizenship at home, no passport, no exit visa, so no status here. There was all the difference in the world between us and them. We got here earlier, with papers, while emigration was allowed, and became naturalised. Policy changed over the next few years, so when they wanted to leave it was so much harder at both ends, but they came: they had to. But being stateless and illegal they can be locked up. And internment is so nasty ...." Her words trailed off, anxiously.

While not surprised by what he was hearing, this was the closest Neil had come to the problems faced by German refugees. He asked: "You say they left later than your family. Can you say why?"

"Well, you have to know them to get it straight. They were proud Germans, and Ab had been a good soldier in the Great War. They couldn't accept there was permanent change around. And when it showed up, there were lots of Jews in trouble, and they helped them, for they're about the goodest people you could ever meet. But after the pogrom last November it was too much even for Ab and Klara, so they left."

"What about migrating to another country, one more friendly than France. Aren't some countries taking good quality immigrants?"

"Well, they looked into that, but very few were taking ordinary Jewish migrants, as distinct from very clever, or very rich ones. But emigration to anywhere is tough. And for my uncle and aunt to get an exit permit they would be disclosing their presence here, which might put them in internment instead. So it's all a big worry. You know, even though we're naturalised we're uneasy about anti-semitism here, not that we let on to them of course. They've been spooked enough already. Now on the brighter side" - and Ana's less serious face showed - "our guests are good company, definitely civilised, and like us, look forward to meeting you. And be sure there's plenty of room in our house. Everybody speaks French, except that my uncle is a bit slow, and as Klara is fast, it works alright."

Neil had listened attentively, and had more questions forming, but let it be, saying, simply: "Thanks, everything sounds really good."

They sat silently for a few moments, each a little self conscious, then arose as one, and left. Outside they entered Ana's car, or rather her father's. She explained she wasn't used to night driving, so wouldn't talk much on the way home. Despite the shadows over Jews Neil found, on arrival, the mood of the hosts was welcoming, quiet, and relaxed, which pleased him immensely. He was also very happy to find the house had ample space and appointments, and looked forward to learning how they came by it. His room was in the ground floor apartment, which was also the main work place. His hosts had planned to scale down work during his visit, so that he had the area mostly to himself. It had its own bathroom and toilet which delighted him for, like many another foreign soldier, he had been appalled by the shortage of them in Spain; and by the primitive habits of many soldiers from poor homes when urinating and defecating, little different from those of dogs. The floor above, forming another apartment, was occupied by the host family, and was the central living area of the house. The top floor, otherwise little used, was given over to the Offenburg guests, where they were out of sight. During his three days there the family squeezed him dry of information about the civil war and their escape from Spain, many new questions having come to their minds since Manny's visit. Ab was particularly glad to find that Neil liked chess, and they played for several hours, along with many questions from Ab about the structure and leadership of the opposing armies in Spain, the way the frontline republican soldiers were looked after, and their weapons; and from Neil about conditions in the German army in the Great War.

Being at 19 rue de la Madeleine was the first time Neil had been in a Jewish home, or in the company of so many Jews. He had ceased to think of Manny as Jewish, for any religiousness he took to Spain was lost there, for there was simply no opportunity for their forms of prayer, food preparation, or dress. Worse, the fierce Leftist commanders of the republican forces had generally been completely irreligious, and also actively discouraged pious observance of any kind. And so it had been very difficult to worship any deity, except in silence and in the dark. Nor did the men in the lines make it any easier. Most of them were as turned off as their commanders and scoffed at, and even bullied anybody who professed belief. Neil supposed religion to be much stronger among the soldiers on the other side, where Catholicism had an honoured place, and he had come across foreign fighters for the fascists, who were there out of religious zeal, like crusaders in early centuries, just as avowed communists like himself and theoretical socialists like Manny had flocked to the cause of the Republic. But he was far less certain about the scores of thousands of Italian and German combatants, given their fascist regimes at home. Then the Moors who made up most of the lower ranks in the African Army of the fascists were presumably Moslems. It was clearly a mixed dish of beliefs and unbelief. What it all meant he could not work out, but he knew Manny's faith had dropped off before Spain, and Neil had witnessed its further waning in the space of the year and more of their close acquaintance. He had once asked: "Manny, excuse my asking, but I wonder how you keep up being Jewish when there are no opportunities for worship."

Manny had grinned. "I've never been asked before, and wondered why. But the answer's easy. I became a reformed Jew when we were in Germany. There was a new young rabbi in Offenburg who encouraged a more liberal approach to worship and ritual, as distinct from our fundamental faith. There was nothing new about reform as it was called. My grandfather, Josef, had met it, as a big surprise, in Dresden on his way west from Odessa, and he had already influenced me. He felt that the Jews did their race a disservice by highlighting the things that made them different from the Gentiles. That was radical talk to traditionalists of course. His father had been killed in a pogrom, and Josef never got over how senseless it was. He just quietly urged change, without expecting a lot to happen quickly. We were all influenced by him, me especially. And it would be pretty hard to be a practising Jew in this army, no matter who your grandfather was."

Neil broke in: "How did the other members of your family take it?"

"My father and my uncle were on his side. The women were

more conservative. My mother put the brakes on my sister getting too slack, and she had to wait until she was older before she could break loose, while always careful not to upset our mother too much. It was easier for me. So don't be embarrassed about asking me what I think. But what about you? I saw a Bible in your gear but you don't seem to read it, or pray. Or am I missing something?"

"Very interesting. I must say I've wondered why some Jews in France make themselves conspicuous by their appearance. That seems to invite attention to how different they are, and goodness knows there are plenty of antisemites in France to use any differences. But I suppose it's faith. As to my own religion, well, it's quite simple. I'm a Roman Catholic through my mother. So is my father, I think only nominally, through conversion on their marriage. He's English you know. I went to boarding school in England for my secondary education. I was one of the few Catholics in a Protestant school. It was my father's old school. They were very careful about keeping the religion you came with, so when I finished school I was still an active Catholic. But the wheels wobbled when I went to university, and fell off completely when I came here. If my mother could hear me now she would cry, and who knows, she might even get me to change my views. But like you I wouldn't talk anybody away from their faith, for they may be right and we wrong."

After that exchange of confidences they attempted to discuss the morality of war and killing, but got lost and gave up. For young men living in a world in a world of killing where there were only two groups of people, each wanting and duty bound to kill the other, talk about love and reconciliation was unreal. Their hearts were not in it, and their minds couldn't handle it.

In Lyon the Mayers adjusted to rising antisemitism by dropping all signs of Jewishness outside the home. In dress and outward appearance they aimed to be anonymous in the street, for their liberty was at stake. They delayed putting on their religious vestments until they were close to the synagogue which they still attended each Sabbath. But they moved to one away from home to reduce their Jewish profile locally. Inside the house Jewish customs were continued, but moderated during Neil's stay. And they explained them, and invited his questions about them, so there was no embarrassment. He relaxed and recuperated in the peaceful and pampering environment of the Mayer home, far from the roughness of the past couple of years. The doctor assessed his body as steadily recovering. With Ana as his guide, he also toured the famous old city. Further acquaintance confirmed her friendly manner, common sense, and quick mind, attributes also noticeable in her parents. She, too, played chess, and was Ab's main opponent usually. He was so grateful for the time she gave him he had made her a complete chess set in a compact carry box, which she proudly showed Neil.

Just as he was interested in his hosts, they also in him. Having a Gentile as their house guest was a new experience, especially one tall and fair and slim, with ascetic good looks and serious air. They saw a multi-talented person, of a higher level of education than their own. He told them he had been a communist when he went to Spain, but went cold after seeing how ruthless and intolerant they were in asserting their beliefs on everybody. "Yet", he said, "if they had been had in complete control all the time we would have been a better match for the fascists. They were very disciplined both in pushing their beliefs, and in fighting."

Klara asked: "Say if you had won. Say if the communists had taken control of Spain. Would that have been alright?"

"The fascists put out propaganda right through the war to frighten the Spaniards of that, and convince them Franco and his troops were there to save Spain. But let's say the communists had taken over the government. Their aim would have been to help the poor people, and that could hardly be worse than fascist control, and continued discrimination in favour of the rich. Remember there was a democratic government trying to improve things when the army rebelled. It's very hard for outsiders to believe the difference between classes in Spain. Franco's army was only one part of the rebellion, the part with the guns. Behind it, equally to blame, were the Church, the grandees, and lots of other Rightists. They're back in power, and I'd bet my life the poor people will have the same bad time as before. So I really think the communists would have been better, even though I dislike them. Maybe I should say I can't see how they could have been worse. We're talking about the poorest country in Europe, as I believe; also the most Catholic; and also where the poor people have been trodden on for centuries."

Klara, listening carefully, showed by her expression that she wasn't quite convinced. She said: "I wouldn't say this only you said you're tiring of being a communist. Actually I'm as frightened of them as of fascists. You might be right, but what I hear about Russia suggests Stalin might be as bad as Hitler. I'm enough of an optimist to think that fascist Franco wouldn't be as hard a dictator as either of those others."

"I understand. I can't say I'm right, but let's say the communists had taken over. Remember they were never a majority either in the parliament or in voting. But say they took charge. They make things better for the poor. I wonder though how far they could go, in the sense of abolishing basic rights, without support from the Church, which would never come. Y'see, Spain differs from other countries in the strength of the Church. It's nothing like France or, as I believe, Italy. It really has a grip on people's lives. It's always been so. When you go there you are truly astonished by it, and communists would have to contend with it. There's nothing in the past to show they could have wiped out religion. Remember the Leftist movements have been going in Spain for seventy years or so, and even when men join and give up on church their women often stay. The Virgin Mother has a big hold on them. They love her, and she is the centre of their faith. *La Virgen* takes many forms and names. Any place, pueblo as they say, can have its own, with her own name. Say, *La Virgen del río del Ebro*, for which there would be a beautiful figure and shrine, maintained faithfully through the centuries, and brought out on festive occasions, and always honoured, and prayed to daily. One in every second community. Now, even though many Leftist men don't believe, they have respect for her. Another thing, the bonds between Spanish mothers and their children are very, very strong, so that maternal influence lasts longer than what we see in other countries. But I'm still serious about leaving the party. If I disappear without trace one day you'll know what communists do to their ex-members." He spoke lightly, but wasn't sure he should.

He kept up with the news, including the French attitude to the Spanish refugees, and the conditions of the internment camps. He was surprised to learn how increasingly antisemitic many French media outlets were, and also the government. He realised those views would naturally influence some citizens. He also became aware of French friendliness toward Nazi Germany. Some commentators went out of their way to praise Germany and its recent economic achievements, and political strength, even suggesting that some sort of peaceful union between the two countries might serve French interests well. Active and noisy fascist and pro-Nazi groupings were prominent. Jews were the subject of many attacks from the Right, so that Neil wondered if they had more enemies than friends in France. Perhaps nobody knew. However, the portents were not good; not that he showed any concern to his hosts. He was assured by Ben that life wasn't as bad for Jews as in Germany, but still bad, especially for the foreign Jews. Ben's family was getting by, while looking at an uncertain future. But above all they were worried about Ab and Klara, being illegal immigrants.

By the time he left Lyon by train for Paris in early June 1939 everybody in the house new more than before about European politics and living conditions than before, and Neil was stronger too. He went on feeling much better. He then stayed for a few weeks with his parents in their pleasant apartment in the eighth arrondissement. His mother, Béatrice, was French, and had met and married Neil's father, James, in 1914 when he was a publisher's representative in Paris and London, his home city. On the outbreak of war that year he had enlisted in the British Army, and served in the infantry in frontline action, then was seconded to intelligence where he spent the rest of the war, including long stints in Paris, where he met Bee. After the war he returned to his peacetime vocation, with reserve status in army intelligence. He was famous in his family for telling them exactly nothing about what he had done or was doing in the army, and Neil would find one day he had inherited much of his style.

Although his parents knew there was entrenched injustice in Spain, they had been against Neil going to war, if not for quite the same reasons. His mother was a conservative Catholic influenced by the Church line of Franco as a white knight saving Catholic Spain from, if not communism, then anticlericalism. She fretted about her son's adoption of a cause that, to her, was worthless. His father held more liberal views, and saw it as the sort of thing he would do if in

Neil's shoes. Both also knew that vigorous opposition would be a waste of effort.

8

With Manny back, and the registrations finalised, and Neil gone, fishing commenced in earnest. They set out to catch whatever was in season and could be caught with the boat and its gear. Setting cray traps was their first priority, as the crays were coming out of their winter seclusion during which they had replaced their shells, and were now filling out with flesh. Locating the sea-grass meadows and reefs that was their habitat was the challenge for the newcomers. Diego also had in mind to trap off the Costa Brava one day, where crustaceans abounded, and sell the catch in France, where they were more popular eating. But in the meantime local crays, and line fishing for prized species such as bonito and even small tunny, were the targets. The small set of nets they carried could not catch much more than bait, which would not matter if the other fishing methods paid off. They would watch carefully the catches of the other boats and where they fished. They hoped to cover expenses from the start, and do better with experience. They followed this routine for several unprofitable weeks, punctuated by a week-end visit from Manny's family to Sète, and a return visit when the two men took the train to Lyon for a few days. And once they fished their way down to Móntago where they disposed of their catch through Diego's father. Eduardo had been keeping up with Spanish events, but there was no good news for his son. It was still a choice of risking prison in Spain, or France on the run. So Diego kept a low profile constantly, as the French authorities were said to be on the lookout for republican Spaniards, particularly those known, or reputed to be, politically impassioned and rebellious. Diego knew he was not of that group, and hoped the authorities would believe him if they met, or that his façade of working gainfully for a French owner would save him should the police stumble across him.

9

When Neil resumed study in London he had been thinking about the difficult step of resigning from the British Communist Party. Its members were not as fervent or aggressive as those of some countries, as he knew from meeting them in Spain. He had been earnest in accepting communism as the way forward for mankind, and sincere in going to Spain in the International Brigade to fight against fascism, and for the downtrodden workers. But the party's methods there disillusioned him, even if its aims were admirable. His former idealist picture of a world being led to justice and equity for all, through the agency of international communism, formed in the conversational style of British communists, had been broken badly. Leftist internationalism had scaled great heights through the creation of the Brigade, thanks to Russia's leadership, yet had fallen away to a shadow thanks to the lack of backbone of British and French Leftists, and also due to Stalinist Russia's typical changes in policies that in the end confused and disintegrated the fighters in Spain, from whatever country they had come. He had seen that no brutality and no subterfuge was too much for Stalinists in gaining power. With international power they could implement their dream of world revolution, leading to the enhancement of the lives of the workers. For them though, he had concluded, the ends always justified the means, and future utopia was worth any amount of present pain and suffering. But to Neil the means were also important, and should carry respect and tolerance for people of different shades of opinion encountered along the way, factors missing among the communists he saw operating in Spain, who had used all manner of lies, deceit and force to silence opposition and eliminate rivals. Whatever communism's laudable aims might be, attaining them inhumanely was unacceptable. But how could he put those thoughts in a letter of resignation? Knocking the party was not sensible. That could incite violence toward him, as even some of the British party faithful were not the gentlest of folk. He did not feel he owed the party an explanation for resigning, but still he dawdled. Then, in late August 1939, on the eve of the attack by Germany on Poland, news broke of the sealing of a surprise Russian German Non Aggression Pact. The linking of communism with fascism threw most communists, including Neil, into a spin of disbelief. It was a signal to him. Russian duplicity had reached its nadir. The letter could now be short and simple, its cause self-explanatory. He sent it on the last day of August.

By invading Poland on 1 September 1939 Germany fell into war with Britain and France. Later other nations would line up on each side. The start of the war was the culmination of aggression by Germany against its neighbours during the latter part of the 1930s, and in view of mounting tension during that period, war came as no surprise. Disappointment? Horror? Yes. Surprise? Not really. Few had expected the 1930s British-French brand of appeasement diplomacy to succeed. Certainly not Germany.

Prior to Poland Neil had substantially recovered from his chest wound but found concentration on study hard going, as his mind wandered often to Spain, to the *Santa Maria*, to Manny, and to the Mayers at Lyon. Them in particular. He had learned the men were master cabinet-makers, and that the women worked in textiles, in any way opportunity came, including seamstress, dress making, and trading in bolts of cloth, led by Naomi. It was her life's work. Klara had come to be her excellent assistant after marrying Ab and leaving Paris for Offenburg. Ana was following in their footsteps. Neil had seen the small signs in the front window showing their services, and had heard the demand kept them well occupied. Their long lease they had taken of 19 rue de Madeleine had been prompted by the ample space of the old three story building, with its handsome and generous winding staircase. And with the garages and yard belonging, it had seemed too large for them at first, but the space had turned into a blessing when Ab and Klara arrived.

But when war came his whole attention was given to becoming a British soldier. It was natural that he would join the army, and he set out to enlist in a university rifles regiment. He was scrutinised carefully because of his past, but accepted, and then his rare combination of education and battle experience quickly brought him a commission as a lieutenant. His regiment was part of the British Expeditionary Force in France and Belgium from December 1939 until evacuated with the last of the Allied forces from Dunkirk in late May 1940. By then his worth was well known to his superiors.

10

As part of its war machine Britain created a special sort of secret service, special in that it was to combine force with secrecy. The names *special* and *operations* were meaningful. So Special Operations Executive (SOE), which was to operate in enemy occupied territories. By late 1940 it was looking for applicants to become leaders of resisters against the occupying Germans and Italians in several countries, and would look further later when Japan entered the war. Men nominated - for long only men - were interviewed, and if found suitable, invited into training in a regime that drew on Britain's defence and security experience and resources, and was designed to turn out specialists in aggressive and secret special operations in foreign countries subjugated by the Axis powers. Failed candidates were carefully placed elsewhere, as in all secret services, aware of the relevant provisions of the Official Secrets Act. Initial approaches to prospects had no set form. For Lieutenant Neil Cameron it came from a naval officer, who offered his name only as Jack, and soon after he was invited to another secretive meeting, with a Captain Martin, in a bare office in an obscure building in London, to learn what to expect. The meeting took place after the Battle of Britain had been won by the RAF repelling the Luftwaffe, and although it was not known yet, Germany had been forced to put aside its advanced plan to invade Britain. Though daylight attacks on London and other major centres had ceased, the German bombing continued at night, aiming to lower British morale, which it failed to do. It would continue for months to come, until Germany turned its attention toward another prospective prize: Russia. By then London and its people and some other major centres had suffered enormous destruction and casualties, particularly during the period of intensive night bombing called the Blitz, and during which Neil was interviewed. The facility of air bases in France and the Low Countries had brought certain British centres within bombing range.

Neil's interviewer was short and rotund of figure, and wore civilian clothes, so that what he was a captain of was hidden. His round face was topped by a bald, shiny head, under which sat two narrow, inscrutable through being deep-set, but penetrating eyes. He shut the door, and brought his chair close to and directly opposite Neil's, so that the two men faced each other, about a metre apart, in which position the captain fixed his gaze on Neil's face and kept it there throughout their interview. He commenced at once:

"To start I must assure you there's no loss of rank, or opportunities for promotion, or pay, although of course you won't be in uniform. SOE is controlled by the War Office, of course, like all the regular armed forces, but it's not structured like them. It would hardly be needed if it were to be only an army look alike, or just a spy service.

"In France it aims to sponsor aggressive resistance, with emphasis on having many trained groups ready for action to help the Allied invaders when they come. Our organisers are to build up cells of trustworthy French, give them weapons, show them how to use them, teach some of them the tricks of sabotage, and get them in shape as a sort of secret army. We're not spies, but if something important pops up it should be passed on. We're not publishers of pamphlets, but will help those in that game if we can. We're not there to help people escape the country, but will cooperate with the people who run escape lines, and also help our own people get out when necessary.

"We must prepare the French for serious guerrilla work when the Allies return to France, gingering them up to take charge of their destiny. We can be anything that kills and undermines the Germans in France. Ah! You might think. What's this invasion talk when we've just been kicked out of Europe? Isn't that a dream, remote from military fact? Might not the reverse happen, and Britain be invaded? The answer to those questions, sound as they appear today, is that we must believe in our survival, and also, one day, an invasion of France. And must fight for it, otherwise the Nazis may rule our world. And we, my friend, are among the fighters.

"SOE isn't political. If we can help the French unite against the Nazis then we will have done our job. You'll find some Frenchmen anti-British, even resentful of us for fighting. Hard to believe, isn't it? But we're basically fighting for Britain, and we want to see France liberated for ourselves, besides them. Britain is running the war at this stage and supplying the money, so we must have our own agencies, besides funding others, while encouraging the French to perform better than they have done so far.

46

"I know you're an experienced soldier and used to danger. As an SOE agent you will find the danger different. You'll be hunted because you are more threatening than any foot soldier. If you're successful the hunting will be more vigorous. The Gestapo is the main hunter. Knocking off secret service enemies is one of its lines. If you do well you serve your country the better, and maybe attract special attention from the enemy. See it a little like a game of chess, with an SOE agent and the Gestapo hunter making the opposing moves. Great care is needed for every move. In the frontlines we have slack times, when our guard can drop. SOE agents in the field don't have that luxury nearly as much.

"Now imagine if there were only one secret service and it was penetrated by the enemy, which is what they try to do, and will keep on, until we kill them. So we don't resent other secret operations, because they use people probably unavailable to us, and the more total damage done to the enemy in France the better. Both SOE and the Free French draw from the same pool of French speakers, so there's a sort of rivalry there. Some people don't want the French working in subversion, considering their record, and Britain paying, but they must be in the fight boots and all, and we must encourage them to get bigger and better. One day they might be able to do without us, but it's not on the radar yet.

"You know very well what an enemy is. You can't pick and choose who to shoot. Anyone in an enemy uniform is a target for us. But here's the rub. SOE agents don't have the same protection as uniformed combatants. So if our people are captured anything goes. You'll see the danger there without me banging on about it, and I'm sure you'll hear more during training. That brings me to chances of survival. Frankly, we're too new to know. Think of the survival rates of our fighter pilots and you might be near the mark. You had some high casualty rates in Spain I understand, so you know the language."

Neil nodded, then broke in: "May I say something personal?" He paused, and taking silence from his mentor as assent, continued, with a hint of anger in his voice: "I know of the Free French, but I wouldn't contact them even though they're the best of us. I'm very disappointed with France's treatment of refugees: I mean the Spanish republicans and the German Jews. Also, too many French people support the Nazis and Vichy for my liking. Too many fascists for me."

After pausing a moment to think about that, the captain continued: "I see. It's a valid attitude. But know that resisters exist all over France, even if you can't see them. It's our job to make more, and manage them all so they become hard nuts, undermining and killing the enemy all over France. SOE's role is to find and organise and lead those people. The numbers will grow, because the Germans and Vichy are in the wrong, and will become resented by more and more Frenchmen as time goes by. SOE must make it possible for them to resist, whether as communists, or supporters of General de Gaulle, or writers, or former soldiers, or any other group, or even if they are unattached. As it stands the Germans have most of the power and guns, so we have a long way to go, but then we're in it for the long haul, and we'll get there, because we have right on our side, and we'll never chuck in the towel. Does that help?"

Neil: "Surely. I apologise if I sounded angry."

"It's OK. Anger drives us on. Now you must know the importance, the very profound importance, of secrecy and team loyalty right through, all the time. Drop your guard, and all other members in the group are also at risk. And just as the organisers like you are carefully selected and trained here in England, so similar care must be applied in field recruiting. You'll need sub-agents, and couriers, and other helpers, who must know something about the group to do their work properly, but never more than just enough. It's very hard for untrained people to keep secrets, and the Nazis are fiends when they capture someone from whom they want information. It's something new and horrible for everybody to know, and fear."

Neil sat quietly, thinking. He wasn't surprised by much he had heard. He asked: "Who makes decisions?"

"Well, we all do at times. As SOE effort is part of the overall campaign, strategic decisions are made in London. Within those limits there's room for initiative, and in fact is needed in all SOE personnel." He paused, sensing a question from Neil. There was.

"I guess the field operatives and HQ keep in touch with each other. May I ask how?"

"Yes. I'll only outline what happens. There's no limit to how, but key factors are the transmission of messages in morse and other codes by wireless telegraphy, by couriers, and by post. Most groups will have a telegraphist with a set to transmit and to receive messages. By wireless – wire less – or radio telegraphy, of course. It's a vital area, and so will be targeted by the Germans. We would be lost without wireless telegraphy and WT operators. The enemy also has it. By penetrating our systems and codes the Gestapo might fool London into supplying secret information, with awful consequences, so safety checks operate. We hope the BBC will get to use its nightly French broadcasts from its powerful transmitters to send coded messages to our people in the field, as a supplement to our own messaging. A message could tell a particular group the place and time to expect something, by air or sea.

"We think that once the tide of the struggle turns in our favour, Frenchmen will come from the sidelines, prepared to risk themselves to take back their country. In other words, the armies, navies, and air forces of the Allies will have softened up the enemy, and toughened up French spirit. Then the organisation and planning we've been talking about will show their worth.

"Expect to hear of other groups apart from SOE. There's no telling how many resisting groups there are, or will be. Resistance takes many forms, of course. Ours is a belligerent one, though we're not assault troops.

"We must get groups going. That means going in cold and starting from scratch. It'll be too hard for some people, which will appear during training. You won't be pushed, but if the experts believe you can handle the job, they'll give you the opportunity. All I'm doing now is raising the possibility, and so you'll have plenty of time to think how lonely a cold start might be, and be sure if it's for you."

He had paused. "That's a big speech, isn't it? Do you have more questions?"

Neil did: "I expect to run across Frenchmen, and maybe others, who were in the International Brigade in Spain. Some of them would come to me, if they would come to anybody, to help, and those would be Leftists right through, and some would be communists. Would that be allowed?"

"Yes. SOE doesn't care who kills Germans or undermines its war machine, as that's all we want. It could give you a great start to have men like them, with their battle experience, especially if they work in crucial infrastructure, such as railways, and canals, and telephone, and electricity. I don't know what mood the communists will be in, though, as there's that pact with Germany, which perplexes everybody. If your French communists toe the party line they might be hard to get on side, even though fascists are communists' natural enemies."

"That's OK. There should be enough brigaders left over for me. They weren't all communists."

That was the end. Neil was ready to head for a preliminary training school the next day.

11

Diego became resentful, and angry, about Conchita's job. The trouble was, he had nothing better to offer. Legitimate jobs for Spanish refugees were not to be had easily, and he had no leverage in that way. Still, her sharing herself with other men left him continually unhappy and resentful, and she knew it. He was plain jealous. She said she would give it up if another job, out of the public eye, came along. But, as he well knew, she had nothing else. He thought about keeping her, but then she would be at a loose end ashore, with increased risk of detection. And she was fiercely independent. She said to him one day: "Try to see it this way. I love you. Those men I serve are nothing but money. If I can get another money supply I'll take it. I can't see one. Can you?" He said: "Say if I supplied the money. You stop work, and until something better comes up I'll look after you." She thought about that proposition, which was not entirely a new one. But she gave it serious thought, the attention it deserved, before answering. She said: "I don't want to sound like I'm making excuses, but help me with these points. What if something happened. Say you were arrested. Where would my money come from? Or say I was arrested, having been seen hanging around doing nothing, and inviting attention to myself. As it is I'm a worker, I earn enough to get by, and

I'm secure in that I'm hidden, and Marta has mates among the *flics* (police). That's a good position for me, as you know. I don't want to lose you, and I don't want to lose myself either. Try to understand that when a horny sailor comes in ...." Here she burst out laughing, thinking she had nearly said 'from Móntago '. Diego asked: "What's so funny." She replied: "I nearly said, from Móntago." She didn't think he would get it, because she knew he sometimes understood fish better than people, so she added : "No, it's not funny. That man comes as a customer, to buy something, like in a shop. I give him a fuck. Not my soul, just a fuck. When you come you're my sweetheart, my lover, and if we fuck it's a love union." At this point she had burst into tears, and embraced Diego, who himself was overcome, and added his own tears. He felt the situation demanded something from him, so he clasped something he felt in his bones was only a straw, but clasp it he must. He said: "Would you come on the boat as crew, if Manny agreed?"

"Of course I would. And I'd sleep on the deck if I had to."

"Well, we can sort that out, but first we'll talk with Manny."

That was a kind of solution, enough to get going with. But Manny was cold. He said, at once, when Diego asked him at sea the next day: "I don't think it's possible. There's no room. And most of the time there's not enough work for three."

"So you won't even consider it?"

"Hang on. That's not what I said. I'll think about it, because I know how important it is to you and the girl, but it seems unlikely."

Diego knew that so didn't press the matter beyond asking: "Would you let me know soon, because I have to work this out? It's one thing for a woman to sell herself in an emergency, but another for her to become a whore as a way of life. And the longer she stays there the more likely it will become a way of life. Then I'm done with her."

"But she wants out, you said."

"Yes, she does, but I don't want to hang around only to find she's changed, and if she did, she'd have no trouble finding excuses."

"It's a tough thing. I want to help you both, and you know that. Let's leave it while I think about it for a day or two."

As a fisher Manny had been exempt from army call up for the war that started in September. But the war ate into his mind. His wish to be there made him look for a way out of the boat. The talk with Diego brought up a solution to consider. So, shortly, he resumed their discussion:

"If I offered her my place as crew, could you both handle it?"

This was new. Diego knew that Conchita did not have Manny's strength and skills, and knowledge of French, so it would take some thinking about, even if very, very attractive. "What would you do? The army?"

"Yes. I'd have to ask them first. Let's do it this way, because we don't want to build castles in the air. If you agree, I'll ask the army if they'll take me. If they will, you put the plan to Conchita. Allow a couple of days for each step, and we could know in a week or so if we have a deal."

Diego slapped his thigh, and slapped it and slapped it, doubling over as he did so. He danced, and embraced Manny. He cried: "You think we could make it, Conchita and me? We can't afford to fail."

"Of course. You and she would be a good crew. She's tough, and smart enough for anything, besides being an eyeful. If I didn't think she could do it I'd say so, and you wouldn't ask either." Diego nodded assent to that.

As a broad proposal it was good for Diego. He had to think hard to be sure he could do all the things Manny did, and quite quickly decided he and Conchita could get by, with talking in French the biggest problem, and that they could work around, because he had noticed hers getting better all the time. Neil's talk with army recruiting went well, though mention of his fighting in Spain as a brigader led to interrogation as to his loyalty, as it was not long since the signing of the non-aggression pact between Russia and Germany, which had caused a rise in France's normal level of suspicion and apprehension. The French, quite rightly, saw Russia's communistic hand in the International Brigade, so brigaders could be risks if allowed into the French army. But Manny was an idealist and a socialist, no more, and was honest and convincing in stating his position. He had good and longstanding reasons to hate the Nazis, and first class battle experience, and was accepted. Now Diego had the very great pleasure of telling Conchita. She, overjoyed, talked it over with Marta. They knew she could - would - lose Diego were she to continue as a whore. She would accept.   Manny never had to put into words how uneasy he would be about a three way relationship on the small boat. The two man arrangement had a special history, and three crew, one being a voluptuous female, might break the bonds, which were stretched at times already.

The army gave Manny a compacted training course, and promptly posted him to a frontline unit. When he saw that his comrades included quite a few men from official undesirable classifications, he supposed their casualties would be more affordable to France than soldiers not so classified. But he did not mind. He had come to fight anyway.

Diego also had considered joining up to serve France when the second world war started, but had been fearful of the eventual treatment of Spanish republicans when their use to France ended. He was right. Those soldiers and workers were not rewarded, but instead would be compelled to stay in the service of defeated France as forced labourers, and later, when Germany ruled all France, even in the service of the Reich. The chances of work as a virtual slave followed by imprisonment in a concentration camp were real, and once there, in France or Germany, death might well follow. Those risks outweighed the inconvenience of being an outlaw. Besides, Diego had a commitment to the boat and another, growing stronger, to Conchita. Would they, sooner or later, be sent back to Franco's Spain? Would the French and Spanish republicans combine to depose Franco's fascist regime? Would internment of the Spanish refugees continue regardless of which side won the war? He had better wait and see. Besides, fishers were scarce, and food were needed. At sea he would be out of the way of roundups of refugees, and earning well, with his woman by his side.

French rules governing enlistments of foreigners varied with the times. Thus it would come about, after capitulation in June 1940, the army would be reduced by an armistice stipulation to a miniature of its once mighty numbers, and most servicemen were discharged, apart from the million and more kept prisoner by Germany, and the smaller numbers serving in France's overseas territories, which remained out of German reach. At all times after war started in 1939, demands for manpower by France were intense, for military service, at least until the capitulation, and continuing through the loss of manpower as POWs; and by Germany, for coastal defence constructions in France, and to fill gaps in the lines of German workers as that nation's losses in combat transformed workers into soldiers. The longer the war went the bigger the pressure on occupied territories for workers in Germany, and France's large population was a natural pool for Germany to turn to in its desperation. France imposed tight and heartless control on foreign manpower within its mainland borders, along with unreal expectations of labour outputs. News got around of the conditions in the French concentration camps, which in a sense included the labour camps, and the emerging German demands for labour from France, and sustained the resolution of Diego and Conchita to stay free.

In this luck would play a role. France had chosen a regime of tight control of suspect groups, effected with neither sensitivity nor common sense. Many people were imprisoned unjustly, while others whose proper place might have been prison were let roam free. The control business was too big and large for the policing apparatus available. At the same time civilian labour was in strong demand. So one policy shift led to acceptance of certain foreigners for work, especially if thought peaceable, and not a burden on the French economy, or a security threat, but only after they had been processed through the refugee control system; yet Diego and Conchita balked at refugee registration. Rather, if caught, they would plead ignorance of the regulations, and rely on Manny's support. They were not prepared to volunteer themselves into the registration system. Given a warning, they could always run up the Spanish flag Conchita and Marta had made for the *Santa Maria*, and head for Spain.

The new plan allowed for Manny to be the apparent owner of the French boat, but away serving in the army, and the others were keeping it going for him in his absence. Conchita kept a low profile until satisfied about the level of acceptance of a woman as crew, for which, fortunately, moving with the times and stresses of war, there were a couple of precedents already in lively, cosmopolitan, Sète harbour, unlike Móntago.

The small French army permitted after capitulation in mid-1940 excluded Jews, in line with the more intense antisemitism brought with the Vichy regime. But instead of being discharged many Jewish soldiers were drafted into labour battalions, as happened also to some Spanish refugees. Manny was one. He had no way or fore-casting this turn of events when he joined the army. But then he and the others had joined up when France was under the Third Republic, and the big changes consequent upon defeat took place under the Pétain dictatorship, in a changed political and military climate. There was ample and immediate evidence that Jews were in for a bad time in France.

In the labour battalion he kept his army rank of corporal. One day he marched a squad of workers out of camp near Toulouse to unload some goods into a nearby warehouse, accompanied by two armed French police. He excused himself to go to the toilet, behind a shed, then kept on going, down the street. As there were vast num-bers of displaced persons on the roads at the time, he reckoned the chances of his being reclaimed were very low. He kept them low through the disguise of workingman's clothes, a cap and spectacles, and made for a lock on the nearby Canal du Midi. There he made himself useful in helping bargemen work through the locks, and after a few days found a single voyage job as a deckhand on a barge head-ed for Sète, the Mediterranean terminal of the canal, from where he went by train home to Lyon for a few days. Back at the coast, he found temporary crewing jobs, and in October 1940 caught up with Diego and Conchita. They were doing well. They invited him to come back but did not expect him to accept. He was pleased their solution was working, and puzzled about one for himself. Wordworking in a shipyard had strong appeal but, given the times, he needed some-thing more combative.

There were few avenues open to young Frenchmen, Jewish or not, for fighting against the Germans in late 1940. They were so strong. You had to go offshore, and getting there was hard. Through Spain to Portugal to England, was a chance, but Manny was troubled by the risk of being picked up in Spain and recognized as a brigader. A long shot surely, but not worth the risk. He had heard of Jewish resistance bands operating in Paris, which seemed like an option, but oppressive German control there, and the difficulty of crossing from the southern, or unoccupied zone, into the German occupied zone put him off. He sensed the presence of resisters around Lyon without knowing any, and of course none advertised for volunteers. He was not at all sure that passive acceptance of the German invader was what people really wanted, though they were scared against saying so. He imagined there were people in France wanting to escape into and across Spain. He knew enough of the geography of the border areas and of the two languages to take on work as a guide, if he could break in. He would look for something in that line.

Under the armistice conditions that set up the Occupation the invaders were in military control of the larger part of France, and this was called the occupied zone, with Germany controlling the lion's share, and Italy a portion near its own border. The French government under Pétain, based in Vichy in central France, exercised parallel and collaborative control in the remaining and smaller area of mainland France, called by various names, such as unoccupied. Resistance of any sort was dangerous, lonely, and unfashionable, because most French people seemed to acquiesce in both the invasion of their country, and its official acceptance of German dominance. Yet resistance was there, in a small and mostly muted way, and its silent potential was greater. It would take time to develop, to attract more Frenchmen, to become organised. The Free French had started, under de Gaulle and associates in London. Certain individuals, including public servants, secretly provided intelligence to the British, and not a few writers colluded with printers and distributors to produce subversive tracts which went some way to countering among the citizens the persuasive propaganda of the Germans and their many French collaborators, and to help keep alive the spirit of a democratic France. Getting out to join Free French or British forces was impossible for most people. Resistance within France, from underground presses to sabotage of installations, demanded the tightest discipline, fanatical secrecy, and intelligent planning. More could be achieved in partnership with others so, gradually, groups of like minded resisters formed and grew, increasing in number as shame grew for allowing the Vichy regime to emerge, a process accelerated by resentment of German oppression. But to actually become a resister, one who did something, however small, citizens had to contend with the personal and family problems that consumed their personal resources each day. Simply surviving in a hostile environment of hunger and rigid controls was a major effort for most people. Yet it would be seen, in time, that permanent German power over France was neither as certain nor as acceptable as it had seemed in mid-1940. And that Britain was not going to yield to Germany in any circumstances surprised many French people who had expected - and even perversely hoped - it would fall quickly, like France. British resolve also provided a signal that, just possibly, a 1000 year Reich for Europe as predicted by Hitler was not certain. And other events occurred, in time, to fortify doubts about permanent German dominance, not least their invasion of Russia in June 1941, as all Frenchmen knew from Napoleon's attempt that the Russian bear could not be easily trapped. The lesson, for those Frenchmen who wanted to learn, was that they could have a personal say in their country's fate. And the men and women of the Left, and the Free French, and the British SOE, and soon its US counterpart, the OSS, were to help show the way. Not least among the volunteers for armed resistance were society's outcasts: Jews, Spanish republicans, and other political refugees from Europe's fascist strongholds, and in 1943, young Frenchmen avoiding compulsory labour in Germany. Although the earnest and skilful propaganda from the Germans, Vichy and the collaborators, greatly influenced French thinking in an era of censorship, enough news of downturns in Germany's military fortunes got through to encourage people to think, at least a little, about Britain and America and, by extension, of the differences between democracy and fascism, including the arbitrary brutality that had been concealed under a veneer of German civility in the early period of the Occupation. So, for some Frenchmen, what had seemed impossible upon France's capitulation, started to be the subject of dreams, even planning, for recovery. Harsh treatment of Jews and Spanish refugees, plundering of French resources in aid of Germany's war, forcing men into working for the German war machine, were coming factors to strengthen French dislike of German and Vichy control of France.

But as regards active resistance, Germany's attack on Russia in June 1941 would change the attitude of the French Communist Party (PCF). Hitherto its hands had been tied. Not only outlawed and officially persecuted in all France, it had been unwillingly constrained in its natural hatred of the Nazis through ideological subservience to Moscow. But the invasion released the PCF to attack the Germans and their collaborators. Its gangs, and publications, made disciplined and militant attacks on the enemy, at the same time encouraging non-communists by example. All the resisting forces would, in time, together grow into the significant anti-German French force called the Resistance, which had many parts.

Extending the escape line notion, Manny practiced, in his mind, with his parents, and uncle and aunt in Lyon. Escapees could be taken out on the *Santa Maria*, or on foot over the Pyrénées, with the prospect of passage onward to apparently reliable departure points in Lisbon or Gibraltar. He started by asking Diego if he would consider sailing escapees to Spain if the money was right. Without hesitation he and Conchita agreed to consider it when the time came. Manny then needed contacts, and started with the telephone book for Lyon, and under *Les Fondations Charitables*, focussed on *La Sociéte des Amis*. His idea was that as the *Les Quakers* were good people, they might know something to help him, and even if they did not, his secret would be safe with them. It seemed worth a try.

Inquiry led him to Marseille, to a Friends' representative to whom he introduced himself under an assumed name, then set to establishing his bona fides, and noticed his contact gave nothing away, though testing him all the while. In the end Manny felt he had failed, but the man took his postal address, just in case, and though suspicious, Manny still gave it. He was glad he had when he received a note, which in turn led to a meeting with one Roger, he with an air of authority, but no details about its source. The secrecy right through was at first annoying, because puzzling, but in time Manny took it to be the hallmark of a secret service, then he understood. He learned that courier and escort jobs could come up at once, and later weapons and explosives training for resistance fighters. His services were wanted, and he would both useful and busy. There were though some preliminary matters to be worked through. First, he needed a new identity complete with a revised story of his life, plus identity and ration cards to suit. He would be supplied with the details. Then he must have a job, a cover, especially one that would involve his moving around the country. Spotting antique furniture for dealers was chosen. So he became Marc Mattisse, a native of a town in northern France practically wiped out during the German invasion, with substantial loss of official records. There was more to the story, which Manny would have to put together and rehearse as he went along, against the day when he might be interrogated by suspicious French police, or worse, Gestapo. While the papers were being prepared, over the next few days, he was to get ready for a courier run. He would be briefed later, but in outline he would take a train to Grenoble, there to pick up a parcel from a man he would sit next to in a park. He was given passwords to exchange. Within five minutes, and no more, the other man would depart leaving his parcel behind, for Manny to take with him when he, too, left a little later. Failure in any detail meant Manny should get out the best way he could, with or without the parcel. In any case he would never know its contents, though better informed people might guess it could be a Swiss made machine tool for a weapons factory in Britain. He must deliver it to a park seat in Perpignan, in like manner as it came to him. There was no provision for conversation at either end. At no time was he to inquire about, or discuss, the organisation he was working for, or anybody in it. Nor would he would be told anything except what was essential for immediate tasks. Seeing how closely information was guarded he did not inquire about his employer, and because of events still to occur, would never do so.

12

In Lyon the Ben Mayer family took comfort in being in the unoccupied zone, for long the safest for Jews. Their new home was a little larger than they needed at first, but as their businesses had taken off it was not too bad, and not at all later, when Ab and Klara came. They then saw their choice of the large premises, giving the refugees their own quarters, as a blessing from God, and they all gave thanks accordingly. Dismay followed soon, when the French lost the war and the Occupation commenced. For the Mayers it was as though the Nazis were on their tail all the time, first Germany, now France. On the other hand, while antisemitism was rising incessantly there, in the unoccupied zone, it was worse in the occupied zone, based on Paris, with relentless German persecution. Nationwide anti-Jewish policies had been applied through laws and decrees forthwith after the armistice of June 1940, and Ab and Klara, as refugees, had good reason to feel especially vulnerable. So they kept out of sight in the top floor of

19 rue de la Madeleine, with the others as lookouts and minders.

By its unnatural nature, hiding from danger is stressful for everybody in a household; and so it was with the Mayers. They all tried to keep Ab and Klara occupied to counter the boredom of confinement and little contact with the outside world. They were the best of guests in this sense. Klara, with her especially calm and loving nature, reduced the hardest of problems to something that could be managed with minimal fuss or strain, and her temperament, as always, kept the more volatile Ab calm. Helping with the work in the small family businesses was a useful outlet, as were the frequent games of chess that had long been a favourite pastime of the two men, and then in hiding Ana played with Ab when her father could not; and later, when house-bound in a flat, she would learn to play against herself.

Klara, technically a French Jew, one born in France of French parents, was not as much at risk as the so-called foreign Jews, at least not until the German attack on the Jews grew more vicious and indiscriminate, and even French Jews then became liable, sometimes by accident, to be scooped up in a roundup with the same dire consequences as for the others. But Klara had no desire to protect herself where Ab could not, so she adopted his classifications as her own.

Hunger was common to ordinary French citizens during the war, especially city residents without farm contacts, such as the Mayers. Most farm connections came through family, so foreigners, of whom there were very many besides Spanish republican and Jewish refugees, were usually in the same boat as the hungriest French. And the Offenburg visitors had no ration cards, for which identity cards were needed, and to get which they would have to out themselves, and maybe land in an internment camp. Therefore some black market purchases were necessary, until Ana forged ration cards for them.

At the beginning of 1940 about 300,000 Jews were living in mainland France, going by careful estimates, which was all there was to go by, as France had never distinguished Jews in census counts. They were not bigger in numbers than others, Italians and Spaniards in particular, but may have seemed so because of their concentration in Paris, their dress habits, and their tendency, common to immigrants, to live in the same neighbourhoods. So when the antisemitism of the French and France developed in response to the nervous

60

times, there may have seemed more Jews in France than in fact, and so more blame could be heaped on their shoulders for poor France's bad decisions and governance, and it would be better that they left. How that could be arranged was a hard question to answer, at least until the deportation era came, and a start was made. France was not as eager to see the end of Jews of long standing as much as the newer ones. As the boundaries of classifications were rough, it may be assumed some French Jews were interned and some died solely through the accidental workings of an artificial system. France had led Europe by granting civil rights to Jews through its Emancipation Act of 1791, and this, in conjunction with a generally liberal immigration policy, had attracted Jews harassed elsewhere. And after the grave losses of French manhood in the first world war, the official welcome continued. The intake rate rose in the late 1930s upon increasing persecution of Austrian and German Jews. The tides of unofficial discrimination that ebbed and flowed through the minds and attitudes of the non-Jewish French were not a deterrent to an influx of refugees from pogroms in countries to the east.

From mid-1940 the new regime under Petain was permissive of anti-Jewish press attacks, and all manner of scurrilous material was published, as in Germany. Those who attacked were more numerous and more virulent than those who defended, reflecting not only the latent antisemitism of much of the general population, but also its preoccupation with the grim business of making a living, and keeping out of trouble with the stern officialdom that held sway throughout the country. From the first days after capitulation and the establishment of separate zones, Jews were taken by both German and Vichy regimes to be security risks, and so regulated. Once they had started upon them, both governments warmed to controls. It was barbaric discrimination, and the more shameful because it happened in France. And it wasn't only the erratic and unjust effects of the laws that was deplorable and fearsome: the internment or concentration camps scattered across France were grim and heartless places, rivalling in their horror some of the aspects of the infamous German concentration camps. They were centres of misery, sickness, stink, callousness, discomfort, cold and hunger. By such means Jews, even some French Jews, were reduced in theory and in fact to stateless status with minimal rights and privileges. More so than the Spanish republicans. They were targets for internment, but if they could avoid it they were not otherwise discriminated against. If, for example, a Spaniard could satisfy the authorities of being in useful employment and was not a political threat then, increasingly, he or was unlikely to be harassed. Not so the Jews. There was though a degree of chance in the application of the property laws that deprived them. One business might be taken over entirely and its proprietor denied a source of income, while another might escape because of perplexing decisions, errors and delays by the bureaucracy. Similarly with Jewish internments. And many Jews took active steps to avoid the worst impacts of the discriminatory ordinances. Non-compliance methods were as varied as the imaginations of the many Jews who sought to protect themselves. They succeeded best when assisted by non-Jewish friends and associates not themselves suspect, or at risk.

Ben and Naomi were not caught by the business aryanisation policy. Their small enterprises were not of primary significance when there were richer pickings available for the bureaucratic leeches who ran the aryanisation system in France. In addition, they gained protection by having a non-Jewish friend take a transfer of the businesses as a blind, which went smoothly enough for them, but did not in all cases.

13

Naomi peeped through the curtain in her work room next to the front door to see who was knocking. Identifying callers was important, given the dangers of the times. She recognized him, and while rushing to open the door she wondered what business might bring rabbi Samuel so far from home. She called to Ben, who welcomed the visitor before surveying the street for any unusual movements. It was clear. As he returned Naomi spoke warmly: "This is a pleasant surprise. I hope you can take tea with us. We have other special guests; Ben's brother and his wife, who will be delighted to meet you. They can't go out themselves just now, being refugees, so company is a joy for them. Come, we'll go up."

Samuel replied: "I most certainly wish to meet your guests, but the business I come on is confidential, so I'd prefer to discuss it privately, then you can decide on the next step."

Mystified, Naomi led them into the work room, and they all sat after Ben closed the door. Before stating his business the rabbi led the trio in prayer, calling for their trust in God in the difficult times in which they lived, and His guidance for the matters about to be discussed. He then said, softly and seriously: "I come to ask if your hearts and strength can cope with another burden. I must present this matter to you, although I'd rather not. I choose this household as a possible solution because of the talents I know you're blessed with, the space of the premises, and the love I know you have for your fellows. I wasn't aware of your guests, and I fear that will make it difficult for you to even consider the matter that brings me here. But with your permission I'll continue." They both murmured requests that he do so. "I have some friends, peasants, Jews like us, who are hiding two English airmen. They came out of the sky by parachute one night after their airplane was hit. My friends took them in and hid them in the attic. One has a bad leg wound. My friends cannot keep them for long. They lack nothing in their wish to serve God by nurturing the men, but are in despair of their ability and facilities to keep them until they are fit enough to move on. They can't put them out in the street, or turn them in to the police, yet the burden is becoming very great. They brought their problem to me. Naturally my first thought was to take the men into my own home, but after prayerful consideration Simone and I decided it would be unfair to our own children, who include foster children, and some have emotional scars from their pasts. Our house is already overflowing, and our hands always full. Besides, it seems to us wrong, even risky, to burden them with secrets they could not understand fully. We believe the men need a safer place than ours. "But I must explain about Leon and Ruth. He is a semi invalid from wounds in the previous war, and Ruth works the farm mostly alone, and it's all they have. Their son is a POW in Germany. Ruth just can't cope with the guests for much longer." The hosts were puzzled. Both wondered why they had been chosen. Both answered, silently: 'Perhaps he has tried others without success. He may be here as a last gasp, asking people whom he knows only slightly.' Then Naomi spoke: "It's a privilege to be

63

asked to help, and we'll certainly think hard about what we can do."
Ben nodded agreement, adding: "When do you want to know by?"

Samuel sighed: "Ah, there's a problem. I must find somebody very soon. They aren't able to handle this burden any longer, having done their best for several days."

Ben continued: "So you'd like to know right away. Could we take it this far today? We discuss it now on the basis of maybe, and we'll discuss it further as a family for a final decision within the next three days. Would that be OK?"

"Thank you, Ben. Thank you. Yes."

Naomi added: "Well, I think we should have tea and talk about this with the others, because they are in it as much as we are. So if we go up you can meet them and we can keep talking."

Over tea the news was broken to Ana, Ab and Klara. All joined in the discussion, and in the end nobody was against taking in the airmen. Ana said she could find out how to move them onward from Lyon, because she knew that escape routes operated for airmen and soldiers. How she would find out was not questioned, but in her mind she would start with Manny. At the end Ben sensed there was no need to delay the decision, so he asked all the family if they thought the rabbi should take a final answer away with him, and all agreed on taking in the airmen. It was then arranged that Ben and Samuel should go to the farm the next day to assess the situation, and work out how to convey the airmen to rue de la Madeleine. Ben's journey to the city outskirts, where the others lived, and return, by train, bus, and foot, took him practically all day. At home he recounted the elation of the group at the farm at the turn in fortune promised by his presence. The Mayers all accepted they were now committed to the rescue: it was their fate.

Finding space for the new guests was not a problem. Bringing them in, and feeding them would be. The Mayer car had been taken by the army at the outbreak of war, and since the armistice they had not asked for it back, not wanting an unnecessary meeting with authority over something pretty useless because of the fuel shortage. How to transport the airmen needed the joint consideration of the whole family. They knew the airmen had neither papers, nor civilian clothes, and the injured one could only hobble. The cover that might come from night travel was lost because of the curfew, which was when the chances of being stopped by the police were greatest. How to move them?

Two days later Ben returned to the farm, driving a small van hired for the day from a friend who was a carpenter, and who used it in his business. Its engine was powered by heat from a towed wood burner. The small tray was less laden with timber, and tools, than normal, and now carried a large bag. Ben picked up Samuel on the way, and they arrived at the farmhouse late in the morning. French civilian clothes, the sizes having been calculated by the Mayer women according to Ben's descriptions, were produced from the bag, into which went the men's uniforms. The passengers boarded with care not to be seen, and after quiet tears and hugs between the farmers and the airmen, Ben drove off, with the airmen in the back, lying low. The trip home was uneventful. They entered the yard of the house from the back lane, the van stopped close to the back door, and the airmen climbed out and were ushered into the house, straight to the kitchen on the second floor, where they sat and met the family around the table. The mutual curiousity was intense. The Mayers saw two very young men of medium height, though both taller than the Mayer men, in ill -fitting civilian clothes and unusual boots. Douglas, the taller and more heavily built of the two, the one with a leg in plaster, had a mop of red hair. Arthur, slimmer, had a thin face, and a ready smile. The women appraised the fit of their clothes fitted, tugging here and there with a view to alterations. Both men knew a little French from school days, and had improved it slightly during their stay on the farm, and so simple, patient conversation could be had from the start. They were visibly dismayed to find out that although they had entered a safe house, it was not part of an overall plan for their immediate return home. It was clear at once to the Mayers, and soon to the visitors, that the farmers had allowed them to think that by moving house they would soon be on their way. The Mayers explained their inexperience with escape lines and the like, and had responded to the rabbi's call as they felt God required them to do, not because of any skills. When the news sank in and the disappointment cleared, the visitors adjusted. They came from the midlands of England. Neither had ever been out of England, or consciously had any dealings with Jews, Germans or Frenchmen before the war. Their hosts were curious about the circumstances of their crash and rescue, plying them with questions. The airmen spoke among themselves, in English:

Douglas said: "They want to know about us and we must tell them all that's safe to tell because they're our only way home."

Arthur replied: "Agreed. But we mustn't give them any details of our mission or our unit, because that sort of stuff could be useful to Fritz if it slipped out. And we don't know what any of these people will be doing or saying tomorrow, next week, or next month."

"Not even the make of our plane?"

"That's right. It wouldn't matter to them anyway. But tell them a bit, if only to show we aren't Germans, or didn't just drop in from the moon. I'll cough if you're going too far."

"OK." Turning to his hosts Douglas continued: "I'll tell you about our crash if you like. It was quite an experience we don't mind saying." Supplementing his words with body language, and with assistance from Arthur, he continued: "To start, remember we're RAF men in enemy territory, so we have rules about what we can say. If we leave anything out it's because of our orders. So there we were, in the middle of the night, in a paddock with our parachutes wrapped around us, and me hurt. We had jumped from our plane, which was going down. Excuse me." Turning to Arthur he asked: "Can I say we were shot down?"

"Yes. It'll sound funny if we don't. Like the plane just fell over."

Continuing: "We don't know what hit us, but we felt a bang, then one of the engines was on fire, and the plane started to lose altitude. We had to jump out in the dark. Then we were lucky to land in a field. We crawled over some fields to a depression surrounded by trees, and parked there. We made a splint for my leg, hid the parachutes, and tried to become invisible. During the morning the lady, that's Ruth, went by without letting on she had seen us, although she had. Then she had to count us, and decide who we were, so looked again while she was working. She was careful, as it's a very small place, and the neighbours are close by and can see everything. Then she said "hello" in French, and when we didn't reply she said it again, so we knew our game was up, and Arthur stuck his head out and waved. He saw this little old lady in farmer's clothes. The big thing was that she waved back, and smiled. Just a little, you know, but we understood she was friendly. It was a great relief. We would have sat up and come out, but she waved us back, to stay hidden. But Arthur pointed to my leg for her to know I was hurt, and showed who we were. She just nodded, but didn't stop. It all took only a few seconds.

"Back home Ruth and Leon had a tough decision to make. They weren't set up for us, and also they knew of penalties for what they were doing, but did it anyway. We couldn't have blamed them had they given us up, and were blessed they didn't. We'll love them for ever for it.

"During the day Ruth came again with a bottle of water and some sandwiches. Then after dark she came again, with their mule dragging a sled which, with a buggy for when they go out, are their only vehicles. I was put on the sled and we all went up to the farm house." Turning to Ben: "You saw it. Weren't they kind, and brave, to look after us? What can you say about people like that? Words just aren't good enough."

Ben nodded agreement.

Douglas paused to drink water before continuing: "Then the next night a doctor came and put something on my leg. He came because Ruth had asked him, and she knew he would be safe. That also was really great. We knew we would have to move on soon, and saw the rabbi come and go a couple of times. We would have turned ourselves in if Ben had not turned up as he did. So that's our story so far. You good people will be a big part of the next bit."

What the airmen didn't say, as being against regulations, was that they were on their first mission, which was the delivery one fine night of two men to a remote, makeshift airfield on a high plateau east of Lyon. On landing by the light of flares a small cargo was unloaded, the two passengers passed out into the care of the ground party, two other passengers boarded, and the aircraft was airborne and on its way home: all within a few minutes of landing. And unknown to the airmen, the flares were extinguished and the ground party dispersed within a couple of minutes more. The airmen thought they were above the range of anti-aircraft fire, until hit in the port wing, greatly surprising them. As stability and altitude were being lost, they had to bale out, and alerted the passengers to get ready. The crew insisted that the passengers, who clearly were men of strong nerves, jump

67

first. The crewmen landed close together in a field, and one passenger was near enough for them to sense his presence. He disappeared, leaving his parachute. The fate of the fourth man was unknown. The plane could be heard flying on at a low altitude, so had righted itself. As the crew made their way toward cover they took the parachute of the third man with them, so as to leave no clues. They never saw or heard of either passenger again. The morning came, but no search party. The fugitives never knew why. It was because the only peasants who saw the landings of the parachutists in the middle of the night chose not to report the incident, but instead to bury it in the backs of their minds. Then, by some aerial mystery, the plane had flown on about 150 kilometres before crashing in a vineyard, to create a local puzzle. It was never linked to the jump, or the strange case of a missing livestock agent.

The other passenger landed safely on the Lyon-Toulouse road. He tied the parachute into a tight roll, placed it in the roadside ditch, and waved down the first slow moving car that came along. Standing in front of it, he showed pain as he gestured toward an apparently damaged foot. The driver, a livestock agent headed for an early market, stopped out of compassion, or curiosity. The fugitive limped to the window and begged a ride to hospital, adding: " ….. but only if you have enough petrol." The driver sealed his fate with his reply: "I have plenty of petrol but I don't know about taking you far because I have another commitment." The pedestrian said: "I wish you would reconsider. It's really important to me to get to Toulouse. Actually, I'm a Free French agent on urgent business."

"But it's out of my way, and I might get into trouble if I'm found taking you. I'm sorry, but try someone else." In response the pedestrian produced a pistol and shot the driver dead. He moved the body across to the passenger side, loaded the parachute, and drove on toward Toulouse. On the way he dropped off the body and the parachute in separate rivers. In Toulouse he parked in a quiet street and left the car with its key in the ignition and the driver's window down. He walked away slowly. He made for a safe house at the university, and on his colleague also arriving, waited with him until their mission to London was rescheduled.

His eventful day had started with him leaving his home on the campus of the University of Marseille for, as his wife explained to her friends, a short fishing trip in a mountain stream. Within an hour the fishing gear had been stored, and he was a passenger in a car nearing a rendezvous between a resistance group and a plane to pick up a companion and himself. The approach of the plane, its circling to identify its reception, its landing, the speed and grim efficiency with which unloading, loading and takeoff took place, were astonishing and exciting events the like of which he had never experienced. He recalled the subsequent disablement of the aircraft, the coolness of the aircrew in trying to keep the plane airborne, their decision to bail out, the firmness of their order to the two passengers to jump, and the wondrous sight of the four parachutes opening, and slowly dropping through the starlit sky. Those were events over which he had no control; unlike his actions subsequently. He carefully reviewed them, and was satisfied. He regretted killing a man, but had been told during training that situations could arise where an immediate and vicious act was sometimes needed to ensure one's own safety, and more importantly, the safety of colleagues. Resisting remorse and possible depression, he dismissed the incident with *'C'est le guerre.'*

The Mayer's guests needing identity and ration cards, Ana had to get in some blanks. She had so far got by with phony ration cards for Ab and Klara, but better materials were needed. She approached a friend from her days in trade school, one who worked in the prefect's office where the cards were kept and issued. After sounding her out she was confident that, at the least, the friend would not harm her. But would she do more? She explained she wanted to help some people, who were not criminals, in avoiding capture by the Gestapo or the Vichy police. To that end she wanted to devise some cover through the use of false papers, and believed that if she could get blank papers and cards she could make up something passable. Her assumption about her friend was correct. After hearing the request the friend said: "You've come to the right place, the right person. I've been wanting to do something useful. You see I have something to make up for my brother. He's a very peaceful man who could only serve as an ambulance driver, and wouldn't carry a gun. His ambulance was shelled by a German tank, and he, and the patients were all badly burned. He's bedridden in the military hospital here and may never recover fully. The Germans didn't have to do that. I would be glad to try to help. You'll understand that I'll risk punishment if exposed. How can I protect myself against that?"

Ana thought, before replying: "I don't know, other than to trust me. I'm in the same boat. Maybe even worse, for betrayal of me could lead to others also being caught, because the Gestapo is smart at links. So though I'd rather not do what we're talking about, I know people who deserve to have the chance to escape. As a Jew I'm well aware of this. You'll wonder for whom I might up papers. Well, I come to you with only two men in mind, not Jewish. I expect there will be others, men who need to get back home to keep on fighting. Also, if given the chance, I would prepare papers for my family and myself. But I came here for the two men only, and since then my thoughts have moved on, so now you know my full position."

The friend had remained silent and thoughtful while Ana was speaking. She reached out and clasped Ana's arm, crying: "I get it. You're a brave one. I must help you. I'll start by looking for some cards for you to work on. Can you come to my mother's home next Sunday afternoon, so I can show you what I've got. Just in case of any change in plans for either of us, please ring me on Saturday evening."

Ana was very pleased. "Thanks. Your brother will be proud of you. But you won't tell him, will you? What we're doing is really very dangerous, and nobody but us should know. Are the cards identifiable as coming from a particular office."

"I understand. No, I won't tell him. Or anybody. No, they're not."

With the blanks in hand and help from her mother and aunt, Ana set to practising signatures, stamps, photographs, and print, on identity and ration cards for Arthur and Douglas. They became Paul, and Michel, respectively. If done well, cards could get through checkpoints, provided they were not interrogated. The game would then be up, as their spoken French was too poor and their English accents too clear for them to pass any hostile conversation, besides which Michel's (Douglas) red hair could be a liability. Nonetheless, she explained the nature and detail of the cards carefully, to help them fit into their new names and identities, and insisted that henceforth each should answer only to his new name, to be used by everybody in the house. If the cards failed in their purpose they would be on their own, as the Mayers had no influence that could be helpful.

She consoled herself that if the airmen caved in under pressure upon capture, they would be unlikely to know where they had been, and wouldn't want to see their hosts fall. She wished somebody would come and explain to them in English how they should behave in the dangerous period ahead. Like Neil, but he, she supposed, was fighting somewhere for the British. She guessed that falling into a virtual police state where discrimination, imprisonment and cruelty awaited around every corner was odd for the guests. It was not something you could see, like the clouds, or smell, like fumes. She must get hold of Manny, because he would know what to do. If she could not contact him she would have to ask a friendly consul in Vichy or Lyon for guidance. She also wanted to get the fit man, Paul, into an escape line because he was becoming restive, and so a potential danger to her family. Manny was due to make one of his occasional telephone calls home, but she would write to him in Sète anyway to ask him to come home. The disabled one should remain until he could move more freely. Naomi thought he'd be unable to walk strongly for quite a time, which could rule out a walking escape over the Pyrenees. Therefore Ana started to think of air, or even sea, but she could do nothing about it without her brother.

Unaware of events at home, Manny was planning a brief visit there on his way to another courier run for Roger. On arrival he did not say what he was doing, nor was he asked, as his family knew he would say if he could. He met the airmen. He liked the papers Ana had made up for them. When asked what to do, he said to leave it with him for a while, and he would work on it. A few days later Klara received a telephone call from Manny. He asked simply: "Is Paul ready?"

She replied: "Two more days."

"I'll ring again." He did, on the second day, and asked Klara, simply: "Yes or no?"

"Yes."

"The lake at three. Wait though. I'll ring again."
Early next morning he rang again, and said to Klara: "Today."

Klara got herself and Paul ready to be at the lakeside as required. She took him, equipped with his new papers, by bus to the lake in the *Parc de le Tête d'Or*, the only park she and Manny had been in together. The ride was uneventful. Paul had been warned not to openly gape at the sights of the great city as they went, but rather to act as if a bus ride on a Sunday afternoon in Lyon was something he was totally used to. At the lakeside they, along with many other people, stood and strolled around looking at the water, gardens, statues and other people, simulating relaxation, then they sat. Soon a young woman joined them, and seating herself with Paul in the middle, said to Klara: "Just sit for two minutes then get up and go away. Don't chat. Don't look back. I'll hold him so he won't follow you."

As she left Klara muttered to Paul, without looking at him: *"Au revoir et bonne chance,"* and left as instructed. She never heard of him or the girl again.

Michel continued his convalescence. The Mayers told him Paul was safe, and on his way home. They were a little glad of the language barrier for he might have asked for details; maybe even distressed at them just leaving Paul on a park seat with a stranger. The Mayer women certainly wondered about such a system, while Ab and Ben assured them it was the only way to do it. The secrecy was exactly what was needed. Paul was in good hands.

Without his friend Michel became more restless. He felt able to go for slow walks, and stated he needed to do so to relieve the suffocating boredom of being enclosed for so long. He understood, so he said, the need for great caution as the security of several people was at stake, but thought that an occasional walk would be harmless. The Mayers said it might well be so, but the risk was so great he must understand that if he went out without their permission he would not be welcome to come back. In the meantime he should build himself up with strengthening exercises so as to have stamina when the time came to move on. Then to make things easier for him they obtained a short-wave radio on which he could listen to the BBC, and on which they could all hear its broadcasts in French of war news. It was a step the Mayers would not have taken but for Michel, as Jews were forbidden to have wireless sets, and even Frenchmen allowed them were not supposed to listen to the BBC, but they often did, which the authorities, French and German, sought to counter through jamming signals and encouraging informers to denounce users. Ab and Ben guarded against detection by constructing a tricky hiding place for the set in the top floor of the house. And at all times it was in use a watch was kept for any unusual activity in the street below, as inspectors were sometimes about. They were comforted by Michel saying that the presence of a receiver like theirs was not easily detected, unlike a transmitter. But the Mayers still had to find out how to get the young man on his way.

14

Early in the extremely cold winter of 1940-1941, Manny and Ana met by arrangement outside a suburban train station near Samuel's home, where she intended to call. She said to her brother: "Michel is restless, but I don't see how he could cross the mountains just yet, especially in this weather, and holding him back is a worry. We can't have more tension in the house, as everybody's stressed already. We tell him about security and he always agrees, but then he says or does something that makes us wonder if he understands. Can you suggest anything?"

Manny thought for a bit, and said: "I haven't forgotten him, but I'm tied to another man who tells me what to do. I've put off discussing Michel until he is better, and you don't think he is yet. Y'know, smugglers have been known to walk away from weak clients, and they then die in the snow. There might be another safe house that would make him happier, but he'd be lucky to get a better one than ours. So what can I do? I'll ask my people if they can find an air passage for him. The trouble in this business is that everybody's so secretive. There's no secretary to telephone and ask for an escape timetable. Air would be good in that his leg wouldn't matter so much. Another thing is that I'm going to talk with Diego about using the boat for a run to Barcelona, which I've heard has a helpful British consulate. This could be more profitable for him than fishing, and suit Michel too. How long before he can travel?"

"He can hobble well now, and his papers are ready, so we need only a few days' notice."

"Good. I'll do my thing right away, because I can see that things could erupt at home, and we can't have that. So tell Michel

I'm busy for him, but keep the boat stuff very vague so he has no way of identifying anything."

"Thanks very much. That'll really give him hope, and make life easier at home."

"Right. Now if we've finished with Michel I'd like to talk about cards. You produce a pretty good article. There's a real need for good ones. Would you be interested in producing more? If so I can send quite a lot of business to you. I guess you'll be getting them out for all the family sometime?"

"Yes, I've started actually. As for doing more, well yes, I don't see why not. I'll need more equipment to be faster, but you're looking at Ana Mayer, professional forger. I take it that Mother and the others – I don't mean Michel – can always help too."

"Why not? They're all good with their hands, and they'll know what you're doing anyway. And why not Michel? He'll know too. He'll feel useful. But there are places around that are better equipped, and to do the job right you'll have to go there sometime."

"You mean presses and things."

"That's right. Faster, with a more even finish. I've seen some. Believe me."

"I do. Tell them I'm open to ideas." She continued: "I'm thinking a new persona might be handy, just in case. I don't need it today, but maybe will another day. I shouldn't tell you I suppose, but these are my new particulars. What do you think of her?"

They settled on the detail. He kept his own alias to himself, and Ana did not ask, though she supposed he had one, especially as he didn't ask her to prepare papers for himself. As they were about to part Ana said: "Papa is concerned to know if you have enough work, and if you get paid for it. He thinks that when French people volunteer to help the Allies almost full-time they should be paid. He fears good intentions can be lost in bureaucratic pigeon holes, and people in the field miss out. He's not hugely concerned, but knows it has cost the family quite a lot of money in looking after the airmen, especially in getting food. He wants us to be paid. He thinks that when the British or Free French send over men and materials and fly planes here, they must also allow money for local services. It's natural for enthusiastic people to volunteer first and think about payment later, he says. Then the local organisers can be so busy they overlook

74

the money part. Papa says the Brits must be paid all the time, just like soldiers, so you should too. He says we should look out for our own interests upfront in any deals we do. He insisted that I talk to you like this, and he's sure to check when I get home."

Manny thought, and said: "Actually, that's good advice. I've been slack, and you can tell him I'll do as he says from now on. I don't expect any difficulty. It's just that the job is more important than anything else at times, so it's easy for the money part to slide into the background. But consider it done."

Talk about names made Manny realise he would be better off transferring the French registration of the boat into his new name, before the rumours about aryanisation of Jewish-owned businesses became a reality. He had his Marc Matisse papers at hand ready, from Roger, so it was only a matter of doing it. M Matisse had also better get listed as a commercial fisherman linked to the Santa Maria.

Ana went on to the rabbi's house, a modest cottage that gave her the instant appearance of being very much lived in. She knocked at the door and introduced herself to the rabbi's wife, who knew why she had come. There were several children in the house. Simone quietened them, and made tea for her visitor, and the two women sat in the humble little sitting-room, clearly normally full of children. She said: "Besides the parcel, something else has since come up. I 'd rather my husband was here to tell you this because it is very sad and he does these things so well. But I must tell you as he won't be home for a few hours, and I know you'll have to get back to town. Now, the fact is it concerns Ruth and Leon, and it is very sad; actually tragic."

Ana caught her breath and sat forward. She sensed what was to come, and exclaimed: "Oh, no!"

"Well, they were found dead in their home a couple of days ago. They were found by a neighbour, who had not seen them around and went to inquire. There they were lying on their bed, apparently both poisoned. He called the police, and later us. Samuel handled the funeral. It seems that running the farm had become increasingly hard for them, especially with Leon's poor health and Ruth getting older. Further, they sold their little surplus produce under the price regulations, when others around them sold half of theirs on the black market, and so made lots of money. But not them. Even had they wanted to it would have been more dangerous for them as Jews, than for others. Y'see, one of the neighbours is land hungry and has been pestering them for years to sell out to him, and to encourage them to do so he has been very mean. Well, they got to where they were close to an agreement, then news of the system by which Jews were to be deprived of their property without compensation got about. The man came and told them he'd be better off waiting for the government to take the farm from them, as after that he knew the right people, and could get it for next to nothing. He knew it would be a gamble, but he was prepared to back his judgement, as the same sort of system had been in force in Germany for several years."

"I know. It's true. It happened to my family."

"Well, Ruth and Leon could not believe what the man was saying, even though they knew things are getting tougher for Jews all the time. He went away. The next day he returned. He then told them that he had been thinking things over, and decided to make an offer now, that would give them a little money which would be better than the nothing they would get later. However, he did not want to haggle about a deal, so the price he would offer would be his first and last. Then he made an offer which was so low Ruth and Leon were flabbergasted. They didn't answer him and he left.

"Later, they told my husband what had happened. They had nobody else to help them. The only people they know have enough trouble just keeping alive themselves. Samuel comforted them as best he could, and we prayed. They were very brave. When we last saw them they were still working it all out, and seemed to be coping well enough. Then we heard they had died. The police are satisfied they committed suicide."

Ana sobbed. She seized the hands of the other woman, crying: "Oh, how simply terrible. What did those lovely people do to deserve that? They were so good, so harmless. OK, OK, it was God's will."

"Yes, my dear, we must accept it was God's will. Nothing else makes sense."

"How long had they lived there?"

"Well, that's part of it. Leon was born there, actually in that little house. He never left except to go to the first war. And for Ruth, who was a farm girl before their marriage, the farm was her life; it

76

and Leon. They must have just decided they'd be better off dead. So we must think of them as being happier now in heaven than they were here on earth."

Ana thought, and said: "I'm sure you're right. You put it so well." Wiping her tears away she leaned over and kissed Simone on the cheek, whispering: "Thank you. And bless you." They sat quiet for a few moments. The children had been quiet but were becoming impatient.

Ana continued: "I must go now. Your husband said there was something for me to take."

"Yes, and it's rather big, even though I rolled it tightly. But it's light enough so I expect you can carry it alright. I've had it for too long, but I've been busy. Ruth said to tell you she burned the rest of it, and you would know what she meant." She left the room and returned with the parcel. It was a bundle rolled in hessian. Ana guessed at once what it contained, and decided not to talk about it. She took it and thanked Simone. Then just before leaving she asked: "May I meet the children?" The request surprised the hostess, but saying they would not look their best, she would be glad to oblige, and proceeded to call them in and introduce them. Ana looked them over carefully, and asked her hostess their ages and sizes. She congratulated her on the job she was doing with them. She then left quickly, as it was getting late in the afternoon, and it would take her a good two hours to get home.

Before moving on Manny rang Marta in Sète, and found that the boat had been at sea for a few days, but was expected back in port very soon. Assuming that Diego and Conchita would take on rescue work, it looked to him that Michel could be offered a berth in a week or so. There was nothing arranged at the Spanish end but that was much the same position that escapees over land found themselves in anyway, and yet many were said to successfully complete their journeys. With the extra knowledge of Spain that Diego and Conchita had, surely they also could succeed. They need aim no further than getting their man into the hands of the consulate in Barcelona. That, Manny understood, had been the first destination of other escapees.

He went on to Sète to wait for the boat. He met it and found both Diego and Conchita agreeable to delivering Michel. They took

Manny's advice and stipulated a fee, to be paid half up-front and half on completion. They were moderate as they wished to keep such French friends as they had, and maybe receive further work. Manny went by train to Marseille to ask Roger to sponsor Michel's escape on the boat. His organization had already managed Paul's return home, and quickly agreed. He was very interested in the boat experiment, and content to meet the fee asked for, and the terms of payment. He also assured Manny of payment, upon production of an account, for all the work done by the Mayers for the airmen. He supplied a neck brace for Michel to wear to indicate an injury, which might divert unwelcome interest in him by officials in their routine checks, some of which were organized, while others were made randomly. The hope was that an ordinary official conducting a routine inquiry or inspection would be disinclined to hurt an invalid, and so might accept Michel's speechlessness, though he should practice a polite and simple response such as: *'Merci beaucoup monsieur.'* If those words came out, only slowly and after great effort, perhaps the official would lose interest, and not even notice his accent.

Ana nervously escorted Michel from Lyon to Sète by train. She did not know whether to travel close, or to keep a distance in case he was caught, as there was no point in her being caught by chance at the same time. And, due to pressure of work and events, she did not yet have false papers for herself, and Jews always had to be careful and try to keep out of official sight because of the rigorous antisemitism of the Pétain regime. She had shut her mind to the risk of her being apprehended, and Michel not. The consequences for both then were imponderable, but all the same she was little concerned on her own account. She was a French Jew, not ordinarily at risk. She did not like to leave Michel alone, so sat in the same compartment keeping a separate profile. It did not matter. There were no checks.

She was surprised at the size and activity of the port of Sète. On locating the fishing boat wharves, she left Michel alone on a park seat making out he was reading a newspaper, and she went to find the *Santa Maria*, or Conchita. *"Conchita! La española. Si;"* said a woman she asked, putting aside the nets she was working on, and pointing down the wharf. Noting that the woman spoke in Spanish and knew Conchita as a Spaniard, Ana assumed she was not a danger to Conchita, and maybe a friend, and that perhaps fishers were a special community. As she approached the boat she saw a woman scraping potatoes on the foredeck, and so stood quietly on the wharf until their eyes met, then she smiled. Conchita had been expecting such a visitor, and the smile told her this was her, and she bounded off the boat to greet Ana with a bear hug. They went at once to the tiny cabin, where Diego, with grease on his face and a spanner in his hand, promptly joined them. He went into a pantomime to show he wanted to hug her, but was too dirty. His welcome was nonetheless warm and sincere. Ana explained what she was doing, and quickly excused herself to return to Michel in the park. Sitting next to him, she spoke slowly to make sure he understood her important message.

"I'm taking you to a boat. It will take you on to Spain. The crew don't speak English but you'll get along in French. They're completely trustworthy, but you must do exactly as they tell you at all times. Do you understand?"'

"Yes, thank you."

"Do you trust me?"

"Yes, indeed. Very much so."

"Right. Then tell me who the third parachute belonged to. Just a description, not a name."

Michel was astounded by the question. His eyes widened and he looked at Ana with a pained, almost angry expression, as if he had lost a secret, which of course he had. He reasoned to himself: 'She knows there was another person. How does she know? Why not ask before now? Oh, I see, we told her there were just the two of us, but she knows there were more: at least three. It's a sort of game. She's just catching up. OK, what's it matter? It can't hurt to tell her something.' He said: "Why do you want to know?"

"It's a matter of trust. You said you trusted me. Don't spoil it with nonsense. Just tell me."

The firmness of the reply caused Michel to think again. 'She really wants to know. If I don't tell her and she gets up and leaves me I'm done for. Tell her, quickly. Be nice too.' So he told her enough to account for the extra parachute, adding, while looking at Ana anxiously. "Is that what you want?"

"Yes. Thanks. That'll do. Are you curious about how I knew?"

"Yes, but I know I've no right to ask?'

"It's OK. Ruth rolled up the parachutes, and before she died gave them to the rabbi's wife for us. She wanted them off the farm, and knew we could make clothes from them. We found three in the bundle, which made us wonder. And, as you know, we made some pretty silk things for customers at home, and got old clothes from them in exchange, and converted them into things for the children, and took them and fitted them up. And, as we told you, they were so very pleased."

Michel smiled as he said: "Me too. And I'll tell everybody back home."

That night she Ana took him aboard the boat, where he was introduced to the cramped hiding place that would be home when the vessel was in port, and when there was any sort of danger. They discussed the plans.

Ana asked : "How will you deliver him?"

Conchita replied: "We're thinking of taking him to the door of the consulate, and watch that he introduces himself, and is taken inside. Then we come back."

"How will you get there."

"One of us - probably me - will get a taxi and take him. We'll make land fall close to Barcelona. Do you have any suggestions?"

"Only about taxis. Would you mind?"

"No, please say."

"Well, you know about Spain and I don't, but I wouldn't use the same taxi both ways. The driver would then know more than he should, and just might tell the police. If he, and they, were quick, who knows what could happen? So swap taxis. Also say you'll pay them well for a good ride and letting you be quiet. The less they learn the better.'"

"I see. What say I make out I'm a nurse, and the man is sick?"

"Great. Do you have a pistol?"

Diego spoke: "No, we think our knives are enough. They don't attract attention, like guns. But we could do with the address of the consulate, instead of relying on the taxi driver to find it. Do you have it?"

"No, and of course you must have it. It's a bad time because offices are closed. I could telephone home, but they don't have a

80

Spanish book. I can get it tomorrow, but you'll be at sea. I can only suggest you look it up in Spain." But Ana then feared that reading telephone books could be difficult, as she knew they were not skilled in reading.

Conchita said: "I know someone here who will have it, or will get it for us. Or else I will get it from someone there. It won't be a problem. Be sure we'll know exactly where to leave the taxi without the driver knowing what we're up to."

"Can I help you get it? I can run a message if you tell me what to do."

But neither Conchita nor Diego wanted Ana to be calling on Marta. One day, but not now. Diego said: "It's OK. We can manage. We'll have the address in good time one way or another. You've been very helpful."

So Ana said goodbye to the crew and Michel, and went on her way. She felt a little empty and cut off from the action after all the Mayer effort for Michel, but now he was out of their care and in good hands, so that was satisfying. Later she recalled she had meant to ask about Marta, as the crew also probably knew her, like Manny. But she could still ask him sometime.

After Ana had left Conchita hurried around to Marta's place in the hope of locating a Barcelona telephone directory. She was in luck. Marta wrote down the consulate's address, and nearby streets, without asking any questions. She hardly needed to, as she knew the boat was about to sail. She took it if she was not told anything it must be on account of serious, secret business.

The boat cast off at first light next morning. The sea was whipped up into medium size waves from a following wind making the boat pitch and roll uncomfortably for a new sailor, so as soon as he had emptied his stomach completely Michel lay down on a bunk, closed his eyes, and hoped for a better future. He wondered if he could ever get used to air heavily laced with fishing boat fumes. Through the nausea he was dimly aware of the pleasant swishing and creaking sounds as the boat pushed forward, but missed out on the crew catching their next fish meal with lines. He spent the day on the bunk, and slept soundly in the afternoon. When he woke up dusk was close, and so was the secret cove. He lay dozing, and recalled that Ana hadn't asked about the fourth man in the plane, so he supposed she was only interested in accounting for the parachutes. Interesting. Practical. The wind had abated, and the inshore waters of the Costa Brava were calm. Michel awoke with a new appetite for life, and for food.

The boat stood off the entrance to the cove while the crew took it in turns to scrutinise the rugged cliffs and shores in the vicinity of the cove. Seeing no signs of life, and knowing that nobody could enter at night, they reduced the sail and slowly moved through the calm waters of the cove until close to the shore, where they dropped anchor. Diego offered to take the others ashore in the dinghy, but they were content to stay on board. Conchita felt instant affection for the place, feeling it to be the headwaters from which her new life stream had flowed. With a light heart she prepared a fish meal while Diego and Michel drank wine, and took in the calm beauty of their surroundings.

Next morning, as the predawn twilight started its daily wrestle with the dark of the night, and wisps of mist joined in the aerial fray, the voyagers weighed anchor and sailed slowly seaward, now under steam, with Conchita lying in the bow to warn of submerged rocks, and push the boat away from danger with a long pole. Outside the cove they turned north, against Diego's every instinct to sail south, to home. But their destination was La Escala. Diego wanted to cover the short distance quickly so that Conchita and Michel could be on their way before people were up and about. Or people other than fishers, because he knew there would always be some activity among them, even pre-dawn. He knew there was a taxi service in the town, and neither resident civil guard nor police. He and Conchita had agreed that delivering Michel in daytime was the best course, as they did not know the office hours of the consulate. By now the passenger was enjoying his brief life at sea, even though he was not sure if he would like coffee with bread dipped in olive oil for breakfast regularly.

They berthed at a quiet jetty on the La Escala waterfront. Diego went at once to find a taxi, and was back with one shortly. A few minutes later Conchita and Michel walked the short distance along the wharf, entered the taxi, and departed. They would leave it in Gerona, and take a different one to Barcelona. When they left Diego stirred the furnace, cast off and steamed the short distance down to

Móntago, for a day at home. Then no trace of the visitors remained in La Escala.

Conchita's return plan was to swap taxis along the line, like going, and meet Diego at the La Escala jetty. The journey passed peacefully, and their shared relief, and buoyancy of success, caused them to relax, and stay on shore for a few drinks and a meal. Then they climbed into the dinghy to return to the Santa Maria at anchor, and on board the celebration continued. At first light their voyage back to France got under way: neither could think of it as going home. They would fish over the next two days and enter port with catch to sell. They did not know it at the time, but the success of the voyage was a milestone in their lives.

Back home Ana had commenced casual work in the large cellar of an unpretentious house at 6B rue des Chartreux, between the Saône and Rhône rivers. It housed a printery staffed by a handful of part time workers, forging identity and ration documents, and printing clandestine newssheets designed to help counter the relentless anti-British propaganda from German and Vichy media, and which was accepted by many Frenchmen for want of alternatives. It was important that news about Allied victories be spread, along with the ruthlessness of the Occupation, and the growth of resistance, as all helped sow seeds of doubt about Nazi worth and invincibility, and touched the chords of latent patriotism in ordinary French citizens, suppressed through the humbling of their nation, and the hardships of life. She also got a job as a seamstress in a local textile factory. She settled into a busy routine of work, some at home, where her family helped, as they all had time to spare because of the work restrictions on Jews.

15

For its clandestine travel - there was no other sort - between Britain and France SOE had complete control of only a very few small vessels, and some aircraft, and so often needed help from the Navy and the Air Force for transportation. Passenger comfort was not a feature of those craft, besides which the seas and skies around France were especially dangerous. All shore landings, and airplane drops of cargoes, were at night, until closer to D-Day when the shift in the balance of power toward the Allies allowed greater use of daylight. Weather was always a consideration, in both planning and execution, and because of its swings many a planned operation was suddenly postponed, or even abandoned. The presence, or absence, of clouds and moonlight had different consequences as between planes and boats. Apart from the navigational challenges of landing an aircraft in a dimly lighted, unknown paddock or rough airstrip at night, or a boat at a point on a strange beach in the dark, those arrivals were of intense interest to the Germans and the French police, who both put considerable effort into detection, even offering cash rewards for reports of suspicious lights and activities. So all trips were potentially hazardous and dangerous, not least for the local reception parties, for all captured personnel were dealt with sternly, and if they came into German hands, brutally. But the supplies were essential for the growth of French resistance to supplement the future major thrusts of the Allied regular forces, and commenced in a small way soon after France's capitulation, and grew steadily, to a crescendo around D-Day. It was as well that France was too big a country for the Germans to police completely, and many furtive arrivals went undetected. Whether the French police could have found and frustrated more than they did is not known, because a policeman could hardly be expected to own up to neglect of duty. Yet it is only reasonable to think of them being influenced by local community moods, and those were increasingly against Germany and Vichy as time passed, so likely the fatalities and disasters at SOE landings, tragically real and many, could have been worse. Widespread admiration of Germany, and disdain of Britain, gave way to resentment of the Occupation, along with other changes in attitude by many citizens as time went by. Slowly at first, and always certainly increasing; shame over France's jelly back acceptance of defeat, shame that Britain remained resolute without French help; resentment that under Pétain and cohorts the government of France seemed almost as much German as French, and shame that French civilisation and honour were being degraded. It was something against which some Frenchmen were prepared to act from the beginning, and their numbers grew. They included those at hand on the makeshift landing strips and deserted beaches in the middle of the night to receive cargoes of people and money and weapons and food sent from London, then distribute or hide them. And as more and more arms came into the hands of resisters, and they became more organised, numerous, confident, and active, French police acquired another disincentive to uncritical support of German and Vichy policies: the risk of being killed by maquisards or other resisters who, as planned by the Allies, slowly grew stronger by the month.

But that growth was in the future when, late on a dark night in November 1940, Neil Cameron landed on a quiet stretch of Mediterranean beach near Valras-Plage, from a dinghy of a very small British warship standing a little offshore. He thanked the naval rating who had carried him through the last little stretch to keep him dry. He stood, holding his suit case, watching the dinghy recede seaward into the dark, before turning to the track over the dunes that would lead to the road into town. He had chosen this spot as one he knew a little. He thought of his safe landing as a seed, from which a useful tree could grow.

For his new job Neil had been given a new persona by London, and like most SOE organisers, he had a cover job to enable freedom of movement. By contrast, WT operators moved less, and then mainly to relocate their transmission points, so as to mislead inquisitive Gestapo people. But they too used cover, and illness was a standard disguise, for it accounted for a person not getting out and about. Neil was a traveller in legal and medical publications for a real firm, well known in France, whose headquarters were in Switzerland. It actually distributed books and Neil was an actual employee. He knew little about the firm, but then he did not need to know either. It had an office in Vichy to use in his job, especially to pick up new legislation and regulations which he could take to customers on his rounds. It would also be a convenient way of keeping in better touch with what Vichy was doing, a matter of continuous importance to London, which took and sifted information from multiple sources.

When he knocked at the door of the bistro in the little port soon after midnight the proprietor was just closing up. Neil did not explain where he had come from, or what he was doing, but only that he needed a bed for the night, and he wondered if mine host could please recommend a place to go to. He was invited in. He wondered if the same man who had served the crew of the *Santa Maria* a year or so earlier would be on duty. Inside, in the light, they instantly recognised each other, with cries of 'Monsieur Neil' and 'Monsieur Jacques', as they embraced.

"Have a drink. What'll be? I've some special cognac that would go down well."

"Sounds great. How have you been? How's business? Things have changed since we met last time."

They saluted and grinned at each other as they sipped. Jacques pulled a face. He said: "Apart from being alive, everything's the shits now. Business is slack, and a man doesn't know who his friends are any more." He paused, looking at Neil, contemplatively. He asked: "But what about you. What a change! Last time you were a crewman and came and went on the sea. Tonight? You dress differently. You're alone. Excuse me if I ask a simple question. How did you get here?"

"Does it matter?"

Jacques scratched his head, and said:" "These are hard times, my friend. I have to know about you. Try to help me please."

Neil did not know the movements of the mother vessel after he was dropped, so he must keep news of it to himself. Yet he must help Jacques, and in doing so, himself also. He asked: "What do you know about me? Or at least, what do you think?"

"What do I know about you, apart from what I've said? Nothing. What do I think? I think that with a name like yours you may be English, even though you act and talk French. Now if the French in you is the main part, I'm puzzled at you being here at this time in this place. A man has to go out of his way to be here. It's a backwater since the war started. The main road doesn't even run through it any more. If though, the English in you is the main part, I would understand you better. Still puzzled, and very surprised, but a better understanding. Like I could believe you are here on a mission of some sort."

"Say that were so. Would you feel you had to report me to the police?"

Jacques laughed. "Me? Me report anyone? Now that shows how much you know of me. So we're both in the dark about each other."

86

"We were. Not now. You just brought the light."

The ice broken, they embraced. Jacques poured them another toast. Neil said: "Man, I was worried there for a bit."

"Me too. I wondered if someone was trying to trap me. But really I knew if they were, you wouldn't be part of it. I mean, last time I saw you and your mates you were Spanish soldiers. I couldn't believe you could change, and also become part of a trapping team here. It was all too odd. Actually, this is the funniest thing that's happened to me in a long time. Now, let's get to business. How can I help you?"

"OK. It's late and we need sleep. I think you can help me. I'm going to ask anyway. What I'd like to do though is to tell you some essentials and see if we can talk again in the morning. Would that suit you?"

"Sure. Sounds good. Go ahead. Another drink?"

Neil nodded and pushed his glass over. There were times for celebration, and this was one. He said: "I've come, alone, for my government. It's going to organise resistance to *les boches*. I'm here to help prepare France for when there is an invasion by the Allies to kick them out. It's a long way off but we have to believe it will happen. I have to organise French people. Not only me, for there are others going in all over France. I need to put together helpers who will feel part of my small team. It's a very serious business, and we must be careful at every point, because we know what the Nazis are like. My people believe that the whole plan will reduce the French casualties that would otherwise occur. If it's alright by you we can leave the rest for the morning. But let me finish with this warning. Secrecy is essential. Without it we all get caught and they kill us. If we are to talk tomorrow it will be on the basis that we both understand this secrecy bit."

"I see. You have to believe I'm in shock. I know what you're asking me and I want to help, it's just that I need to have a long talk with myself to make sure I'm up to it. So sure, let's sleep on it."

"Can I get a room for the night?"

"I reckon so. The best place will be my sister's. She has rooms, and I know she has space at present. Also, it will be a safe place for someone your size. If you're ready we can go now. I'll ask you tomorrow how you got here, but I think if I looked I'd see some sand on the bottom of your case."

Neil looked, then laughed, exclaiming: "Ha! That's a useful lesson."

His first task in France was to start collecting locals into small resistance cells, all part of his group, to be trained and, if necessary, paid by SOE. With more staff he could take on more work, but size was not as important as security. During training he had had that drummed into him, and he felt he learned better because of his father who, as his wife and his son believed, worked in secret intelligence. And Neil's group could not function without trustworthy, fired-up people, and could only do what they were capable of, individually and collectively. Actually Valras-Plage was outside the territory he had agreed upon with London for his efforts, but it would certainly be within the area of another group, and that matter would be sorted in time. In any case Jacques was set to be Neil's first sub-agent, which was a milestone for the new organiser.

Neil brought to his SOE role the aim for his group members to resist everything that was part of the German war effort, and support that of the Allies, especially by sabotage and, one day, by armed insurrection. Like others throughout France their activities would, whenever possible, be filtered and coordinated through London, for which purpose a means of prompt and frequent communication, supplementing visits and coded mail, was therefore essential. For Neil's group it came, substantially, within the fortnight after his evening with Jacques, in the form of a WT operator, called Santo, who was equipped with a shortwave morse transceiver, which weighed about 12 kilograms, and was portable in a small suitcase of standard appearance. Its frequency range was quite wide, but the signal was not, so optimum transmission conditions would be needed at all times. The set came with a long aerial cable desirably laid outdoors, and moved frequently, always placing it as far as possible away from unfriendly eyes. His favourite places, for secrecy and also for enhanced transmissions and receptions, would be in the countryside. And he would add to the security of his fellow workers by brevity in transmissions, and changes in frequencies and transmitting times. All messages would be in code, incidentally disguising the names of personnel being referred to, the better to prevent repercussions for family members of a captured member, as the Gestapo's reach knew no limits. Neil's disguise included a pseudonym, Pasteur, by which he would be known within SOE, and by members of his group, which was to be identified by the name of Silence.

Slackness in the work load was not good for agents. When spare time was linked to the restricted social contact that was part of SOE service, boredom and loneliness were close behind. Restlessness might follow, in turn leading to indiscretions, and exposure to enemy attention, initially through spies and agents, official and otherwise, who abounded throughout France, and in the occupied zone especially. So wise members of groups kept quiet and kept to themselves. At least Neil would not be troubled by any looseness on Santo's part, as he liked writing, and was content with solitude.

The Silence territory was Lyon and environs, without precise boundaries. Group organisers were given programs for some targets, and used their initiative for others. The first challenge was to set up a tight, secure and effective team, looking for quality more than numbers, the better to plan ahead. Finding helpers was a function of organisers like Neil, and group members were also clever scouts for new recruits. Some recruits found in the field proved so able they were sent to England for the extensive training available there. SOE personnel were not necessarily members of the armed services, and their range of vocations and prior experience affirmed that SOE was a separate service, and not a shadow of any other.

Neil lived like any other young business man, but without making close social contacts, on the grounds that a veneer could be cracked by an inquisitive intimate. He needed his old friends though. First he called on the Mayers. He already knew that Manny had given up his crew position to Conchita, and was told he was back at war somewhere, and that Diego and Conchita were presumed to be fishing. He did not disclose anything about his reasons for being in France, nor did the Mayers inquire. They insisted he stay with them for a while, and he gladly accepted while settling into his own flat. He learned, with admiration and astonishment, they had harboured the airmen, and of Michel's passage to Barcelona by boat; although nothing had been heard since. He had looked forward to renewing acquaintance with Ana, but was not prepared for the impact she would have on him. He remembered her as a rather serious looking girl with luminous brown eyes, and brown hair. Now he noticed that her expression was frequently relieved by smiles, made the more pleasant by a wide mouth and white, even teeth. But above all her eyes displayed attentiveness and calmness that he had not taken in previously; it was as if his own eyes had been partly closed on their previous meeting. Fascinated, he found himself inclined to stare at her, even when he knew he should not. She caught him at it at times and was a little embarrassed, as he could tell from her blushes. But they did not indicate resentment.

Neil checked over the Mayers in his mind to see who among them he might approach for his circuit. Taking everything into account, including command of French, and accent, and SOE's policy not to employ females in the field in France, only Manny would do, and he would do very well indeed, if only Neil could find and enlist him.

Since Neil's first visit all the Mayers had changed to standard French dress styles, and so were saved from special attention when in public. It was clear they - and Ana in particular - had also compromised traditional Jewish habits, in order to appear non-Jewish French as possible but, unlike Manny, they had not turned their backs on their faith. Ana readily passed as an ordinary, short, and sturdy young French woman. If she looked a little serious it was in keeping with the looks worn by many other French citizens besides, for those were serious times.

Part of Neil's plan was to look up Frenchmen in the Lyon district who had served in his battalion in Spain. All were ideologically Leftist, and some actual members of parties of one or another name. He had an important calling card: he had been in Spain with them. He would find the leaders and talk with them. The help he needed would be of more use if driven by a hatred of fascism, which had characterised their presence in Spain. He knew the difficulty of the Germans and the Russians being together in a pact would make some communists aloof, for the French communists generally followed Moscow in their thinking and loyalties. But maybe not all would turn him down, and there were still those who were not communists, and to whom the pact would mean nothing.

16

Although keen to have Diego in the Silence group, Neil was puzzled by the boat. His brief did not take in a boat and its crew, but he saw it as a unique opportunity, which he would grasp, and leave the details for London to sort out. He went to Sète and found the Spanish couple, somewhat transformed from the pair he had last seen some twenty months earlier. After a little time with Conchita he thought: 'She's a different person. Alert, confident, content, and clearly a fisher through and through, she's very much at home on the boat and the sea. Both the boat and Diego are cleaner and brighter looking than before. These are fine people for SOE. They know how to handle trouble. They know what secrecy is. I wonder if their refugee status would be a sticking point with London. They might be wanted in Spain because of the wide-sweeping Law of Responsibilities passed by the Franco regime in February 1939, making criminals out of many republicans. Would that be a stumbling block? It shouldn't be. They're not going to work in Spain. And after all, Spain calls itself neutral, though good friends with the other dictators. And since the war started Britain's foreign policies are more positive and more democratic than its appeasements of the 1930s. Surely London will see their value. If the fishers show interest in joining Silence I'll push hard. Sure, they're French is pretty weak, but they'll not pretend to be anything more than Spanish refugees, fishers. There's no reason for France to lock them up, because it's showing signs of releasing Spaniards where it can. And their work is needed. If they're willing I'll put their names in.'

It was already clear from the voyage with Michel that the *Santa Maria* and its crew boat had potential for clandestine marine action. But Neil was obliged to sound out Conchita for her loyalties and discretion. He already knew her background from Diego, although he could not let on to her, and she must tell him herself. As he expected, she hated Germans and Vichyites as fascists, blamed the Nazis for Franco winning the civil war, and disliked the France that placed Spanish republican refugees in primitive concentration camps and treated them as enemies. Her story fitted what he knew.

He apologised for having to tell her the work ahead would be of the most secret nature, where any slip could seriously endanger not only her, but associates besides. He was glad he had apologised first, as he was sure from her looks she might otherwise have blasted him for lack of tact and trust. He was satisfied, and even more eager to enlist the pair and their boat. He undertook to contact them again, soon, more definitely, after discussion with his bosses. He hoped SOE, or a spy service, would see uses for them in coastal surveillance, and in smuggling people and equipment, possibly from a larger vessel standing offshore. If so, the work would be spasmodic, well paid, and sometimes dangerous. Diego thought a false internal hull could be added, in which to hide passengers temporarily, but getting the work done would not be easy. Surveillance should be possible, if the means for reporting could be set up. If the boat was required to watch close inshore, with slow movement, they would have to adapt fishing effort accordingly, which could mean pretend fishing, because the fish mightn't be there, so no fish, no money, and then then they would need compensation. Neil already knew that SOE paid well for services rendered, and that the last thing it wanted was arguments about money in the middle of a war. He assured his friends of proper remuneration. They made a verbal agreement, subject only to HQ approval, and to Diego talking things over with Manny, who had an interest in the boat.

Neil now had to locate him. As a French soldier with frontline experience and knowledge of weapons and explosives, he would be another excellent addition to the Silence group; but how to find him? He went to see Marta to explain his position. Three days later, when he rang her as arranged, she said Manny would be home the next day and would await a visit. They met in a park near Manny's flat, the same park in which the siblings would meet another time. Neil put to him the same general proposal as he had made to the fishers, but with heavy emphasis on a prospective role as a weaponry and explosives instructor for resisters who would, one day, take up arms to help liberate France. Manny's position was complicated by his current attachment to Roger's secret group, who had treated him well, and were expert in style. In addition, Neil's offer sounded conditional on London's approval, and Manny felt that if he were to move from Roger he should do so at once, or not at all. Neil cursed his luck in meeting this problem. He reflected on it: 'It's not for me to tell him he's wrong in that thinking, because I'm not sure it is, and it wouldn't help matters anyway. What are the chances of London declining him? I know I must get their approval for an important appointment, and I don't like going against their rules when I'm so new, but I don't believe SOE, or my group, can afford to pass on him, and if I'm to be trusted as an organiser whose job includes recruiting, it's reasonable that I put him on, and that London accept that. If he were to seem unsuitable during training, then of course he would be for the chop, just like any other candidate. But I'd better not tell him that, in case he jibs. But how could he be knocked back? Will him being Jewish be a problem? Not a bit of it. He's probably broken some of the anti-Jewish laws, like most Jews, but that's not an area of SOE concern. He's an illegal for deserting from the labour battalion. Is there a real risk of detection? Or are there just too many deserters from various forces all over France to be concerned on that score. Being wanted by the enemy is not a barrier surely. We're all wanted. But with a new name and identity won't those objections dissolve? SOE could make him into a non-Jewish Frenchman. But say they lost their brain in London and rejected him. Would Diego stay? I'd better make him an unconditional offer, as if I were Mr Churchill himself.'

He engaged Manny with his eyes, and his hand on his arm, saying: "Manny, my friend, I have authority to make appointments, and I'm a little nervous when I'm so new. But if I waited ten years I couldn't do better than go ahead now, and ask you to join me in SOE, with immediate effect. It's an unconditional offer. I hope you'll accept, for there's nobody I'd rather work with. But even more important is the special help you can be for me. You know your way around Lyon, you know people, you know where the important places are, some of which we'll attack one day. And above all, you know from your school days and from your socialist connections some of the brigaders we knew in Spain. We need to bring some of them into SOE and resistance, and it's going to be easier for you to flush them out than for me. It's one thing to have fought with them, as we both did, but another to have grown up with them. Even if they won't help they won't turn you in. Not you, and probably not me, but the chances are better with you. The first contacts are most important. You can't ask men to join something without telling them what it's all about. So we should only ask reliable men, whether or not they accept. Their selection is a vital thing, and maybe I can do it alone, and maybe not. With you I can."

Manny saw Neil's difficulty. He was embarrassed about the competing positions, but supposed and hoped Roger would understand he could not refuse Neil. He faced him, saying: "You're convincing, and put things well. I want to help you. Of course I do. You say I know my way around the place and know people, but does that also mean I'm more likely to be picked out and betrayed and arrested? For me to really help you I must live locally, and that brings closer the day when I'm recognised and targeted. I can handle that risk for myself, but what does it do for you and other people in your group? What do you say?"

Neil didn't know what to say. He had to think first. He answered: "Before I answer there's another point to cover. You may not know, but I resigned from the Communist Party .... " Manny broke in with: "No! You weren't too happy with them in Spain, and you weren't the only one, but to resign! And you're still alive too! When? And what did they do?" Neil answered: "The tipping point came with the Pact. I was disgusted. I resigned at once. Carefully, of course. No big speeches, or moral rantings. Very simple. 'Count me out'. I've heard not a word since. The war came immediately so they must have had other things to handle – maybe the timing saved me. It certainly was timely for me going to enlist in the army, and to be able to say I was out. That stuff doesn't worry me in looking for help here, but you would have an easier way in sometimes, which could make the result better."

Manny nodded. "That's interesting. Now I've some news for you. Some of those guys, including commies, are my mates. We socialise, drink together. Go to the football. Muck around. I would bet my life if someone I asked turned me down, he wouldn't squeal. Not if he valued his own life."

Neil continued: "As I thought. Y'know, I could speculate about this profile thing but really I don't know what to say. Maybe though London will, because what we're talking about is not new and they can assess it and tell us how to counter it. For the moment though go back to the time we were teaching Diego not to be Spanish." Manny interrupted, laughing: "Now that was a real challenge. If you could do that, you can do me without much trouble! Sorry. Keep on."

"Well, all I'm thinking is disguise, or anything that gives a person a different look. Can we try it this way? You come in, on the condition that this identity thing is sorted out to your satisfaction. Remember, it's not only your skin being protected here, so HQ will be concerned to see the best result. From my experience during training every problem that is new to people like us has been seen and dealt with back there, and the aim of training is to produce an agent who is going to be effective. Let me come at it another way. Frankly, I'll be lost without you. Stay with me until I get off the ground. Stay with SOE even if they tell you to relocate. I know you won't get a swelled head when I say this, but I must say it, because it's so true, and so important: I need Manny Mayer."

At this Manny looked Neil in the eyes, and said: "Count me in. I understand. We understand. I'll drop Roger and I expect he'll understand; sure hope so. Let's shake on it while we're in the mood." They embraced, and shook hands. Neil thought as they parted: 'Who is Roger. Who is it behind him?'

And that was how the Silence circuit got off to a brilliant start. Neil reported on his actions to his commander, through Santo. About Manny there was no hesitation. He would be invited to England for training as an instructor promptly. In time there would be a supply of resisters for him to teach. They would include men who had some military training under France's longstanding conscription system, but they would need to be trained to use British weapons when the time came. They would also require training as saboteurs, in guerrilla warfare, and in the use of the new plastic explosives. Neil was congratulated on finding him. They would disguise him. But there was a snag about the Spaniards, arising from the military aspirations of a group of Spanish republicans in France. They wished to attack Spain, a treasured notion of loyal republicans, but Britain could not afford to fall out with Franco at that time, when he was postulating that Germans might cross Spain to seize Gibraltar, or that Spain might join the Axis powers in the war. Republicans did in fact make an unsuccessful thrust into northern Spain, at the Val d'Arran, but Britain had not supported it. These activities made Britain occasionally nervous, a condition that affected SOE's consideration of the *Santa Maria* and its crew for a short time, but in the end had no impact on the decision that they were very welcome. Neil had pointed out that the boat was French, and the nationality of the crew from to time should be of little concern to London, especially as he would be at hand. There was a place for another marine entry and escape line to supplement the existing air, land and sea lines. And the Allies not only had an insatiable need for all types of information about the enemy, and life and activity in and around the territory it occupied, but coastal surveillance craft were rare, and one with a hardened crew was of particular interest, not as much to SOE as to the Secret Intelligence Service. The risks about Franco in this instance were therefore far outweighed by the potential benefits to the Allies. The decision was the easier for SOE because it had a freer hand in sea matters in the Mediterranean than along the Atlantic and Channel coasts where, in the interests of overall strategy, the British Admiralty exercised tight control over seaborne ventures. For the time being at least there were no Mediterranean naval activities with which the proposed work of the *Santa Maria* could be in conflict. The dual nationality of registration was a useful feature for a vessel that could be in the territorial waters of both France and Spain at different times. While the delay in considering these matters bothered Neil, he was glad to know they had no impact on the crew, who had no idea of time in such a matter, and were not in the least put out.

Manny was soon in England for a few weeks of intensive training at the range of specialised schools run by SOE, not only for France, but also the other countries where it worked. He was more advanced at the start than most others because of his experience as a frontline soldier, in two wars, in Spain and in France, he was French, and had practical experience in courier work for Roger, and in avoiding trouble within France. This compared with some trainees who were civilians. His training concentrated on the use of explosives, weapons, combat tactics, sabotage, and the training of resisters in weaponry and guerrilla tactics. Helping Neil for a time was to be his first purpose on taking up duties. They had in mind he would soon turn to training resisters in guerrilla warfare, which would take him away from the city a lot of the time, and then they provided him with tips and gear for disguise when needed.

Neil's immediate further targets were ten men to be sub-agents, each to lead a cell in the Silence group, and each to build up his cell to ten reliable men sharing a passion for undermining both the Occupation and the Vichy regime. Neil particularly looked for men with experience as Brigade fighters, as railwaymen (called *cheminots*), as canal workers, as telephone technicians, or as trade union leaders, as having future value. But not only them, for he knew leadership came in many different cloaks. Given the right men, plans they were capable of implementing could be made, and the necessary weapons and equipment and money, over and above the substantial funds Neil had been entrusted with, sought from London.

The nucleus of sub-agents established, Neil worked out with them an overall plan for sabotaging railways, rolling stock, canal locks, barges, bridges, electricity substations, factories making German war gear, and telephone lines in the Lyon district. The aim was to disrupt or destroy selected local targets near Lyon when the time came, and to hit some early for practice, and to train the saboteurs. And setting up fighting cells, to be trained in guerrilla warfare and the use of appropriate weapons, was also important from the start. He knew many of the Silence men were by nature belligerent, and he did his best to curb the urge for immediate action, while allowing there had to be some from time to time for experience, and to make the training seem worthwhile. One problem about precipitate action was that the Germans inflicted savage reprisals randomly, on the assumption that as the culprits could not be caught, the local community that housed them should pay. Yet attacks had to happen, or the German war machine would not be slowed, or its soldiers know fear in France.

Later, short of workers at home, the Germans would persuade France to swap French POWs for French male and female civilians to take jobs in Germany. It started as a voluntary scheme, and when it failed expectations in 1942, Germany applied pressure on Vichy, which then introduced compulsory labour in Germany for large numbers of workers in several categories. But great numbers of those chosen made themselves scarce, aided by French sympathisers. Many took to the bush, and hills, and forests, of which there was much, particularly in the central and southern districts, and where it was hard for hunters to find them. They also became available to join bands intending to fight the Germans sooner or later, as soon as they were trained and armed, and the time ripe. They acquired leaders, from several sources; natural selection, SOE, refugees from fascism such as former brigaders from Spain, and from the tightly organised communist party. As with all bodies of human beings a pattern of order was required, and it evolved in the bands, or at least in those that survived. It was these men that SOE instructors such as Manny would teach to become guerrilla fighters, to kill the enemy and survive, and to damage the things it needed for efficiency and smooth movement. They were called maquisards, as belonging to the bush, or *maquis*. They were frequently on the run from one or other enemy group, and as great harm came with capture, they quickly learned the worth of secrecy and discipline. SOE supplies, training, and money, helped them survive with a purpose. When D-Day came the maquisards were not the only French resisters to emerge with gun in hand and hate in heart and sabotage in mind, though a significant proportion of the total.

But back in early 1941, Neil was content with the way the Silence group was taking shape.

17

The Pyrénées route out of France had ample hazards. If an escapee fell into the hands of a rogue smuggler he was in danger. Physical strength and stamina would be fully tested on the way, as in any weather the terrain was rough, and travellers were very heavily clothed, and few had enough reserves to assist laggards. In winter there was ice, snow, rain, and intense cold, which only the strong and clever could manage. Language was a frequent problem, so body language was heavily used. A sea line for smuggling munitions, and even people, had appeal for SOE. It would suit all if Diego would work for SOE on demand, leaving him free to take on other jobs that might come along.

Secret escape lines, of which several existed, might be customers, depending on weather and traffic loads, even though the land route was something more readily understood by many escapees, and their minders. Similarly with surveillance activity: it would have to be arranged in London so that instructions would come from SOE to Neil, and results returned in the same way. Those arrangements would be hidden from the crew, who would only know they were working for Neil. Soon they were given false French identity and ration cards, which were not necessarily a waste of effort, as many random checks consisted only of a request to produce a card, a quick look at it, and the affair was over, often without any need for the targeted person to say one French word, but if questions had to be answered by voice the game might be up. Arrest would probably follow, with consequences that varied with the current rules which changed from time to time, and luck. Refugee Spaniards might be pressured to go home, or arrested and interned, depending on French political nuances and manpower needs at the time.

SOE left in Neil's hands the details of the deal about the boat and its crew. SOE groups being the personal creations of their organisers, and their daily responsibility, there was no other way. They had to find within France trustworthy sub-agents to join and contribute to the effort that SOE wanted from the group. While the broad aims of sabotage, and preparing resistance bands, were constant, the circumstances of the growth of all groups and their activities varied greatly, so no single template applied. Many groups managed to succeed and produce useful results, while others fell by the wayside due to several causes, not least human error, a term that included betrayal. As the risks of infiltration of groups and denunciation of agents were ever present, it was wise to impress on all members of each cell the purpose of and need for security, and this was something ceaselessly in Neil's mind. He would spare no effort to that end. It became his obsession.

France's harsh treatment of the refugees and others it classified as undesirables ran through several regimes. First, the government of the Third Republic until its defeat in June 1940; then that of Vichy that came in its place, and which itself had shifts in attitude, some of its own making, others largely forced upon it by Germany, but for the worse always, until its inglorious life ended with the liberation of France; and harshest of all, the German control which spread territorially and in rigour during the Occupation. Those regimes savaged those who at one time or another they classified as undesirables: Spanish republicans, resisters, Jews, political activists forced out of their own totalitarian countries, freemasons, homosexuals, gypsies and communists. The *camps des concentrations* used by France for their internment or imprisonment from early 1939 were unfortunately of a low to extremely low standard, and blighted its sometime reputation as a compassionate carer for refugees. The vigour of the hunt for undesirables varied with the times, while consistently mean. Inhumanity toward prisoners was common to most camps, to a level as low as those of the Nazis, except that the French did not actually kill their prisoners as a routine matter, unless allowing people to die from neglect, or deliver them in sealed railway cars into German hands, was to kill. As the war developed the intensity of persecution against the Spaniards waned, while increasing toward the Jews.

A change of identity not only hid Manny Mayer, former French soldier, Jew and labour battalion deserter, but also had the effect of heading off any possible impact on him of Vichy's developing policy of excluding Jews from the economic life of France. This, a copy of a like policy in Germany, and there called aryanisation, a form of official theft, would be authorised in the unoccupied zone by a Vichy law in July 1942, following an earlier regulation affecting the occupied zone. Compulsory transfer of Jewish businesses and other property in France to non-Jewish ownership was the intent with no, or only trifling, compensation. But the *Santa Maria* was never listed as a French business owned by a French Jew, for Manfred Mayer had never registered as a Jewish property owner. And by the transfer to Marc Mattisse it was out of the reach of aryanisation.

SOE wanted a two-passenger capacity for the boat, allowing for one possibly disabled. It would need a refit to be suitable, and this at SOE's expense. It was quickly learned that the materials needed were in short supply, and that some of the work would be too private for any but the most discreet shipyard, and require special expertise. Besides, there was the problem of basing Diego and Conchita ashore during a refit, for both were fugitives in both France and Spain.

Part of the plan was to relocate the home port to Valras-Plage, because the refitted boat might attract interest in Sète, when the aim of all was the opposite. And the smaller port, near uninhabited dunes, would fit in as well, or even better, for smuggling, the land end of which Jacques was ready to handle. There were though, several points of quiet coast between the mouth of the Rhône River and the Spanish border to choose from. A particular task of the boat would be to land cargo from a larger vessel standing out to sea. But first it became clear that refitting could not be undertaken promptly, if at all, in French or Spanish shipyards, and Diego was advised a different venue for the work, and for instruction of the crew in their new range of tasks, was being sought.

The naval shipyard at Gibraltar was chosen. It would be a very long voyage, and a challenge for both boat and crew, but the location was not unexpected, so they were ready. Thinking of the refitting work, Diego and Conchita suggested to Neil that Manny, the woodworker, should go along with them. Neil, not wanting him out of circulation for the several weeks that would be needed, agreed reluctantly, swayed by Manny being a part owner. But when he was approached, Manny requested Conchita to stand aside as crew, as he feared their mutual friendship might not survive the long voyage on a small boat. She was disappointed, and resisted the change, but Manny persisted, politely. Diego was keen to humour both, and yet needed him more than her in Gibraltar, and came up with a compromise plan, saying: "We should contact the consulate in Barcelona so that when we bring someone another time they'll know who we are and won't keep us waiting outside where the police might pick us up. That needs talking about on the spot. So say we drop Conchita at Móntago where she can meet my parents, and go on down to Barcelona when it suits her, and we can pick her up on the way back."

This was seen by all as a practical solution, although disappointment remained for Conchita. However, to stay in France on her own, an unattached Spanish republican, and an escapee from French custody to boot, would be unwise. Meeting Diego's family and the villagers was not such a bad idea considering that one day she and Diego might return there to live. And making the Barcelona contact would be a challenge.

18

The *Santa Maria*, under French markings, steamed out of Sète harbour as pre-dawn twilight gently pushed aside the clasp of night, to reveal a sea that was also a mirror, and on which the ancient boat was the sole voyager. Landward, occasional little spots of light in the gloom were the only signs of port and coastline. Seaward, as the light spread, the mirror extended, as if to the horizons. Light rays reached up from the east in advance of the sun, their feathery touch extinguishing the twinkle of the stars, and dimming the moon. Seeing nature at work entranced the crew, who felt they were alone on a calm and private lake. Then, as the golden sun rose through the dark blue of the horizon, the few wisps of morning mist were dissolved, and a gentle offshore breeze, being the cool air from land flowing seaward to take the place of the ascending sea air as it warmed, bore down upon the mirror, breaking it into tiny ripples, soon to grow larger, intending to become the small waves that were as much a part of the water as the mirror had been. Nature was starting another day's work at sea.

Half an hour into their voyage the breeze was strong enough to unfurl the patched triangular canvas which was the boat's single sail. The crew continually moved its heavy boom to catch the best winds. The present following wind had originated in the French hinterland. Should it continue strong, and breezes from the Pyrénées added, the boat would have used little fuel on arrival at Móntago, but they would still try to take on more there, in the hope of sailing straight through without making port again. With fair sailing the 650 nautical miles to Gibraltar could be covered within five days. The first leg, was completed as dusk was closing in. The next would be started early the next morning.

Disembarking at Móntago, Conchita put on a brave face and resolved to make good friends with Diego's family. She expected questions about her antecedents, and particular curiousity about a woman being crew aboard a fishing boat, something unheard of on the Costa Brava, where by superstition a woman on board would drive away the fish on which life depended. She supposed the locals would have but little idea about conditions in France, and no means of checking anything she might say. "Expect an old fashioned place with its own customs," Diego had said: "My family will be friendly in a suspicious way, but that's just how my people are. Keep in mind they haven't travelled. Their world starts and finishes in Móntago. Don't expect more of them than they're able to give. They run the place in a cooperative way a bit like the anarchist communities you saw in Aragon, and which the communists destroyed. They may not tell you, but the village isn't pro-Franco, nor are many people along the coast, as the fascists bombed us to frighten the Republic into surrendering, like they bombed Guernica. The worst raids were on Barcelona, where thousands of people died. Móntago was hit too, and a few people killed. The others don't forget. People will stare, because few outside women come, and even more so if they think you were a soldier. You'd better not let on to anybody you carried a gun, as that's the sort of stuff to make the authorities more interested if they came to hear of you. The best thing is to tell my mother you were a soldier because she'll get it out of you anyway. Then leave it to her to work out a story for the others. She knows how to do that."

During the brief stopover Diego told Eduardo and Alicia, his parents, about Conchita, omitting the parts about sexual harassment of vulnerable females by *macho* Spanish soldiers, arrogant French camp guards, and proprietorial French farmers. And the pressures that could force females into prostitution. Those matters need not be known to the fisher folk, who would like as not attribute fault to the victim, even if they tried not to. Conchita's had been such a different world from that of the pueblo women. It would be better if the difference was noted without trying to reconcile the two, or judge the one by the standards of the other. The rest of her life was interesting enough without the detail that could cause harm if known, without any prospect of good. That Alicia might guess bits were left out was certain, but so long as Diego and Conchita kept their mouths shut she need never actually know.

When it came to disclosing that both were working for somebody mysterious, Eduardo broke in: "I won't ask who you work for, but I must know that it's neither Hitler nor Mussolini."

"No, I don't, we don't. And please don't talk about Conchita having been a soldier. You could say she came north as a civilian to find her husband, not knowing he was dead, and got caught up in the rush to France to avoid the fascists. For all we know the fascists are still looking for people like us."

Eduardo continued: "What's Neil doing these days?"

"I'm not allowed to say. But I see him sometimes and he's well."

The parents drew their own sensible conclusions from that and were content. Neither needed reminding of Franco's wish to capture former republican soldiers, nor of the interest that the civil guard could take in people suspected of harbouring fugitives. Nor did they need reminding of the Spanish dictator's connection with the German air force during the civil war, and his later support of the German army through the so-called Blue Division sent by Spain to fight for the Nazis against the Allies.

Diego continued: "Conchita has some business to do in Barcelona and would like your help, mamá. She has no papers that would pass, and the police wouldn't be interested in her if she was with you, going to market if you like. Conchita will act like a sick one if you're stopped. But if it would worry you she'll go alone. She's done it before, but it's better with cover."

Alicia replied: "I'll take her."

After Móntago the voyagers kept close to the three mile limit off the Spanish coast so to be able to claim the protection of Spain's territorial waters if a German or Italian foreign warship should approach, and kept ready to run up the Spanish flag to bolster the proposition. And, flagless, they would claim to be in the international waters of the high seas, and so beyond the Spain's jurisdiction, should it be a Spanish warship. Diego knew the ploy might fail, if things became serious, but he had to try. The western Mediterranean Sea was a war zone in which the Italians for long rivalled the Royal Navy, both powers using surface craft of all sizes, and submarines. The Germans contributed from time to time, at differing levels of intensity, through the Luftwaffe, U-boats transferred from the North Sea area and, later, patrol and torpedo boats including those called E-boats. Until the British got on top in that theatre from late 1942 onward, British and neutral shipping was at constant risk of attack. Traffic between The Rock and France was muted in 1940 and into 1941, but as the seas became safer and, at the same time, demand grew in France for materials including weaponry and explosives, and for infiltration of instructors and other resistance figures, more runs were needed. On this particular voyage there were no encounters, until entering the Strait of Gibraltar, while riding the high swell formed from the clash of the outgoing flow from the Mediterranean with the inflow from the Atlantic. There the *Santa Maria* was challenged by a small British warship. As best they could, in both French and Spanish, the crew explained their destination, adding they were to meet a Captain Ramsay of army intelligence on their arrival in Gibraltar Harbour. But their story was treated suspiciously, maybe in part because of an acute communication problem. In the end the skipper of the warship sent a small, armed boarding party to search, and stay aboard while the warship lead the way into harbour. The Rock lay ahead to starboard, an impressive, exciting spectacle, and clearly strategic, for Africa was visible on their port side. The sight signalled not only the successful end of their voyage, but their entry into British territory where fascism, Germans, Vichy police and the Spanish civil guard had no place. Both felt lighter in spirit as they recognised all life need not be lived in a nest of vipers as had been their fate for the past few years. It was not something to talk about, or explain, but only to be glad about, while treasuring the feeling that one day they would live where freedom and fairness were normal. It was only when they turned north to Gibraltar's harbour in Algeciras Bay that they began to truly feel there was another dimension to the war. Ahead, the naval panorama of the large harbour unfolded. It was home to scores of warships at moorings and berths right around; in addition to many merchant vessels which the visitors later learned were forming into a large convoy to proceed, escorted, into the Atlantic, then to double back to Scotland, so avoiding the most powerful parts of the German naval blockade of Britain, and there to land valuable supplies. The visitors had not thought there could be so many ships almost in the whole world, let alone in the one harbour, flying so many different flags, not least among them being those of Britain and Free France. It was an enormously encouraging sight for men whose daily lives were clouded by the success and domination of the Germans and their associates in the Vichy puppet government. Their hearts swelled with joy and hope, for here was evidence of the forces the Axis would have to conquer if it were to dominate Europe. But even so, the struggle clearly remained, for several vessels bore the scars of serious battle. And that the Rock was in a war zone appeared from bomb damage, the result of occasional futile aerial attacks by Axis planes, none of which disabled any of harbour, airfield or human spirit that together were its essence.

The fishing boat was directed to a mooring, and soon their contact came. Satisfied about their bona fides, he welcomed and assured them of all possible assistance. Their boat was allowed to tie up later at a wharf next to damaged warships, and its crew were given good quarters ashore in naval barracks. They were given the standard warnings about behaviour as for all visitors to the port, it being a politically sensitive spot on the Spanish land mass and over which Spain wished to assert sovereignty. While they appreciated the Spanish wines and beer and food, they avoided the Main Street prostitutes, in Diego's case because Conchita was the only female he had room for in his life, and in Manny's case because he was cranky about having once been infected with the pox in Barcelona, the treatment for which in pre-penicillin days left painful memories for countless victims.

The Rock, whose strategic value was well understood, was on permanent war footing, and its people were concerned that Spain might join the Axis, to be followed by an invasion which the British just might not repel given the pressures it faced on other fronts; for those were the days before America's entry into the war, and although Russia had been drawn in, it was embattled with an unknown future.

The visitors were impressed by the naval dockyard at work, but there was little time for gaping. Their main link became Placido Rodrigo, a shipwright who, with many other Spanish workers, came in daily, and were trusted, at least while the two countries were at peace and the Spaniards needed the work. He was to supervise the refit. The plan was to build a false, hidden inner hull for hiding either people, or stores, such as weapons and ammunition. It was work that intrigued Manny, and in which he joined with skill and enthusiasm. Later, Diego would require all secret passengers to hide there for a trial so as to be better prepared in case of emergency. A slab of plastic high explosive was being sent to the Silence group, and the *Santa Maria* was to be its storeroom until Neil found another storage site, or used it. The crew were alarmed at the proposal, until assured it was new substance that was not at all volatile unless abused or detonated. So informed, they marvelled at the convenience of explosive with such valuable qualities. It took up but little room in one of the new spaces. Under the fish hold a hinged false floor was installed to provide extra space for secret cargo. Improvements were made to the galley, and the bunks enlarged. Under the wheelhouse ceiling a storage space was provided for the indicia of Spain to be hidden when the boat was French, and vice versa.

During three weeks of constant work the hull was cleaned, caulked and repainted. The engine was tuned and the transmission tightened. The wireless set was upgraded. The electrical system was checked and a new battery charger and reconditioned batteries fitted. Charts of the western Mediterranean waters were updated, and more powerful lens installed in the telescope. The crew's knowledge of navigation and chart reading, and of devices such as dividers and plotters, was tested, and Manny was briefed on weapons and explosives. It was important that the boat be able to rendezvous with the British supply ships that occasionally carried secret cargoes to France. Those larger vessels, submarine or surface, had to stay in the deeper water, so that a smaller coastal vessel was a necessary link in the delivery chain. As equipped the crew would be able to find the boat's direction via a hand compass; calculate the allowances to be made for compass variations; reckon boat speed in knots by timing by stop watch the movement of a floating object along a known distance, which for them was from bow to stern; plumb the depth of water with a lead line; ascertain the existence and nature of a current by reference to both a dead reckoning position and an observed position; provide steering compensation for the pushing sideways of the boat by wind, or leeway; estimate an approximate distance from the boat to a fixed object; and, not least, have good reference charts. Thus informed and equipped, the boat and its crew, and especially its skipper, were in good shape for the work ahead. All the works were carried out by and at the expense of the Admiralty. At the end

Placido went with them to sea for a few hours for trials. Out there Diego said to him: "It beats me how my father and those before him survived without the gear and learning that we're getting here."

Placido replied: "You're so right. But it's not just them, it's also sailors and fishers right around the world ever since boats went to sea. They developed systems and skills that they needed, but they got lost in fog and capsized in storms much more often than we do today, so while the oldies were good, you're safer. My ancestors fished for cod out on the Dogger Bank in the north Atlantic, and many never came back. They would have survived better if they were set up like you are. Then of course the Mediterranean is a safer sea generally than the Atlantic, though big storms and rough water can come from nowhere." Patting Diego on the back he continued: "But, *mi amigo*, you and your boat are ready for anything."

The evening prior to their departure a naval officer visited them to explain that SOE was sending two agents with them, and a quantity of Sten guns and ammunition. Diego and Manny quickly adjusted to the news, as that was exactly why they were there and why the boat was refitted. They were not asked their opinion about anything, only that it was required that the voyage commence at 2200 hours the following evening, with a view to arrival at a destination off the French coast at midnight five days later. The passengers would not be discussing their mission or destination with the crew, or disclose their identities, but were to be known only as Tom and Dick. Diego would be given a sealed note to be opened only on arrival in French waters. It would be written in both French and Spanish for better understanding, and was to be destroyed forthwith once read. The passengers could be shown the note for their information. Diego explained he had to pick up Conchita at Móntago on the way back and also may have to refuel somewhere, so that the passengers would, he supposed, have to take up their positions at those places. The officer thought not. He could not see any problem about the passengers being on deck. The boat was in transit. Those on board were not going ashore. The passengers carried French passports and there was no war between the two countries. If there was a special problem for Diego, say at Móntago, he could decide what to do on the spot. Anything that would get the passengers safely to France.

19

Conchita was at a loose end often because the younger women, her natural associates, had little time to spare from their chores. And chatting with older women, even if less busy, went slowly because their respective dialects had little in common. To have the company of the younger women she joined in their work, and in doing so learned about the fishing gear used on different boats for different catches, the repairing of nets, the seasons in which different species were best caught, the ways they marketed the catch, including barter, why the winter months were lean, and how fish were cured and salted and put by for use in winter. Every kitchen always had a supply of dried fish hanging from a line. If times were good there might also be a few sides of imported salt cod, *bacalao seco*, much prized by Catalonians. A valuable sideline for the women was collecting from the hills the plants from which they made a wide range of baskets. They earned but little, but everything helped in a subsistence village economy. Conchita knew this work from home, where the main plant, esparto grass, grew just as well and prolifically as in the coastal hills.

She noted a difference in family planning. At home large families were desirable as a means of support for parents in old age, in a society where there was no age pension, and the subsistence wages of agricultural labourers allowed no retirement funds to be set aside. Basically it was a matter of eating. The Montagons differed through having fish and the sea, and the fishers being self-employed, old men could work longer, if not as vigorously as once, and nobody starved. But the bodies of the landless labourers of Andalucia gave out sooner, and without their manual work they had no income, and commonly, little or no savings. Hunger, near starvation, and actual deaths from it were well known there, but not in Móntago. There the custom was to have no more than two children, as more would be a present day financial burden for parents who could expect to get by later with a little communal assistance and the perpetual bounty of the sea. Families among Conchita's people were very much larger. So was the child mortality rate, but four and more children usually survived. The difference seemed to Conchita economic rather than tenets of the Church concerning birth control, and stemmed from economic factors. It was no wonder, even to Conchita, a new observer, that the seeds of anarchism, communisim and socialism had sprouted far more vigorously among Andalucian landless labourers than Costa Bravan fishers.

The matter of Conchita being crew on a fishing boat caused local anxiety, as it was contrary to local lore, and had not been dealt with by Diego before continuing his voyage. Conchita was then left to argue, mainly through his parents, that she would not be crew on a fishing boat out of their port, and that Diego would handle any questions on his return, he being of the pueblo and also her employer. The small amount of tension the issue had raised then diminished, because the question had been answered, and so could be put aside, at least for the present.

As the sea and its fish dominated life in Móntago, so the senior fishers were dominant in civic affairs, and controlled the cooperative, which managed the small communal cork oak forest and olive grove, coordinated basket sales, and other small communal enterprises and services. But the fishing effort was not one: it was not socialised. There would be no tourism, and little commercial enterprise independent of the cooperative, or that was not dependent on the patronage of the fishers, for many years ahead. Apart, that is, from government services, such as those of visiting health professionals, and the mayor 's office. Education was available in La Escala at the parish school staffed by nuns, but attendance by Montagon children was generally poor, as village parents mostly saw no need for more than a basic knowledge of the three Rs. The spiritual needs of the villagers were met by a resident priest who lived with his housekeeper in the presbytery adjoining the church, both handsome and ancient structures. However, the spirituality of the fishers – as distinct from that of their women – did not extend to church attendance. The sea was their god, around which traditions and taboos foreign to the lore of the Catholic Church had become entrenched, so that to identify with one was to exclude the other; and the fishers invariably chose the sea. However, they neither forbade nor encouraged their women concerning adherence to the Church, and in fact most village women belonged, without trying to change their men; a position the priest regretfully accepted. The split in beliefs also had the effect of keeping the local Church poor, as the fishermen had little money to spare for its work. But all the same it was a successful and respected institution in the village.

Apart from necessary contact with La Escala to deliver fish and attend to material matters beyond the resources of the village, contact with other communities was only occasional and occurred mainly through the likes of an occasional fair, bartering, selling fish to hawkers who came for supplies every few days, family visits where there was intermarriage, and medical attention in Figueres or Gerona. The villagers could rarely afford extras. They had no motor vehicles, and bicycles were impractical. The cooperative's few mules and donkeys were not available for private expeditions, so a proposed visit farther than walking distance would involve unusual expense, the prospect of which often put an end to a journey before it began. Yet the quality of life in Móntago was well sustained by the beauty of the sea, its abundant fish, the mild climate, and the plentiful rain that helped keep the land clean and green.

As part of her purposeful identification with the village, Conchita learned Catalonian cooking, played their card games, worshipped with them, sang their songs, and danced their regional folk-dance, *la sardana*, notably as one in a group from the village at a festival in La Escala. In the dance male and female dancers moved alternatively to left and right in a circle, with body movements and music that reflected moods that varied from happiness to deep sadness. She, in turn, introduced her friends to the rudiments of the flamenco and other popular Andalucian dances, and songs. The tempo of her activity became enough to keep her fully occupied during the day and tired at night. She would wake early and be ready at once for another busy day.

The time went so quickly that the second week had passed before the proposed Barcelona visit was discussed in detail. Diego's mother was to go too. So on the Wednesday the two women set off to a background of wagging tongues around the pueblo. What was the big secret? The villagers would normally expect a full account of every aspect of a visit to Barcelona; before and after. This time they had little information, so were puzzled, and most curious. Why were they going? Not shopping. That was not Alicia Gómez. Nobody was ill. No, there was something mysterious going on, something to do with the war in France. What else could it be? And where was Diego? Alicia knew how intensely interested the villagers would be, as she would, but could say little, a painful situation for her. She would like nothing more than to tell all and sundry the whole story. Conchita fortified her in the painful silence by pointing out that the Germans had plenty of agents in Spain, and information about the *Santa Maria* might interest them.

Conchita carried a shopping basket, like Alicia. They took the bi-weekly bus from La Escala to Gerona, where they boarded a third class carriage of a train that stopped at all stations. The constant movement of passengers and their goods gave Conchita a glimpse of the way other Catalonians lived, while the gentle pace of the train afforded a panoramic view of the countryside; a more pleasing and relaxed one than when she had been fleeing from the fascist enemy. She was saddened by the sight of missing limbs and disfiguring burns and wounds on some men. As the limbless had little in the way of prostheses, their resulting awkwardness in movement was piteous. She reflected that for every one seen in public, there would be more at home or in hospices, for some wounds were totally disabling, or grossly disfiguring, and she had seen soldiers on the battle fields alive, but with parts of their heads or faces missing, and such were unsuited to appearance in public. She knew most of those casualties to be the poorest of men, which was often the reason for their being frontline infantrymen, and the same poverty condemned them to lives of misery when disabled. She saw passengers look hungrily at the baskets carried by the women. Some were out-right beggars, although many of the people they begged from had but little. The sadness of the adult passenger scene was offset a little by school children with their books and chatter, men and women carrying baskets of vegetables and fowls to or from market, and the alertness of men and women clearly on their way to or from work. All in a Spain in the grip of bad seasons, suffering from the gross destruction of the recent war, friendless beyond the cold skirts of the Axis powers, and governed by a regime whose functionaries were notably inefficient and corrupt. It was also the era of retribution and discrimination against the losing republicans by the victorious fascists, as the devout General Franco, successful in war, was unwilling to lead his subjects toward Christian compassion and forgiveness in peace. His was a conditional, even grudging Christianity. This was unremarkable in a scion of Spanish Catholicism, for it was a special subset of the Church, and a grim and unjust one for underprivileged or vanquished Spaniards. The national malaise was shown as well through the Falange as any other group. That movement's sometime ideal of power to fairly serve all Spaniards had been corroded and transmogrified, with silent assent from on high, into continuous clutching by its members for influence and secret commissions. It was an unstated trade-off: Franco's connivance in their corruption in exchange for their political subservience. But one could not learn those things on a train to Barcelona. She took from the evident poverty and distress of many passengers that official checks were unlikely, as unrewarding, and noted that the off duty soldiers on board were not at all curious about other passengers.

Alicia filled in time by asking Conchita further questions, including how she had become an anarchist. She was glad to be asked, because to talk of the past took her into her childhood and home and many happy memories, alongside the others. Alicia hadn't expected as much as Conchita gave, but was glad to know. She wanted to ask about France too, but decided to leave it for the time being. For her part Conchita sensed what was going through Alicia's mind. She would be ready when the time came.

At the consulate Conchita explained to a doubting officer the purpose of her visit, requesting they check it out with SOE through an officer concerned with the Silence group. She reminded them of her delivery of Michel, the British airman. All she wanted on this visit was a password or some other future introduction, that would another day put her, or a colleague, into contact with an officer rapidly. Her interviewer left her alone in a private room and soon an officer came and introduced himself, added a few questions, thanked her, and gave her the name 'Jeepers' to use. She collected Alicia from the waiting room, and they were led out the back way by a cleaning woman who was just leaving, and who took them to a market where they bought vegetables before going home by train, and then a taxi, for there was no evening bus. It was Alicia'a first taxi ride.

When the *Santa Maria* made port at Móntago on its return voyage the villagers looked on Conchita's imminent departure in different ways. On the one hand the women, especially those she had worked with, and Diego's family, had come to admire her and see her as a brave and intrepid person whose life was coloured with much more adventure than their own. They would miss her. On the other hand the fishers looked forward to the departure of a woman whose vocation was to be crew on a fishing boat. The sooner she went back to where she had come from the better, summed up their attitude. To avoid any embarrassment Conchita did not meet the boat at the jetty, but waited for Diego at his home. Their unusually long separation had tested their love, which was proved the way they flung themselves at each other as soon as Diego entered the door. They went on board very early next morning, the others having slept there, and after refuelling, and after talking on board some ice and bait, the crowded boat set off for France. The crew hoped that with the power of both sail and engine, a rendezvous would be possible that night at the place to be disclosed in their orders, to be read *en voyage*. After exchanging news about the past few weeks they were all content. The voyage had been a success, and all had contributed something useful.

Their destination turned out to be a quiet beach north of Perpignan, marked on the coastal chart which came with the orders. On arrival it was light enough to cruise by to get bearings. Now, soon after midnight, the boat drifted shoreward quietly until about half a nautical mile offshore. Manny shone a flashlight which drew an immediate reply, and after a brief exchange of lights in code, he and Diego were satisfied enough to lower the boat's tiny dinghy and send Manny and one passenger in it toward the beach. As it pushed off Diego handed Manny a Sten gun. Smoking and talking were not allowed. The landing of the passengers was to be swift. Both Tom and Dick were only too pleased for the voyage to be ending, as a smelly and crowded fishing boat was not their idea of comfortable travel. There was a shore party of four men waiting. Close up they could see each other well enough. Leaving Tom in the dinghy Manny approached the group, saying: "I don't know you, and I must be satisfied you're the right people to take my friends. This is how we'll get this over quickly. I'll ask questions, each of you, and let him answer alone. Speak quickly."

All members of the waiting party were astonished, and angered, but their leader cut them short, saying: "Don't get excited. This man is just protecting his crowd. He's making sure we haven't been infiltrated. And we must show him, in case he shoots us. Remember that's an automatic he's pointing. So let's do it his way. Answer his questions as best we can. He'll soon sort us out." Turning to Manny he continued: "You heard me. You go ahead. We're ready. But hurry, because we're all pretty nervous here, and if we can't get it over quickly you'd better go back to the sea and we'll go home."

"That's a good plan. I don't want to lose you and I don't want to lose my friends either. I'll be quick. I'll point to the one I want the answer from. Just one, y'know. Remember this is only business, and nothing personal. I know how you must feel. All understand?"

They all replied they did. He proceeded with a series of connected questions, and if the men were genuine the answers would flow quickly, and if they were not he might shoot them. He started at once, and was quickly satisfied from the replies they were genuine resisters. He could do no more. He called Tom over and introduced him, adding: "I'm as satisfied as I can be that these men are loyal, but you also have to be satisfied, so talk with them if you wish." He stood aside while the discussion continued. Shortly Tom turned to him, saying: "I'm satisfied."

"OK. Good. Stay here and I'll get Dick." Taking Tom aside he handed him his flashlight, saying: "If anything goes wrong and you want to tell me to head out to sea, flash this slow and long. If you do that, we're away."

He took off in the dinghy, all the time watching the shore. There the leader was busy calming down his men, who were offended by Manny's style, and Tom was comforted to see their resentment, which to him supported their claim to integrity.

The rest of the unloading was uneventful. Diego handed down to Manny in the dinghy the weapons and explosives brought for the shore party, and Dick took with him the small parcel he had been given for the leader. The mission complete, the shore party very quickly took off, after smoothing over the footmarks in the sand, with Tom and Dick working hard to convince all members of the reception committee that Manny's attitude was his way of keeping everybody safe. Their leader joined in, and the grumbling abated, with help from the praise Tom and Dick heaped on them for a smart reception.

The task done, the *Santa Maria* steamed seaward and away from the drop point, then it drifted while the crew took turns on watch and in sleeping the few hours until dawn. By then the boat was French, bearing no Spanish signs. It would spend a few hours fishing before returning to Sète late in the afternoon with some catch. Back in port, and after selling the small catch, Manny took his leave of Diego and Conchita with a view to meeting Neil to report and be assigned some work. He would also find time to dream of repairing and building boats, as the shipyard at Gibraltar had inspired in him a feeling for a future as a shipwright after the war. His friends were sorry to see him go, yet glad to have the boat to themselves again.

Observing while fishing, was the new role of the *Santa Maria's* crew. The boundaries of the surveillance area were the Spanish border one way, and the Carmogue wetlands the other, beyond which lay the delta of the Rhône River; in all a long and difficult shoreline to guard and police, for which France had little cause, although after the Germans took over the unoccupied zone in November 1942, their fear of invasion stimulated a higher level of watchfulness. Busier areas, of which Marseilles stood out, lay to the east, where guarding was more intense, and restrictions on sea movement meant economic disadvantage of fishers out of ports along that section of coast. So the *Santa Maria* stayed away, and with a new home port at Valras-Plage well to the west, it was able to both fish and observe, not that there was ever much to see, which for the intelligence service was itself useful information, if not understood by the crew. They felt more useful when smuggling, for which there was a steady demand, both to and from the coast: materials one way, personnel both ways.

20

When Germany unleashed its awesome war machine on France and its northern neighbours in May 1940, after several months of relative calm, people had been terrified, and fled south. The blitzkrieg smothered all opposition, so that everybody quickly knew the French were no match for the Germans in this war. French soldiers knew it better than anybody, and some got out of the way almost as fast as the civilians. Those who stayed to fight were killed or captured, a million and a half men being taken as POWs quickly. Whole towns and Paris substantially emptied. The roads and accommodations in the south were quickly filled up. The stream was enlarged by refugees from Belgium and Holland, to whom France had seemed safer, and once there safety seemed south again, which upon the armistice that followed capitulation became the unoccupied zone. Some, a lucky or rich few, continued on, through Spain, or by sea, to other places. Jews in particular were keen to escape, especially those who had already fled from the Nazis into France. A new French government had taken over at the time of the French surrender, headed by Marshall Pétain, who had served France well during the first world war, and would serve it badly during the second. After trying other places, the new government found its home in the town of Vichy in central France, within the unoccupied zone. As Paris had long been the central city for government and administration, a country town was a poor substitute, and a grave loss of prestige, and was said to have caused past patriots to turn in their graves. Yet it could not be helped. Paris was a German prize, and the Occupation was centred there. A distance from that atmosphere was necessary for administration of what remained of the broken nation. From Vichy the new government managed the whole of France, but in a conditional manner, for its activities were subject to the terms of the armistice, and the fact of Occupation of most of the significant parts of mainland France, and most of its land area. France's overseas territories were unaffected by the Occupation, and so Vichy ruled there too.

The relatively loose German hand on the unoccupied zone has been explained in this way. Germany had hopes of France coming over to its side, turning it from enemy into friend. Those hopes had been sponsored by a considerable degree of cordiality shown to the invader by many influential French politicians and writers. In addition, Germany simply did not have the manpower to garrison all its conquered territories, so that the more French administration it could leave to Vichy the better. But by November 1942 adverse turns in the fortunes of war had combined to change German attitudes. It had become clear that France was not for turning, unless it were in the other direction, for the French people had started to show signs of resentment of Vichy, and resistance to Germany.

21

An alert, composed, competent woman could do valuable things to harm the enemy, even succeeding where a man might not. There was room, and a need for both sexes in the SOE field, and there were never too many of either. The special qualities needed were most often met by men, as SOE personnel were in a front line of the war, no less than those who wore uniforms. In a sense though all France, and its streets, were part of the front line. Yet excepting when animal strength and aggression were needed, women were as well suited to SOE work as men, though their admission was bureaucratically long delayed. Brains and bravery were essential for all SOE agents. A woman might beguile an enemy where a man might attract suspicion. But every agent had also to be passable as a French citizen; real or pretend did not matter.

SOE controlled and funded two branches, one being for the Free French who wanted a degree of autonomy in secret operations in their own country. They wanted much more, but had ground to make up before they could be trusted as equal fighting partners, and this was postponed until close to D-Day. Appointments of official SOE agents required, usually, more than the say-so of an organiser in the field. An error in selection could mean an inefficient group, or worse. An agent was certain to meet checkpoints, where papers and appearance always, and sometimes answers, had to satisfy police. So the native French had an advantage, but many candidates with a French mother, or suitably long residence in France, also spoke French well enough, and weaknesses were addressed in the SOE training schools. Besides, many different accents were always to be heard in French streets, and the most dangerous interrogators, the Germans, were out of their normal language tree anyway. Alongside SOE's official agents were many French men and women whose local knowledge and ad hoc assistance was indispensable for operations, and allowed SOE to be so much more successful. They, appointed and employed by the official agents, were resisters of the first order of quality. They contributed by providing safe houses, carrying messages, finding information, printing propaganda, working in smuggling operations by land, sea and air, as team members in sabotage activity, and by numberless acts that undermined the German war effort. And, always, and increasingly as the war years rolled on, and essentially, killing the enemy.

Some Frenchmen wished to keep apart from the ceaseless tumult of French politics, and some did not like de Gaulle, so in addition to half-French like Neil Cameron there was a pool of completely French people to serve in SOE, but not in the Free French arm. More came forward to SOE generally, and to other resistance entities, as the fortunes of war swung toward the Allies. Seeing Britain remain defiant of the German spread of power gave heart to many Frenchmen, some having too readily written Britain off as another German conquest by the autumn of 1940, so its survival and resolution were beacons of inspiration and hope for those who could see.

When Neil met Ana in a park after work on an autumn day in 1942 he was clearly excited, so she was keen to know why. He said: "My news is that SOE has decided to accept women as agents on the same level as men. A legal technicality, now past, prevented this before. I'm ready to put your name forward to London at once, if you're willing. I needn't tell you what the work would be, because you've been doing it already in your own way, as much as me, but having the recognition, and being on the payroll, are good things. I expect you would be called to England for formal admission, and entry into training, for there's actually more to the job than you've seen, or indeed than I could tell you." He paused, looking at her face, and asked: "Do you want me to go on?" She replied: "Yes, please do." He continued: "There's not much more, but I'd better treat you like a stranger, at the risk of stating things you know. You know the risks. You know the enemy. But there's this too: you have to disconnect from your family, who mustn't know where you live or the work you're in. Then we must be careful about socialising with other members of a circuit, but instead, aim for personal isolation. Think of yourself and your work as a link in a human chain, the other links being unknown to you, just as you would be unknown to them: this for everyone's safety. If an agent doesn't know then he or she cannot tell, be it just chatting, or under interrogation by the Gestapo. That fear, and intense loneliness because of the nature of the work, come with the job. I'm sorry, I know it's a gloomy prospect."

"I can keep my chess board?"

"Yes, if I may drop in sometimes for a game." They both smiled. He continued: "As you know, we're finding new people all the time. Now there are ever so many people who would rather die fighting the Nazis than to live under them. Eventual victory for the Allies will mean a free Europe, and an end to antisemitism. Armies alone might not be enough to win. People like us can also play a part."

When she became a candidate for SOE, Ana's experience in clandestine work and association with her brother and friends were attractive qualifications, as was her German background. Her application was considered at an initial meeting between Jean Amery from FANY, the multi-task British women's service, and George Martin from SOE. Jean stated her view: "Going by her dossier this girl knows no English, and is fluent in both French and German, which would be enough. I like that she is single, has good reason for hating Germans, and is nobody's fool. Does it matter she has no English?"

George said: "The other things you mention more than make up for it. All the people she works with will know French, so it's all OK. If she comes in for training she would be in the same boat as many other foreign agents, and as you know we can accommodate them all through our linguists. So yes, for her limited operations, it's not a problem"

Jean thought about that, and said: "Good. By the way, in the snap she looks well, even pretty, so I suppose we know she's healthy too?"

"That's all we have, plus the organiser's recommendation, and he would hardly want a disabled agent. But she'll be checked if she comes. By the way, she's Jewish, did you know?"

"Well, no. She didn't strike me that way. It's funny, isn't it? You don't know something about someone, and when you find out, it's all so obvious. So now you tell me she's Jewish I can pick out those features, and if you hadn't told me it would never have crossed my mind. But that's all nonsense. The big thing is that she didn't come across to me as Jewish, so she won't attract particular attention anywhere. And so there's a good reason for anti-Nazi feeling. You don't have a thing against Jewish agents in SOE, do you?"

"Heavens no. We have them already. Much of the resistance in Paris comes from young Jews, who are quite aggressive. Hopeless stuff, but great spirit."

"Maybe she doesn't know of them. I've heard they're like suicide squads."

"I don't know she's even been there, but anyway it would be hard to get in because of the zoning, and besides her family are in Lyon. She'd be lost. Street guerrillas depend on their local knowledge for escape routes. That's one area where they have an edge on Jerry."

"I see. So I don't have any objections to this girl. None at all."

"I'm glad to hear that. If she comes for training you might like to meet her. But there's another point. Her brother is already serving with us. Quite an experienced hand. His chief - that's Pasteur - thinks the world of him. Weapons instructor among other things. Was briefly in one of our groups as a courier until Silence started, and he moved to be with its leader, who is his old friend from the civil war. Roger was sorry to see him go."

"We don't mind siblings in the service?"

"No. We have a few, and a married couple."

"So the girl's application is independent, but she has connections to our people already?"

"Yes, we believe. Don't ask me if there's something between Pasteur and her. If they were engaged or married we would have been told."

"My guess is that something is brewing there, but then I'm a romantic. Would it matter?"

"I don't think so. They'll know we deal with agents as separate people and not twosomes. All the same, I would hope that unless they asked for it, they wouldn't be separated, or the girl moved from Lyon, which is her home town, and an important resistance area."

"I suppose the main thing is to keep from becoming pregnant. As you know, my people give them plenty of advice, and the rest is up to them."

"Quite so. It just occurred to me that if she and her brother grew up in Lyon, and work around there, maybe they'll be safer if our disguise people worked them over."

"I agree. One more thing. Remember please I would like to meet this girl if I'm around when she comes."

"I'll minute it."

After being chosen for training Ana travelled to England by secret ferry plane, her first flight. The RAF was highly skilled and usually successful in this daring business, dodging bad weather and darkness and even, occasionally, hostile ground receptions variously comprising French police, collabos, and Germans. On arrival she quickly sensed London's age and size and centripetal role in the Allied war scheme, and was astonished at the extensive damage to the city from German bombing, which had occurred before the RAF had conquered the German air force. She knew that if admitted as a candidate she would go into training at once. Her final interview took place at an office to which she was taken by Monica, a FANY officer who had been put in charge of her, and where she met an interviewing panel of three, a woman in uniform, and two men. She was surprised at their questions about Manny and Neil, and replied without pretending she knew everything about them. The panel members knew that passions had run high before and during the Spanish civil war, and that the men and a few women who had fought in the Brigade had been mainly driven by high principle, whether they were communists, as many were, or only antifascists, like others. Those issues were in the thoughts of the interviewers while Spain was under discussion. Ana knew the fighters there had felt let down by Britain and France, and especially by France, where there had been a socialist government at the critical time. She was pleased to see the panel taking an interest in the subject. Turning from the two men and the civil war, the senior man asked Ana:

"We know you're Jewish. I suppose it's a pretty hard life in France now?'

Ana replied: "Yes. It is." She paused, and the others waited. She wondered how to proceed. "I suppose you all know that Jews are persecuted almost beyond endurance by both the French and the

Germans, and for us it's hardly believable that France in particular would do this. As it's getting worse all the time, and as Germany's policy is to do away with Jews, we can only suppose we have worse times ahead. Generally we are powerless victims, with little support from Gentiles." Pausing, she looked directly at each panel member in succession, then resumed: "Would it be out of order for me to say something more?"

The panel members looked at each other, and as none signalled against it, the senior man said: "Please, go ahead."

"Well, thank you, and I know this is not why I'm here, but we wonder why nobody helps us. And of course it's not only France, but that's my home."

Senior spoke again: "As you say the problem is also outside France. And it's a gross wrong, and many outsiders are sympathetic." Here he passed, and his colleagues murmured sympathetic words before he kept on. "But it's beyond the control of the Allies. Think about it. The only way we can get into France today is through special effort, and then only in small pieces. We'd like nothing more than to turn France and Germany around, and that's our target, that's what we work and live for, and many of us will die along the way. We think we're winning, and that the future belongs to us. But until then the Jews in France, as everywhere, are on their own."

The other man on the panel added: "Ana, that's true. I wish it were not, for I too am a Jew." Ana gaped, then looked at him gratefully. Addressing all, she said: "Thank you. I'm better off for your advice."

Then she sat, waiting for a lead from the panel, but there was nothing left to say, and the senior man suggested to Jean, that if Ana could wait outside they could deliberate. There, Monica took her to the tearoom to wait. After a while time started to drag so that Ana started to feel she was headed for rejection. She did not let on though, and instead plied her friend with questions about the Blitz, and Monica was only too pleased to talk about something so frightening and harmful, realising that this girl from France knew practically nothing of the awful events that every Londoner had experienced, and were still suffering through occasional bombing raids. As there had been much propaganda in France against Britain, and little about scores of thousands of civilian bomb deaths and massive damage,

Ana got a new vision of war and a better understanding of how pro-paganda distorted facts.

At length she was recalled, and was at once comforted by the cordial expressions of the panel members. Senior spoke: "Please forgive us for taking so long. We have some procedures to follow. We are delighted to offer you a candidate position, which y'know means that you're invited into training and assessment, and if found satisfactory will be returned to France as an accredited SOE officer. Your actual work and its location will be worked out during training. Those are not matters we decide. However, we don't doubt you'll be in France."

Ana asked: "Does that mean SOE operates in other coun-tries?"

The Jewish member replied: "We thought you would have known, but yes, that's so. But what happens in one country has no bearing on another. And in France other secret services are also active, and they have no bearing on SOE's work, nor we on theirs. Ours are special operations, like sabotage and active resistance. It's something like what commandos do, except we aren't in uniform, and aren't part of the regular armed forces. But you'll still be part of a noble cause."

He stood up, and all followed. They came to her with con-gratulations. Senior said: "Ana, Monica from FANY will look after you until the call comes for you to present for training. Don't ask her where that might be, because even if she knew she couldn't tell you. You might never know in fact, because these places are remote and confidential. But she will get you the clothes and gear that you'll need when you go into training. You can ask her questions, and if she doesn't answer don't press her, for she will only be doing her job. Above all, remember she's your friend."

Monica told Ana much the same, adding: "So we understand each other from the start, my job is to be with you all the time until you're called. We'll return to my barracks and stay there. There's no chance of sight-seeing, not that there's much to see just now. But we'll make you as comfortable as we can. You won't be allowed out without me, or someone in my place, and then only if my superior gives leave. Sorry, but they're my orders."

Ana laughed: "I don't mind, but it sounds a little as if I'm a prisoner. Am I?"

Monica also laughed, saying: "I apologise that it can sound that way. It must be they don't want to lose you, maybe a foreign girl in a strange city thing. But they're serious, and so I must be, so everything will be OK, won't it?"

"Of course it will. I'm here to do as I'm told, so don't worry."

"Good. If anybody asks you who you are or what you're doing here, simply say your orders are to refer the inquiry to Lieutenant Monica Hampson – that's me. Now where we're going is our headquarters, and I'll tell you more about us soon."

"That'll be lovely. I'm looking forward to it. I'm so interested. This is all like a big dream for me." She wondered if she had better have said bad, because in truth she wondered what was happening to a girl from Lyon. Her loneliness and wonderment were exaggerated by the language. Even the simplest things had to be translated for her, and the people who could do it were not always available. So soon she made a conscious effort to keep close to Monica, who never let on that the caring role was at times taxing. She consoled herself by the thought that at least the authorities need not be concerned about losing Ana.

The barracks were large, old buildings joined together, secure through fences and guards and checkpoints, in which many uniformed women lived and worked. Although their purpose was not clear to Ana, she could see it was a serious one, as was the demeanour of the workers, at least until they went off duty. It was there that Ana had some fun. The girls did not know what this pretty little French girl was doing among them, and presumably had been cautioned not to ask, for none did. Yet through Monica's attachment to her they understood it was something out of the ordinary. They were obliged to confine their interest to improving their own French through banal conversation, which was enough for Ana, because any warm, human contact was most welcome.

Ana had wondered about her family worrying about her, and was relieved and happy when Monica told, on the second day, that someone in France known as Pasteur had been briefed on her safe arrival and her being in good hands preparatory to training, and that the person had undertaken to pass this news on to Ana's family promptly. Ana toyed with the idea of explaining something of the setup in Lyon, and while to do so would have been an emotional release for her, she recalled Neil's words about secrecy, which she translated as keeping one's mouth closed, so she would wait until Monica questioned her, which she never did. She guessed, and it was a good guess, that Monica would report any lack of discipline or looseness of tongue.

She dined with Monica in an officer's mess, and played cards and other table games at night. Everybody listened to the BBC news in both English and French. Ana had the feeling that she was different in a nice sense, not like being a despised Jew in France. Yet she was lonely in a way she had never known before, and although not in the habit of bedtime praying, she waited until lights out each night then told Monica she was getting up to pray, and knelt by her bed and prayed for God's support and guidance so that she would carry out her duties with honour and courage, and never be a sook. Though comforted, she still cried herself to sleep, on the first night, and awoke restored and ready for whatever might come.

On the third and last night in the barracks, Ana felt at home enough to ask Monica about the organization, FANY, and also how she had become so proficient in French. Ana heard that FANY was an acronym with a long history, and was women who served as required by the government, although it was an independent service. It had started up in a British war about fifty years earlier, through women retrieving wounded men from battlefields, and had extended its activities into other non-combatant activities in wartime, especially during the Great War. For example, she herself had served as a telegraphist in north Africa, along with other women, working with Army Signals. She was an instructor here in London for the time being. She said: "Those of us who know what you're here for are very interested because SOE excluded women until very recently. Some are asking how it is they can't serve in SOE, and French women can: not just you, for there are a couple of other cases. Maybe some serve in other countries besides. My commandant, whom you met at interview, is looking for an explanation, so as to answer questions like that, but she said the answer can come only come when SOE is ready, which is fair enough for a secret service."

"You were going to say how you got to speak French so well." It was a timely issue, because it gave Monica the chance to talk about her upbringing, and in doing so found Ana a ready listener. In turn

126

she asked Ana about her own history, and Ana was also glad to talk about that.

Late next afternoon Monica took her by train to the outskirts of London, and there, waiting outside the station for a car to take Ana onward, the women took their leave of each other. They knew their meeting had been something special for both. The French woman had been entranced by the blonde hair and fresh, fair complexion of the sturdy English girl with smiling grey eyes, and she in turn had been taken by the darker complexion of the pretty visitor with the big brown eyes. Above all, each liked the other for what she was doing, and the way she conducted herself. They parted as the best of friends.

As dark was coming in, the car came, and with another passenger Ana was driven for some hours to a place she learned was her first SOE training station. Training varied by country and by individual, building on experience and skills already held. Ana's training, during four weeks late in 1942, at different venues, included the information that SOE stood for Stately 'Omes of England, and it was not until later in France that Neil revealed it was only a play on the use for SOE training schools of many grand, and spacious, and remote, country homes commandeered for the purpose. Her training emphasised small arms, in addition to building on her existing skills in courier work, and forgery, where her tutors included professional forgers, amnestied from British prisons to serve the war effort. She noted her fellow students were nearly all male, and spoke different languages, so she had little idea of who they were or where they had come from. Yet language barriers between students and teachers were broken down expertly, so it seemed nobody was held back on that score. There was but the merest amount of leisure activity, and there was little demand for it either, as all trainees knew they had to succeed in the courses if they were to be placed as agents. The trainees knew the pressure was deliberate, for if a person was likely to crack, better at training than in the field, where lives could be at risk.

The serious nature of her future work was underlined by her course leader, on the day after her training finished, giving her a small suit case neatly filled with the forgery gear of the type she had become familiar with, and a small revolver, and a cyanide pill. Then she was told to pack and be ready to be picked up at dusk. On arrival at an airfield she was one of three passengers brought together to be briefed on the flight they were about to undertake. All were searched to eliminate any English signs such as coins, or tags on clothes, or scraps of paper in English. They heard there was bad weather about, and in fact it caused a two day postponement of the flight, which Ana filled in with forgery practice. When the weather and the moon were right the plane left without ceremony. On some flights the passengers were dropped by parachute, providing they had made practice jumps beforehand, but none had, so all were to be landed. While in-flight they could not see out, and were apprehensive about landing and what might follow, and conversation was not possible because of the engine noise. This gave her the mental solitude to reflect on her now being a combatant. There was no turning back. The passengers had been warned to prepare for bumping and noise on landing, and it was as well, otherwise they might have supposed the plane to be crashing. On landing she was ordered her to grab her bag and run, as for her life, because they must clear the landing area and the goods the plane had brought at once, in case the enemy was closing in, but she took care to call out her thanks to the pilot. They kept her in a safe house for a day to see if the flight had attracted unusual police interest, and once satisfied that it had not, she took a train to Lyon, to her new apartment, pre-arranged under her new name. She had stepped onto French soil as a different person from the one who had embarked a month or so earlier. In the train she again reminded herself that she had taken this new direction in her life willingly, and she accepted her destiny.

22

Ana became a pretend Protestant as part of her new persona after England. The worship style involved little learning. By going to church a few times she felt able to answer any questions that might be asked of her by possible interrogators who, as Nazis, were unlikely to know much anyway. She could also show ID, and give accounts of her invented antecedents and place of birth, which would get through any but the most exhaustive examination. Her cover was as a commercial traveller in fabrics in southern France for a Lyon firm, where she was allowed generous discretion in her movements. Her main work as assistant to Neil was wide ranging, including courier runs, spotting future hit points, occasionally escorting escapees of special interest to SOE on a stage in their trek out of France, and she helped with the very important planning by the Silence team for the blowing up of strategic railway lines, and bridges, and canal locks, and the cutting of telephone lines leading out of Lyon, when the time came for the Resistance to support the expected Allied invasion. Charting hit points, and the caches of war gear sent from London, was also her work, besides which she went along as lookout and guard for Silence sabotage operations, as even before full-scale battle commenced the German military had to be diverted and made uncomfortable, and this was done through relatively small acts of sabotage at strategic locations. The targets, being significant, were often guarded, and close study of the quality of the sentries and the tightness of security was carefully undertaken before action. They were hit-and-run affairs, and the escaping was often hair-raising, and occasionally fatal. Whenever possible care was taken not to unduly damage civilian insfrastructure, or injure French citizens, which were among the reasons for night attacks being favoured, along with darkness being the saboteurs' friend. On one occasion Neil arranged with a trade union leader for internal sabotage of a local ball bearing factory serving the Germans to be carried out so that the RAF abandoned a scheduled bombing and so civilian lives were saved. Yet many times civilians suffered because industrial bombing work was of great strategic importance, and the air forces very often could not wait once a target had been listed. And civilians also suffered when sabotage involved deaths of Germans, and their forces conducted reprisal executions and harsh imprisonments.

Forgery was also Ana's work. Everybody required an identity card, and to buy basic foods in the open market a ration card was also needed. The quality of the ID cards came under scrutiny, at checkpoints, some of which were static and hence predictable, such as railway gates at big train stations, and others random. And special passes were needed when authorities restricted passage into a particular district. Authenticity depended on details such as appropriate paper and ink, neat content whether typed or printed or photographed, and signatures and stamps that looked authentic. The raw materials came from diverse sources, including London, and thefts and gifts in France. The stamps had to be made up, but experts like Ana, starting with a sample, tracing paper and a drawing compass, could quickly produce a document good enough for the many officials who were not experts. Ana's products carried several escapees along their ways. However, if a bearer were suspected, the forgeries might not stand up, and the game could end there. She was extremely busy sometimes, and rarely slack, and then she kept to herself in view of Neil's instructions.

SOE's local helpers were clearly essential for the success of its clandestine activities. And once they became disengaged, from whatever cause, their standards of secrecy might wane, and the security of a group undermined. If a sub-agent knew nothing beyond his or her special duties, and no more people than essential for those duties, the risks upon disengagement would be less. And if one were captured, it was hard to know how brave he or she might be under Gestapo interrogation with torture. So the less a sub-agent knew of anything past the job in hand, the better and safer for everybody. Fortunately helpers did not disengage readily. The spirit that drove them into resistance tended to strengthen as the truly brutal traits of the German occupiers became evident, the Allies showed they would fight until they won, and the France of Vichy showed up as false and unworthy.

SOE was not a general provider of safe passage out for escapees, though it cooperated with others, on a case by case basis. As escape was a very private and secretive matter, most of what happened in the escape lines went unrecorded. After the war it would appear, to those who looked hard, and knew where to look, that Britains's Secret Intelligence Service had been prominent in setting up and managing escape lines in several countries and localities, without ever being the only body active in that work. So Ana often had little background when she was told to escort an escapee for a step in his stage-by-stage progression toward Spain, and each escort would have the merest contact with those before and after. It was to be an impersonal affair all the way. Her escort journeys normally started at a quiet train station in the Lyon area, and ended in a pre-arranged place, such as a park, near dusk, or at a safe house, down the line, where the handover would depend on coded mutual identification between the new and old escorts. One spring day in 1943 she was instructed to pick up a downed RAF air-gunner who had escaped to Switzerland, from where an RAF escape line had escorted him to Lyon. She took it she was being lent by SOE, for the next leg, to Narbonne. She was told to carry a gun, which conveyed to her that special alertness would be appropriate. She was impressed on meeting Henri Rée: neatly dressed in modest civilian clothes, quite handsome, and fit. His watchful look was normal enough for escapees, even after being told that a relaxed demeanour was safer. He was a native of Belgium and so spoke French. They ran into a checkpoint at the train station but had no trouble passing through. In the compartment on the Perpignan night train they sat apart and avoided mutual recognition, both pretending to be sleepy, and the airman to have a sore throat, so as to head off unnecessary discussion with other passengers, one of whom was a German soldier for an intermediate section. On leaving he left behind a German newspaper, and the reading light on. Then Ana actually fell asleep. In the course of awakening, but without showing that she was awake, she surveyed her surrounds with narrowed eyes. She noticed the newspaper had been moved. It was now right alongside Henri, who was looking down at it intently, with occasional glances at the sleeping Ana. Later she indicated, by body language, that she was waking up. Then she saw the paper had been moved back to its earlier position. She drew no immediate conclusions from those observations.

At Narbonne train station Henri went to the platform toilet. While he was away Ana moved to drink from a nearby fountain tap close by. She saw a German soldier going in as Henri was coming out, and as they passed a brief exchange of words took place, which sounded to Ana as though the soldier had asked: "Pardon me, but do you have a light for my cigarette please?", and Henri had replied, instantly and almost without stopping: "I'm sorry, but I don't carry them. I don't smoke." For Ana the puzzling thing was that the exchange occurred entirely in unhesitating and fluent German. If Henri had been known up the line as speaking German she should have been told. She was jolted into thinking her own German background had been a factor in her being chosen as escort for this escapee, and maybe he was suspect as being a plant, part of a plan to infiltrate the escape line. This was a new experience, though she knew the Gestapo was constantly at work in that area, and any time they succeeded then pity help the members caught in their net. It was the sort of thing that always happened to somebody else, and the revelation it could also happen to her was at first disturbing, as a prelude to her grim alertness. She saw clearly her duty. She remembered what Manny had once told her: 'Don't be afraid of being afraid. Everybody is when they might be killed or captured. Tough people get on top of it.' She recovered quickly. She knew she was entering danger, alone, and that it was just not possible for her to put her colleagues at risk, especially Manny, and Neil. She turned away and was walking slowly back to their starting point when Henri caught up with her. She supposed he would not know of her eavesdropping. They walked out together, hand in hand, giggling as if they were sharing a lover's joke, while trusting the train station officials to respect the privacy of the young lovers. Outside, with an hour to fill in, Ana led them to a café, where they sat and ate separately. Later, Ana used the excuse of borrowing a spoon to tell him it was time to leave. Out in the street she led him to a park. The atmosphere between them was calm and cordial. Their journey was nearing its end.

They sat on a park bench, a little apart. It was close on 10 o'clock. The park had no lighting. Ana explained that as they were a little early she would wait with him for a while. While chatting she had opened her shoulder bag and placed her hand on the butt of her gun. Then, looking at him, Ana asked: "By the way, where did you learn to say in German you are sorry you cannot provide a light because you don't carry matches?"

Henri was taken aback. The implications hit him hard. This woman knew he could speak German, and she could also understand it. But he reacted coolly, with the question: "How is it, I might ask, that you understand German words."

"Because I grew up there. Now what about you?"

Hans suddenly felt a chill in the air. He said: "A friend of mine in my squadron was part German, and taught me a little. It filled in time and he kept his hand in, so to speak."

Ana continued: "What nationality is he?"

"Belgian, like me. I find German an interesting language, and knowing it might help me get a job one day."

"Very sensible. Can you read German too?"

"Not really, only a few words."

"Did you tell the escape line that you know German?"

"No, but only because I wasn't asked. I would have told them I knew a little had they asked."

"Of course. Why not. Keep it up, because having two languages is good. I hope it gets you get that job one day."

Conversation faltered, but the atmosphere had become softer. An approaching train wailed its warnings in the distance. Ana said: "Our relief should be here. Maybe he or we are at the wrong seat. It'd be easy to get it wrong in the dark like this. I'll just have a quick look around. You stay here though so we won't both get lost."

With that she rose and slowly walked away, thoughts flooding through her mind swiftly. Henri had not told anyone he could speak German, yet certainly would have been asked about his languages. She was sceptical about tutelage from the Belgian friend, for his fluency was higher than that of a learner. And he had seemed at ease when reading the paper, which the woman next to him had told Ana with her eyes. Moreover, and above all, he showed no interest in Ana's German background. His lack of interest there showed a wariness that was inappropriate when she was helping him. He could have something to hide. She saw more clearly why she had been chosen for this escort, and also why carrying a gun had been suggested. Thoughts streamed through her mind. 'Do I have to be detective, prosecutor, judge and executioner? But how can I allow him to get away from me? Oh, how I wish Neil or Manny was here to deal with this. What would they do?' She prayed for guidance. She decided the way forward was clear. She could not take him prisoner, for she had no prison, and could not let him go, so she must kill him. Unless she was quick and ruthless he might take her prisoner, and he would have a prison at hand for her, which would suit him well if he was planning to bust the escape line, or even more. Or he might simply become suspicious, and get up and go. That could mean the damage was done. Maybe that's what he was about to do.

Meanwhile, Henri remained seated, disturbed by the tone of

the discussions, and uncertain about what to do. Ana had seemed quite relaxed as she got up. If he left now, his mission incomplete, he would have provided good service to his country. He had learned a lot about this escape line, and also more general information about other lines. There was enough information for several arrests. But he could do a better job by waiting for his next escort, arresting him, and taking him to the nearest police station. Or even just going with him on the next section, and then further down the line, which would make his efforts so much more fruitful. He sat and busily weighed up his options. But in doing so he was unknowingly at a grave disadvantage. He did not know there would be no escort. This was not the park Ana's instructions had specified. She had decided on the switch before they left the café. This park was much closer to the railway line. She could tell when a person was fluent in German, which had seemed to be what the woman in the compartment also thought. She felt sure Henri was a plant, and so she would be saving the line, and maybe the Silence group, by taking him out. It was a ghastly thought, yet her job required initiative. It would be better that Henri die rather than her colleagues. Like him, she knew a quick decision was to be made. His was to wait. Hers was to kill him. She took out her revolver, already loaded. Hands shaking, she released the safety catch. With her bag on her shoulder and her hand inside it holding the gun she walked quietly back toward the seat. From the cover of a tree a few metres back his outline was visible against the faint light from the station. Ana knew the express train would pass soon, and that it blew its whistle loudly to warn level crossings and signals ahead. Now it was coming, its shrieks piercing the calm, cold night air. As it thundered by she moved swiftly behind Henri, and shot him twice in the back of the head. He groaned loudly, then slumped forward, half on and half off the seat. Ana was appalled at the great supersonic noise of the gun firing, and knew it would rise through the subsonic sound of the train, but it might not be easily identified, and she was consoled by thinking that there weren't many people about, and even if curious, few would want to plunge into a dark park to investigate. She pushed him hard, and his body moved sideways without resistance. Still holding the gun toward him, and shaking all the while, she reached into the pocket of his jacket where she had seen him put his personal papers, and withdrew them. She quickly touched the other pockets but they yielded nothing significant. She put his case aside, stood back, replaced the safety catch of her gun, blew down its barrel, and returned it her bag. She also placed in it the papers she had stolen. Then she took Henri's case in her hand, and walked away, out of the park, into the main street. At a taxi rank she tried to stand but her legs kept buckling under her so she sat. Her first thought had been to proceed to a friendly *pension* to hide, but now she decided to try to get out of the town, lest she be trapped. That, and shed Henri's case, preferably after she had glanced at its contents. She understood the German presence locally to be on the small side, so it would take a while before there was any alert from that quarter, and be it the German or the French police, reconstructing Henri's assassination would take time, enough for her to be out of town if she acted swiftly. So she would try for a train out, preferably up the line, but anywhere for that matter. Carrying a lot of luggage to or from a train station was not unusual, but she couldn't walk around town that way. So she took a taxi to the station. If there was to be a train out within two hours she would take it, and if not she would go to the *pension,* and hide for a while, and burn the incriminating case in the furnace that supplied the hot water. She was in luck. A slow night train to fit her plan was passing through soon, and she took it. On the way she went through Henri's notebook and effects. He had recorded his travels on the escape line in a mixture of French and German, showing clearly his grasp of German. Names and places were listed methodically. As she read, Ana's blood chilled. She had been mortified at killing him, and had dreaded the chance of finding she had made a mistake. Her relief was immense, only equalled by her anger at what he had been about. Now she could deal with the affair as a matter of work. She had been trained to kill, and had been diligent in her duty. She left his case on the train when she left it at Montpellier.

Later, when inquiries were complete, Santo received a coded message from SOE London on his transceiver, which he passed on to Ana. It said: 'Subject took the identity of a deceased RAF member, a Belgian, not listed as speaking German. Subject a plant.'

Ana was consoled, but the hurt of having killed remained, at least until other events hardened her heart toward the enemy even more.

23

The Axis powers entered and took control of the unoccupied zone on 11th November 1942, in response to the increasingly threatening presence of the Allies in north Africa. They did it in two parts. The small existing Italian zone, nestled up against the Italian border by the mountains and sea, was expanded westward toward the Rhône River, so taking in the Côte d'Azur and its well-known towns. Subtracting that zone, the rest of mainland France was now under German Occupation, and would be governed through two layers; a military Occupation, mostly German, above a French civilian administration. The Vichy regime's pretence of France being a sovereign State was shattered. Not that the occupiers wanted to run France in all respects. They relied on the French for the bottom layer of control, so sustaining the traditional public services on which France's functioning as a civilised State had been made possible at other times of disruption through political tumult, war, defeat, and occupation. With the partial exception of the Italian zone, the effect from November 1942 onwards of German military control throughout mainland France was to put at risk of arrest and imprisonment anybody classified as Jewish, whether French or foreign. Once imprisoned all were liable for deportation, as keeping to a German deportation train schedule could outweigh the merit of a case for release. But those most at risk were the foreign Jews, because both the Vichy regime, and individual French police, were often uneasy about taking French Jews, and those police were essential for success in roundups.

It was clear that with more Germans and more resolve there would be more arrests in the former unoccupied zone. The Mayers in Lyon decided to consider a move to the Italian zone, without applying for the permission that Jews required to change address, as such an application would invite delay, and probable refusal. Moving was not simple. To leave legally, with proper papers, would lead to Ab and Klara being outed, with dangerous consequences for all, as both harbouring, and being unregistered foreign Jews, were offences, and any offence at all by a Jew might lead to prison, and worse. A furtive escape out of France would risk rejection at the border. Manny's advice would be welcome, but he was always busy, and remote.

Klara took the lead. With the assent of the others she went to Nice to look around. She located a cottage outside a village called Bevile, in the Alpes-Maritime department. The village was at the dead end of a rough rural track, and the cottage was only accessible by a long further walk, a view of which was commanded from the house. The whole area was hilly and forested, broken by small valleys both arable and productive. The village lay a few kilometres north of Puget-Théniers, on the Nice-Digne railway line, which led to an inland route that Klara saw as an alternative to the heavily policed coastal line. It seemed that as long as the Italians were in charge they could be safe there. So she negotiated with the owner, whose farm adjoined, for a lease of the cottage for a year, with an option for another year. The cottage walls were stone, and the roof slate, giving it a deserved air of strength. It was basically just a single room, with a stove and open fireplace in the centre, and from it a stone chimney rising through the roof. The clay floor showed no signs of roof leaks. It had neither toilet, nor electricity, nor running water. Klara knew she could not ask for everything she would like, but insisted that the rain water tank be repaired to receive roof runoff, and be filled with water to commence the lease. Also that she should have the right to draw water from the farmer's wells in an emergency, the further rights to take timber from the trees around for repairs and renovations for the cottage, and to use fallen timber for fuel. Satisfied with the assurances of Jean-Paul, the owner, the lease was settled, the rent reflecting the tenants' obligation to repair any defects in the building. During the negotiations he had said that farm work would be available, as there was a grave shortage with so many young men away, at a time when produce was needed badly and profits from it very good. In all, it was a deal with prospective benefits for both sides. Klara noted that the farmer did not ask about the origins of his pending tenants, so took it he had guessed, and if not would soon do so. Home again, she stressed to the others that by accepting her plan they would be moving into a house of genuine discomfort, which could only be changed with considerable effort by all of them. They would all need to find compensation through being out of harm's way.

Ben and Naomi disposed of the lease of 19 rue de la Madeleine by leaving behind most of their furniture for the landlord to dispose of as he pleased. He was content, as the furniture was of good quality, and he expected to let the premises again soon, at no less rent. For the Mayers the less hassle and delay about their departure the better. In any event they could not take much furniture with them, and selling publicly could create suspicion.

The migrating party, with their household effects and personal possessions, still substantial after rigorous culling, was met by Jean-Paul at the local train station with a heavy ox cart in which he carried the travellers and their gear to the cottage, where they arrived in the dark after a slow journey. Inside they found piles of straw for mattresses, and a wood supply by the fireplace, gifts from him. Still, they had never seen a domestic set-up as primitive, and it was an effort for all to comprehend it was now their home. Soon though dismay was overwhelmed by the freedom they felt around them, and the challenge of adapting. After Jean-Paul left them, with their grateful words ringing in his ears, they all knelt and offered up thanks to God for what they had been given, and called down His blessings on their new home.

The identity papers used in the Italian zone did not mention if the bearer was or was not Jewish, unlike the German zone. Klara stressed they must all act as if they were not Jews, a pretence they had learned at Lyon. People might well suspect, but without evidence they could not be certain. And uncertainty could forestall adverse action, or gossip, which might otherwise lead to betrayal. Ana had coached them on how to project themselves, as far as each was able, as non-Jewish. Success could one day mean the difference between life and death, she had said. Klara's was an influential voice alone, but she knew that the message would be stronger for the calling in of Ana's views.

Using considerable energy and their various skills, the settlers made the cottage tolerably comfortable. They all obtained food ration cards through the office of *le maire*, the mayor, of the small commune centred on Bevile, one of many of only a few hundred hectares which abounded throughout rural France. Most administrative matters for the tiny commune were processed in the department office in Nice, but the food coupons were a local affair. The official rations for all the French at this time were little enough, and if a local supply were deficient, as happened frequently, the more vulnerable citizens went from extreme hunger to starvation, and for those doing hard physical work the problem was greater again. But the Mayers were able to trade their work for food, so ate reasonably well. While being courteous to everybody they met, they all knew their protection depended considerably on the goodwill of the mayor. They supposed he sensed who they were, and what they were doing. On the other hand, they did not know he could not bring himself to turning over Jews to the French police, who in turn could not or would not do what the Vichy government and the Gestapo wanted without his co-operation, and the assent of the Italian military. He and his wife, fortified by the local priest in an intensely religious Catholic community, knew enough of how Germans and Vichy police treated Jews not to denounce them. Without local cooperation the police did not have the resources to search and inquire everywhere, even when they had the will. And if the police were to muster enough men to surround a rural area and conduct house to house and farm to farm searches for refugees, they might be, and had been, denied Italian permission to take away any they caught. Moreover, when raids were proposed in rural areas, when planning brought several people into the loop, leaks were common, such as an anonymous call from a police station, or a mayor's office, and so many birds had flown into the woods before the catchers came. The towns were different. Everything there was more compact and concentrated. But even there, including Nice, the Jews were relatively safe while the Italians were in ultimate control. So, for these reasons, the senior Mayers lived in peace for several months.

For Ab and Klara in particular, victims of Nazi oppression throughout the 1930s, and in hiding in Lyon since their arrival in France, it was a time and place for unusual relaxation. Nowhere they walked was threatening. Nothing made them hurry or hide. They could talk aloud to the birds and animals and trees and flowers and hills, in Yiddish or other, without looking over their shoulders. They decided early on not to tempt fate by wondering about the future.

24

Although the elder Mayers were satisfied with their hill retreat, Ana was not. Fearful of the increasing intensity of antisemitism, and the deportations in full swing by early 1943, she worried that the frail shell protecting her family would crack, with all the bitter consequences that were increasing apparent in the rest of the country. She finally convinced them to aim for escape to another country, whatever the difficulties, with Palestine as the primary target. Her plan was to keep her family from the hunters in France, remove them to Spain, and wait there for an opportunity to migrate further. She said it seemed Spain did not have anti-Jewish laws, even though General Franco was reported to have made occasional antisemitic speeches, but fairly mild in tone, and possibly reflecting sympathy for Nazi fascism above anything else. Ideally the émigrés would acquire appropriate French papers such as an exit visa for Spain, then a Spanish entry visa. The first may have to be forged. With it the Spanish might be coaxed into issuing a conditional entry visa. Failing entry with documents the option of entering clandestinely remained. It was not obvious, by 1943, that an illegal political refugee would be returned to France when he or she was only using Spanish soil as a staging post in a larger move. So far as Ana could tell it was one thing to be caught at the Pyrénées border, and another if you were deep inside Spain. She hoped the consulate in Barcelona might appreciate the work being done by the young Mayers for the Allies, and it did not seem to her impossible that communication, and perhaps more, existed between it and SOE. That British policy made it very hard for refugee Jews to enter Palestine was unknown to her, but had she known it would not have changed the Spanish step, as there were other later destinations to be considered, all seemingly more accessible from there than from France. To ensure deep entry a sea voyage should be considered.

Settling in Spain was not much of an idea for those who knew very little of its culture or language. They did not know that in fact it had commenced to protect and save those descendants of the Jews expelled in the 16th century, known as the Sephardim, who were at risk from the Nazis in various countries. They were being offered

Spanish citizenship, even though very few had ever visited Spain, or spoke Spanish. It was an anomaly, an attempt by this Spain to make amends for pogroms by its medieval predecessors. As Spanish citizens the Sephardim were technically entitled to exemption from deportation, and if the ruse did not always work, failure resulted from the antisemitic deportation zeal of the Nazis and their cohorts, and not Spain's sincerity. And in parallel with that scheme Spain's attitude to other Jews who entered legally, or otherwise, softened. It did not want them to stay in Spain permanently, and if other destinations were being searched for, some were allowed to live outside prison under a range of controls. But these facts also were still to be learned by the Mayers.

Ana undertook to escort the escapees within France, but not beyond, where she could make no special contribution, besides which she had work to do for SOE. They were dismayed but not really surprised. They asked though how she would avoid imprisonment, and she replied that it was all taken care of, an answer which contented them. They had noticed she had changed her appearance, which they took to be for her protection, and even though Naomi preferred her previous appearance, she kept it to herself, and pretended she had noticed nothing. Manny had mixed feelings about the plans but could not offer anything better; and after all the older people knew what they were doing. Ana asked her parents how they were off for money, in response to which Ben simply pointed to his boots. As the granddaughter of Josef she needed no more answer. His descendants were doing the same as he had done to bypass the banking system in anticipation of the authorities in his home town of Odessa confiscating Jewish bank accounts.

The war was going badly for the fascist regime in Italy, under devastating attack from the Allies by land and sea and air, the success of which encouraged the army and the king to overthrow Mussolini and the fascists. Concurrently a plan was being hatched for the emigration of thousands of Jews from the Italian zone of France into Italy proper, and which might have included the four hill refugees, close to the border. Such large-scale acceptance would reflect the humane attitude of the Italian government toward Jews, at a time when everybody knew of their vicious persecution in France, and elsewhere, by fascist regimes. The émigrés would go from the several border departments, but after a hopeful start, it all came to nothing. Failure was due to bungling by the political and military heads in Italy, which were in disarray at the time, yet France maybe could have seen the project through to completion had it acted quickly and waived its antisemitism, if only for that special purpose. But under Pétain, Jews should leave indeed, and deportation was a convenient device.

When, in September of 1943, Italy's zone in France was taken over by Germany, it was all bad news ahead for Jews in the south, as arbitrary arrest and imprisonment were more likely through heavier attention from German forces, suddenly thicker on the ground. The simple fact was that the Italian government, as then constituted and under its then policies, was not drenched in hate for Jews as was its German counterpart, which had commenced its monstrous program of Jewish deportations well before taking over the formerly unoccupied zone. Even a relatively humane Italian administration could not always save the Jews in its zone during the final months of its control there, yet it was still the best place in France for a Jew. When the Italians left those living in the haven became an endangered species, being prey for the human vultures who denounced them, assisted in their capture, and relentlessly stole their belongings, or what was left after the Gestapo had picked over them. The Mayers never knew, and had they known had not the means of taking advantage of the situation, that the departing Italians had afforded cover to many hundreds of local Jews when leaving France. They left with them. It was an opportunity confined to associates of the Italians, and of them mainly those who could ski, and so take advantage of the unpatrolled, high, snow country. Their fates in Italy varied, for they entered that part of the country still controlled by fascists, with strong antisemitism and a deportation regime developing.

Ana found she could arrange for her family to stay in a safe house near Sète, while she worked on getting them into Spain. The elder Mayers discussed the idea and were reluctant at first to leave the security of their mountain cottage, which they had repaired and improved and where they had been at peace for several months, yet it became apparent very quickly that purging the area of Jews was to become a serious business, so they would leave in two steps. First Ab and Klara would go, then Ana would return for her parents. They would travel by train via inland Digne to Montpellier, then by bus to the safe house. To limit Ab's need to speak in the event of a challenge he would look ill, which in fact he was. Ana would escort them, but not appear to do so.

Arriving at Montpellier train station at dusk, they debarked, with the safe house now not far away. As the passengers filed off the platform, Ab and Klara together, and several passengers removed from Ana, it was apparent that a French policeman was checking passengers' papers, with a German officer looking over his shoulder: they had run into a higher level checkpoint, such as came randomly from time to time. Ana saw Klara and Ab pass through, but then was horrified by the sight of the gate being slammed shut, and Ab being recalled. The policemen fired several questions at him to see if he understood French, but he failed the test. He was arrested. Klara tried to intervene and was warned to keep out of it. She would not, so they arrested her too. Both were made to sit while the rest of the passengers filed through the gate. Another man was arrested. Ana decided to avoid the gate, and slipped out of the queue, and went to the dark end of the platform, then along the rails until she found a way out into the street. Severely shaken, she asked herself: 'What could I have done to save them? What can I do now to get them released?' But no answers came. She walked along in tears. She had warned everybody of the risks, but had not admitted to herself that disaster might strike. The reality now engulfed her, yet she must not show it, in case by doing so she would attract attention. She recalled Ab's words to her as they parted company just before boarding the train at Digne. He had said: "You're less likely than us to be caught, not that we expect it. But in any case I want you to hold these items until we're safe." He had handed her a cloth bag in which she could feel hard objects, so she guessed she was holding valuables. He then handed her a bundle of bank notes with the words: "These too."

She had demurred: "Do you think you need to do this? It's a responsibility for me, and nothing will happen anyway." Then, twinkle-eyed: "Actually I could have a good time with this, so you might be picking the wrong person."

But Ab had insisted, saying: "Well, you can if we get caught. The police would steal it anyway. Please take it, just in case."

"Shouldn't we check everything so we both know what there is?"

"Only if you insist. But I promise you'll have no trouble or questions from me later."

So she had taken the money and valuables, which obviously were too bulky for his boots, unlike her father, and the weight of responsibility that came with them. Now she wondered if by doing so they had tempted fate. 'No,' she firmly thought: 'That's superstitious. They would still have been caught, and the Gestapo would have stolen everything. Ab will be satisfied with his planning. But oh, the poor people!'

She went on to Sète, where she was not due at the safe house at any particular time, but where she could look for Manny to share the awful news. He had a small flat from which he worked in his cover as an assessor of antique furniture in the countryside. It was on the second floor. Ana was wary about entering the building. She waited until a light came on, then threw stones to attract him. As she did a man came out of the building, and asked what she was doing. He was pushing a bicycle. She felt from his manner he was not dangerous so she told him she was looking for her brother, adding that she did not like stairs. The man replied: "Oh you want Marc. I'll go and see. Please hold the bike. What's your name?" He pushed the bike to her and went inside. In a minute he was back saying: "He'll be right down. Now I must rush. If I hurry I'll be at work on time." He rode off as Ana called out her thanks.

Manny came down right away. Thrilled to greet his sister, he wondered as they embraced: 'Why is she here? This sounds like bad news. She doesn't visit me like this. Agents aren't allowed to socialize.' But he hoped he was wrong, and did not show his concern. He said: "What a nice surprise. Why are you here? But come up and we can talk over coffee. No, we'll go for a walk first, and talk as we go. OK?"

As they went Ana's distress showed. In the shelter of a dark spot she burst into tears and threw herself on him, while she sobbed her heart out. He soothed her with words and embrace, hoping to calm her down. Realising she must be stronger she took some deep breaths and simmered down. Then she told him, exactly and without tears, what had happened. He was shocked by the news, concerning as it did the couple who were as dear to them as their parents.

144

Indeed, for a young boy growing up in Germany, especially a Jew-ish boy, to have an uncle who had been a war hero was an inspiring thing, and also a comfort at school when bullying of Jews increased. He kept his emotions in check in view of Ana's state. They agreed there was nothing to be done, as the jaws of internment were known to be ever so strong. And who among their family and colleagues could approach the authorities for clemency without risk of arrest? So what good could be expected from intervention? None, they con-cluded sadly. As Manny said: "We must get used to it. This is a Jew's life in France today." Then they worried about how to improve the plan for their parents so they would be safe. But there was no magic wand to be waved. There were risks whether they stayed in the hills, or took the train out. If they decided to move the same train trip still seemed the best, followed by sea to Spain.

Manny escorted Ana toward her safe house. Passing through a park near the railway line, they sat to continue talking. A south bound train roared past, with long, penetrating blasts that filled the air and stayed Manny's talk. Ana realized it was the Perpignan Flyer. She hesitated. She understood he did not know about Henri, and wondered if she should tell him. But Neil had not, so should she? It was part of SOE secrecy that you didn't give in to the urge to talk. There was no need for Manny to know, at least just now. She would leave it to Neil.

Manny said: "Conchita rings a friend here to say when they'll be back in port, or to ask for news. The friend tells me what I need to know and I pass messages to Diego through her. We have a careful system. I think you're right about the boat. Our parents should get to Barcelona faster that way, with less hassle. I think the risk of being turned back, or returned, is greater if you're caught near the border, where they have special patrols. Anyway the mountains are pretty cold. But any way you look at it, you need luck, don't you?" Ana nod-ded agreement.

He continued: "If we can land them in Barcelona and if Neil can get the consulate on side, then maybe they'll be able to live there out of prison. If they can show the Spanish they have, or are get-ting, an entry visa for somewhere, and can support themselves, they could be left in peace for a few months. It would be lonely for them but nothing they couldn't handle. I say get them to Spain then find a further destination. Maybe Palestine, but beggars can't be choosers. First though, the boat. Let's talk to Diego."

Ana's normally calm brow puckered. She said: "This is a new line, but say Diego came to the coast near Nice, and I took Mum and Dad out to him in a little boat, then they go off to Spain. That way they could stay in the hills where they are safe and would avoid the train. Is that a good idea?"

Manny frowned in turn: "Yes, like everything is. Why don't you go back to them and break the bad news, while I look out for Diego. I'll need to know how to contact you."

Ana said: "I think the best idea is for me to stay here until Diego comes, otherwise I'll be making too many train trips through nasty train stations."

"OK. Stay around. Have you got things to do?"

"Yes, I can make some visits, so I'll be out of touch for a couple of days. I'll contact you then. Now I'd better go. I'm really washed out." They rose, and walked on. After parting near the safe house, Manny's true feelings took over as he walked home, lurching from grief, to anger, to despair, then intensified hatred.

25

After their arrest Ab and Klara were taken in a van to a police station where they were ordered into a room to stand before a German officer seated at a desk. He interrogated them in German. He looked at their papers which showed their correct names but, having been made up by Ana, were not stamped to show the bearer was Jewish, as official papers would; but he had no doubts. He snapped out: "Are your real names Abraham Mayer and Karla Mayer?" He started to make written notes about the answers.

"Yes."

"Are you Jews?"

"Yes".

"Why is that not shown on the cards?"

"We don't know. We didn't prepare them."

Kara added: "I'm a French citizen. I was born here."

"But you both came here from Germany?"

"Yes."

Then, in rapid succession: "Where from?"

"Offenburg."

"When?"

"Early 1939."

"Where have you lived since?" At this point the prisoners slowed down. Each had instantly felt that truthful answers could mean risks to others. They could not allow that, so framed their answers accordingly.

"Near a village north of Nice."

"Its name?"

Ab: "I don't remember that"'

Klara: "The name didn't matter to us."

"The name of the mayor?"

Both: "I don't know."

"You rented a place?"

They nodded.

"The name of the owner?"

Both: "I don't remember." Ab added: "Wait on. Wasn't he Paul?"

Klara: "That might be it, though I'm not sure. We paid rent to a shop in the village."

"Which shop?"

Klara: "I don't know its name. We knew it, but not its name."

"Who got you the house?"

"We looked around for ourselves."

"Where were you going?"

"To near Sète. It's on our tickets that you have. May we have them back please? We need them to go on."

The officer smiled, saying: "I think we can arrange for you to go on." But his look became severe again at once. He continued: "Why there?"

"To stay with a friend who lives there."

"Friend's name and address?"

Ab: "I don't remember."

Klara: "They are to meet us at the bus stop, then we'll know."

The officer became silent, looking at the ceiling while thinking: 'They won't give useful information without pressure, which only the special interrogators can apply. And I don't want them hanging around here for too long, because I'm busy and they're a distraction. They can wait with the others until the train arrives.' His decision made, he stood up, walked around to face the visitors then, without warning, punched Ab in the face, knocking him to the floor, saying: "That's for lying to me, you filthy Jew scum. Liars deserve to be deported." He called in an orderly and gave the order: "Keep them with the others until we find room on a train for Rivesaltes. I'll send all the papers with the escort."

The guard escorted them to a large room containing several prisoners, all Jews as they soon found out, sitting on the floor looking miserable. They had been arrested over the past few hours on trains and platforms, or in the street. There were men, women and children, all of grave and fearful countenance, for all knew that arrest by the Gestapo was a first step to deep misery, of a sort they could only guess at. They had all been arrested, interrogated, and locked up, and refused permission to contact anyone outside. It was after midnight and everybody was tired. Children, and a few adults, were asleep on the floor. Some, the newcomers were told, had been in the room for several hours without food or water or toilet access. Requests to the guards for relief were futile. All baggage was withheld from its owners. As their bladders and bowels hurt a spontaneous wailing commenced, which brought shouted threats from the guards, but the station commander came to investigate, and then they were allowed to visit the lavatory, and given water. Their baggage was still withheld, and for some was never seen again.

In the early morning most of the captives, 14 in all, were given back their baggage, and all were embarked on a southbound train, which delivered them to Rivesaltes, in the department of Pyrénées-Orientales, the most southerly administrative department in France, and whose boundaries included the Spanish border from the Mediterranean Sea to Andorra in the heights of the Pyrénées; and a fifty kilometre stretch of the sandy beaches, coastal lagoons and fishing villages of the Côte Vermeille north from the border. A little to the north of the main centre of Perpignan lay Rivesaltes, and a large concentration camp, one of several along the coastal plain of the department.

The camp had been established as barracks in the first world war, and by 1943 had become a very large complex of wooden huts on an open plain close to the sea. Frequent cold winds from the mountains with strong gusts up to 120 kmh tended to freeze the poorly clad and ill-fed prisoners in winter, while creating tiresome clouds of dust, and in the calmer weather of summer the heat was another form of misery. From early 1939 onward Spanish republicans were the only inmates, to be largely displaced by Jews by the time of the arrival of Ab and Klara. For all those inmates the prison had a continuous and deserved reputation for being a dirty, unheated, insanitary and sometimes brutal place, where malnutrition with high adult and very, very high infant mortality rates, were well known. It was entirely a French affair, and showed the capacity of the French State and some French people for inhumaneness in creating outcasts, then treating them as pariahs. The extreme nature of the treatment was slightly relieved by the open-hearted ministrations of volunteer social workers oriented toward children. Those, mainly women, came from French and Swiss welfare organizations, performed nobly in an atmosphere of dirt, despair, and official indifference. They softened, as far as they could, the cruel blows of fate on little children, who included many orphans. In many ways though Rivesaltes was a transit camp, from where inmates were moved to Drancy thence deportation. And after a few days the roundup that included Ab and Klara was added to from other inmates to fill a freight car, which took them to Drancy, in squalor and deep misery. On disembarking there they were again segregated by sex, and taken to different dormitories. Some only had the clothes they were wearing when arrested days before. From their luggage Ab and Klara were allowed to take some items of clothing which they gave needy companions, and their main luggage was taken into storage.

26

Early in 1943 the Vichy Government formed a paramilitary force, a militia known by its French name of milice, for better collaboration with the Germans, and for hunting down French resisters, saboteurs, Jews, and other undesirables. This new creation had evolved from another conservative, but less violent body. Its members were well qualified for this work because of their local knowledge, and they were successful in German eyes, being ruthless in true Gestapo style, with which it soon came to work closely. Its ranks included criminals, thugs and other mean men, for some of whom the chance of loot from victims was a reason for membership, and for others it was a way of avoiding compulsory labour service. They became hated by those with cause to fear them, and a mini civil war developed between them and resisters, and was fought at high levels of bitterness and atrocities, and as such was self-perpetuating.

Ana became a little concerned that the factory she worked in was located in a district where she had been to school, thinking that the chances of her recognition as a Jew might be greater there than in a different locality, even with the changes in her appearance by mild disguise. So she started thinking of leaving that job, though mindful of the effort that some unknown people had made to set her up. In the meantime she would keep as low a profile as possible so as to minimise the risk of recognition and betrayal. But one autumn morning in 1943, as she got off a bus, she almost walked into a young man whom she recognised from her school days. She walked on without stopping, looking straight ahead. She remembered him as Jean-Pierre, but nothing else about him. She felt fairly confident he had not recognised her, but the encounter troubled her. Then a week or so later she noticed him in the long street in which her factory, one of many, stood. He was strolling, appraising the several factories along the street. As that was the sort of sniffing around miliciens were known for she took notice, and went to Neil for guidance. He said the two risk points were her home, and the factory. There was nothing to suggest that either was being watched, but she should find a new residence promptly. As for the factory, Neil thought she should leave, which was regrettable since it was good cover, but the proprietor should have a say in the matter, so she should tell him everything before making a decision.

A few days later, as she neared the bus stop after work late one afternoon, and before she had spoken with Felix, the factory owner, Ana noticed a police van down the street just past the stop. She turned back, but as she did two gendarmes came up to her and one said: "Excuse me please Miss but we would like ...." and before the request was completed she knew she was a suspect and was to be interrogated. However, as she turned to the men she displayed and expressed surprise. In a friendly tone she asked: "What can I do for you?"

The senior gendarme replied: "It would be better if we went somewhere private to talk. Our car is just down the street. We can walk there quickly, but please do not do anything silly like trying to run away."

Ana said: "Well, if I must come then I will, but I hope it won't take long, as I must get to work, and I haven't the faintest idea how I could help you. But no doubt you will explain."

"We will, we will," both replied.

The car took them to the police station a few doors to the north of the *préfecture de police* building on *Cours de la Liberté*, which name seemed to her a bad joke in the circumstances. She had seen German uniformed personnel going in and out of this station, so took it be a centre of collaboration between the police forces of the two nations. This led to the thought that the Gestapo might interrogate her, at the thought of which she went numb. It was the dread of all resisters. The Gestapo were known to be highly experienced in torturing their victims in both mind and body. Ana's mind flickered over the especially sensitive parts of her body and shuddered. But it was not new. She, and all people in her line of belligerent effort, knew from the beginning they were engaged in a merciless struggle against a ruthless and depraved enemy. Death, injury, transportation to a German concentration camp, all could happen to undercover agents. Not that their superiors dwelled on those prospects, for to do so could restrict the numbers of recruits, of whom there were never enough for the task, except later when the tides of war were running out fast for the Germans, and being an active resister became more fashionable, and less dangerous.

The police car entered a yard at the rear of the station, from where she was led inside to the reception desk and the duty officer took her particulars, and belongings, before sending her, under escort, to an interview room on the first floor. Alone, she collected her thoughts and prayed for strength to cope, and be brave, drawing comfort from the fact that she still had her suicide pill to use if her spirit failed. But first, could she escape? A glance around the tiny room showed there was one window, high in the wall, barred, and inaccessible; and one door, which she found locked. She decided against picking the lock, a matter she had some training in, because were she to fail she might add to her problems by being charged with attempting to escape. So she sat mute, waiting.

As the fortunes of war swung firmly towards the Allies and the desperate and ferocious barbarism of the Germans occupying France hurt citizens more and more, some French police became less inclined to follow their leaders blindly, but instead began to exercise a private, unofficial, discretion in some situations. Moreover, the Vichy edict that they hand over certain suspects to the Gestapo for interrogation, without even preliminary examination by the French police, didn't go down too well, for it made them, in effect, hunters for the Gestapo, which worked outside French rules for dealing with suspects and criminals. Those rules contained an element of respect for individual rights and due process and the rule of law, if muted where Jews were concerned. The Station Superintendent was especially cautious about handing suspects over to the Gestapo. He had discreetly told his inspectors that certain cases should be brought to his attention, or in his absence to one of a panel of names chosen by him. This meant that on the evening Ana was brought in after a tip off from a milicien, an Inspector Clement had to be informed, and that proceedings should not go further without his express instructions. It was not for the duty gendarmes to query this procedure, but only to report the occurrence to the inspector's office, and appoint a station guard to stand outside the door of the prisoner's room until given further orders.

Marius Clement had been ready to go home when he noticed

on his message pad that a female was in custody for interrogation on suspicion of espionage. There were two annotations, reading respectively: 'M tip-off', and 'Jew?' He knew from experience that such cases were considered by the Gestapo to be its special province, as affecting affairs of State, as distinct from breaches of the criminal code. He wondered if the Jew question underlay the matter. He knew that the milice of which, and its members, most police were contemptuous, sometimes presented cases that were not in fact proper subjects for French police inquiry. Yet it was a law enforcement arm of government, and so he must deal with the complaint. His first step was to check if Ana's name was on the Gestapo 'wanted' list in his drawer. It was not. Now he could appoint one or more gendarmes to interview the suspect, and decide upon action when he read their report, probably the next day. It would be difficult for him not to act on their report. Or he could deal with the matter himself now. Not very happily, he decided to do that. It should not hold him up for long.

On coming to the interview room he dismissed the young gendarme seated outside, and entered. He saw, seated at the table, staring straight ahead, a neatly dressed, small, young woman with colourful brown hair tied in a bun, large brown eyes, and sharp features. Her complexion was fair and unmarked and her demeanour calmly serious. On his entering, and recognising him as a senior officer, she stood up and said: "Sir." He replied: "Good evening. Please be seated." He sat opposite her. She waited for him to speak.

"How old are you?"

"I am 23."

"Are you French?"

"My papers are at the reception desk, and show I am." She paused. The inspector took it she had something more to say, and waited, but she didn't speak.

He asked: "You have a slight accent. Could you tell me a little more about yourself?"

Ana thought. 'This man is not the Gestapo, but if I lie to him he'll send me there. He might, no matter what. If I go there they'll treat me like a Jew, and find out I am. He's likely to find that out anyway. If I lie to him there's no chance of him being kind to me. Perhaps not even if I'm truthful, but that's to be seen. A lie to the

Gestapo is something I think I can handle: I'm uneasy about lying to him.' The inspector had no idea what was racing through her mind, but was not especially surprised when she continued: "There's something else though. My family came from Germany. I'm Jewish, and French. Some of my relatives have been deported, and I believe they're dead. I think I'm only here because someone I was at school with is a milicien and saw me in the street. Please be kind to me and let me go, sir. I'm very frightened about my fate otherwise. Please sir." Her eyes grew moist and she hung her head, pursing her lips to keep control of herself.

Marius Clement listened impassively. He looked away from Ana while she was emotional. He thought about his wife. She had strong views about the way Jews were being treated in Lyon, as elsewhere in France, and she was well informed about the conditions of their detention camps here and the trains in which they were deported. Like him, she wished they had not come in such numbers, but that was no excuse for treating them as subhuman. And neither of them liked Germans, as both had relatives who had suffered from them in both big wars. But agreeing with his wife at home was different from carrying out his official duties, even when personally distasteful. Here he had to make a decision. He sensed he was at the edge of more information from this suspect, the possession of which could make it difficult for him to help her if it came out. Yet he recoiled from referring her case either to the Gestapo direct, or to the Germans in charge of Jewish affairs. In either event a young, apparently decent human being would be turned into a physical and mental wreck awaiting death. And this without any more of her life being revealed, for he did not overlook the possibility that somebody like her might be engaged in activities of interest to the Gestapo, if not to him. He decided not to go into more detail. He thought: 'Whatever she is she hardly deserves to be a Gestapo victim. If I give her up and the Superintendent finds out about the case he'll be disappointed in me. If I give her up I couldn't honestly tell my wife that I do what I can. She's never said, but I think she prays for that a lot. I'll be home soon. If I'm in a funny mood because of sending this person to the Gestapo my wife will surely try to get it out of me, and if I don't tell her she'll be sure I've done something wrong. Not that I could bear to tell her. The last thing I want is another lecture on moral cowardice.' He looked at Ana impassively, and spoke deliberately: "You claim to be a French citizen who has not broken any laws, so that your arrest is apparently a case of mistaken identity. You say you're disappointed to be kept here and interrogated. It seems to me there's nothing in your conduct that amounts to a breach of the laws of France. In those circumstances, and without evidence to the contrary, I'm obliged to apologise to you and allow you to leave. The record of interview will reflect those matters." Pausing a moment, he spoke slower and more deliberately: "However, your particulars, including your current address, are entered in the station records in accordance with normal procedure." He paused again, and looked at her as if to have his words sink in, then continued: "Do you have any questions?"

Ana sat numb in mind. She had been very fearful that she was for the chop when the inspector looked so serious before he started talking. As he went on her heart lightened, even though she had trouble following his formal manner of speaking. But the gist of it was clear. She was to go free. She felt like hugging, or kissing him, or both, but knew not to. She knew he had spoken good news to her, so she would like to hear it again, but she wasn't going to tempt fate by asking for that. Instead she kept quiet, while struggling to hold back her tears that were close to pouring out. Then, looking at him, she cried: "Thank you. I understand. I thank you with all my heart, sir."

They both got up. He opened the door, saying: "Come with me for your papers, then you may leave."

They went to the ground floor where the inspector spoke to the duty gendarme and pointed to Ana. Then he came to her, and said: "Wait here, and in a few minutes you'll be called to sign for your papers. I'll leave you now. Goodbye." He turned and left, making a mental note to remind his staff tomorrow that being a Jew was not of itself an offence; at least at present. Ana waited in fear that someone would intervene to change what she had been told, and that the inspector would then not be at hand to help her. But it was alright, and a few minutes later she was outside. She stood and breathed in the sweet, free air. She shook all over. She thanked God. She found a taxi and arrived home about midnight, quite exhausted.

Next morning she woke with waves of exhilaration surging through her, and forthwith applied her mind to the future. First, she must consider leaving the factory, in case she attracted official attention to it. She knew nothing of her employer's political leanings or private activities, and did not need to know. But in case he was vulnerable she must tell him the facts of her arrest. And she must change her identity again, and her address, as they were now in police records, which could be but a step away from the Gestapo. And also she would look out for piecework, where she could work at home for part of the time and be paid only for output, as was a common practice in the industry. But she would seek Neil's advice and instructions in all those matters, not least because she might need more SOE pay if she changed work. She had lots to do, but since she was alive, free, and unharmed, she was confident she could handle everything. And as she prepared for the day she made up a little song to sing to herself:

"The papers say you're the King, Monsieur le Marechal Pétain,
And that you are the best,
And us will sustain,
And lead to glory,
But when it's all put to the test,
It will be a different story."

27

Drancy lies some six kilometres to the north east of central Paris. When Germany invaded France it was an outer suburb. Its most prominent feature then was a group of five storey residential buildings, none with a lift, the whole being part of a public housing scheme near a train station. Although partly unfinished, it was empty, and taken to be fit for use as a prison camp, and as such received its first inmates, Parisian Jews, in August 1941. Their roundup was a joint exercise of the French and German police targeting males aged between the ages of 18 and 50 years, most of them found at home in the early morning and selected, ironically, from their responses to official demands, introduced in late 1940 throughout France, that all Jews register. Previously, as registration of faith had never been required, officials could not distinguish them, nor had they the need, so those who complied made it easier for their hunters. Their favoured arrondisements were now surrounded and methodically combed. This was a German sponsored event, an extension of its official policy of rounding up and imprisoning Jews so as to aryanise the territories under its control, just as had happened in Germany. With about 3000 victims it was the largest of the early roundups, and a harbinger of many more throughout France. As strangers, the Germans had relied on full cooperation from the local police, both for compiling lists, and during the house-to-house roundup, and would do so in subsequent roundups no less.

Drancy was one of many concentration camps of the French government, which had proliferated since 1939 with the incarceration of Spanish republican refugees - when the government of the Third Republic was in power - and seamlessly continued into 1940 and beyond, after the Vichy government took over. Prisoners then came from an increasingly wider range, many being Jews fleeing the Nazi terror. From the beginning the internments provided convenient supplies of potential victims for the Germans to sift through in searching for those whom it saw as its political enemies, and those selected were taken away with little ceremony, or objection from the French. Later, as Germany's labour needs increased, and as a separate matter the Final Solution was developed, substantial human cargo was required by Germany, so the institution of French internment camps and prisons was again useful, now more in the same style as livestock holding pens. For many non-Jewish French men and woman deportation was their being ordered to work in Germany, where the pay and conditions were not unreasonable. For the Jews deportation had an unknown, yet sinister purpose, and the destination was not clear. Quite early in the Occupation the stateless, or foreign Jews, took over from the Spanish republican refugees as the main group of internees in France. Room was made by dispersing many Spaniards variously to forced labour for either France or Germany, to Spain to home, to isolated French communities where there was spare accommodation and little opportunity for subversive activity and only loose supervision, to a few sympathetic countries led by Mexico, and some to the emerging resistance groups soon to be called collectively the maquis, and later, the Resistance. The Jews were not given as wide a range, as French hatred and contempt toward them was on a different level. The Spaniards who had been fellow prisoners with Ab and Klara'a Jewish group in Rivesaltes were remnants, women and children, and the aged and incapacitated. As the war progressed the shackles of the Spanish refugees loosened, and those of the Jews tightened.

The numbers of Jewish internees jumped with the extension of German military control to the whole of mainland France by successive steps in 1942 and 1943. In German eyes being Jewish was a crime, and all Jews were therefore criminals, and enemies of the Reich besides, so all, without either exception or mercy, were to be accounted for, and controlled, and reduced as far as practicable to animal status, with their complete elimination from society as the final target. Had they the necessary clairvoyance, learned observers of an earlier age, even if antisemitic, would have thought such a series of events improbable, or even impossible. Not because mankind was incapable of such persecution, for there had been past instances in Europe and Asia and Africa that amounted to mini genocide. But our hypothetical soothsayers would not have expected such leaders of European civilization as Germany and France to have been parties to genocide in the 20th century; at different levels to be sure. That the wipe-out was not achieved in full was in no sense to the credit of either nation, joint perpetrators of the wicked scheme, but due only to what, to them, was the unexpected: the Allies winning the war. It was that alone that saved the Jews of France, and indeed of all Europe. And that was not the main aim of the Allied war effort, but merely a fortuitous consequence.

French contribution to the Final Solution of the Jewish problem – to use the heartless language of the Nazis – was complicated by the French perception of two categories of Jews. It is not to be supposed that the boundary was as sharply etched in the way a coastline puts the land to one side and the sea to the other. Yet, after allowing for tattered edges, on one side were the French Jews, being those well established in France, and on the other the foreign Jews, being recent refugees whom few people, French Jews or Gentiles, wanted to remain. In the majority French view, citizens and Vichy politicians alike, the French Jews were not to be forcibly sent from the country. They could be plundered economically, demeaned socially, and discriminated against politically, but not deported. But the State had no reservations concerning the foreign Jews. If Germany wished to deport them France would help. It had no deportation program of its own, and hardly needed one with that of Germany at hand. It was content to give them up to the Occupier whose longstanding object, constantly affirmed by word and deed, was their elimination.

The early roundups in Paris were never completely successful, even with earnest French police support.   Human affairs being dynamic, many dodged the net before it reached them. The difficulties for the Germans were greatly magnified when it came time to seek out all the Jews in the whole of mainland France, after Germany's takeover of the south. The Germans never had enough men on their own, so in searching were always very heavily reliant on the French police, and miliciens from their start up in early 1943. The level of assistance afforded the Germans by the French at all levels reduced as the war went badly for Germany, and the ruthlessness of its troops and police showed increasingly. Yet for all the difficulties, the ingrained antisemitism of the French allowed a degree of success for the deportation scheme our observers of a century ago would not have expected.

Then the further question surfaced. As Jewish internees were seen, and known to be treated badly, in France, what worse treatment might befall them upon deportation? Although citizens had little direct power to change matters, their country being governed by the dictatorship of Pétain and the ruthless German occupiers, voices could be raised and, when those came from influential persons such as a few leading churchmen, complaints started to make news despite rigid censorship. The effect was to make more Frenchmen aware of the inhumanity of the treatment of foreign Jews, and more inclined to help them evade arrest. To a certain extent, though falling far short of rejection of the scheme, France became less supportive of deportation. The net result of mixed influences was that deportation train schedules became progressively harder to meet, to the chagrin of those in charge. To go ahead of events, the end result was that many thousands of Jews were not clawed into internment, but lived through the considerable privations of the ordinary French people, the more profound for being Jews, to be still alive in France at its liberation.

Although not extermination camps in the German style, thousands of people died in French internment camps from disease, medical neglect, starvation, and in some cases, bashings. The regime of misery at Drancy was typical of the general run of the French internment prisons, with the added feature of it being the main holding and departure camp from which Jews were taken into the special trains that carried pitiable human cargoes to inhumane endings far away. From March 1942 onward over 70,000 victims left it for death in places such as Auschwitz in southern Poland, then occupied by Germany. So several thousands of Jews and other victims such as political enemies of either the Nazis or the Vichy regime had been imprisoned and deported from Drancy before Ab and Klara Mayer arrived there, and many thousands more, again mainly Jews of all ages gathered from all over France, would follow until the last deportation train on 17 August 1944. They entered, resided in, and departed from Drancy in subhuman conditions. And this was so, regardless of age, frailty, or sex. Drancy was a French shame. And it was not less so because a handful of brave and compassionate women, and fewer men, called social workers, were able, despite official obstacles, to push themselves into it to ease a little pain at the edges of the great mass of hurt.

28

Soon after her brush with the police Ana had taken a new name and address, and had the cover of pieceworker for the same establishment, allowing her to minimise her attendances at the factory, and so her profile was lower. She trusted her factory boss, and being convinced he was a resister, felt safe in explaining her status and the encounter with Jean-Pierre and the police.

Felix Briand employed a few score garment workers. His brick, three storey, 1880s factory building was located in an old part of Lyon, easterly from the left bank of the Rhône River. However, the machinery inside, and the production methods, were as modern as the owner's energy and money could make them. The staff, mainly females, included out-workers in the suburbs and near countryside. There were constant comings and goings to and from the factory as goods were brought in and out, and workers and contractors came and went. The firm had been started by his grandfather, a tailor, and through family affairs the business had devolved on Felix. He and his wife were thoroughly, but quietly, anti-German and anti-Vichy.

Felix became involved in resistance activity through a friend, a lawyer. Both believed they could serve the cause of resistance best working to plans made up by experts. As he knew that in the course of their ordinary business lawyers had to make all manner of inquiries, and so had access to information that was not readily available to laymen, Felix took him to be well placed to locate resistance organisations, and told him he would be open to suggestions. Some weeks later the friend had telephoned him to be on the lookout for a female salesperson who would identify herself in ways he described. The meeting with her led to Felix employing various people nominated to him from time to time by or on her behalf. He treated them like other employees, and never inquired into their activities. He knew his business was now a front, and that besides himself, only the secretive woman knew. He was content. He did not, for example, arrange for searches of materials going and coming to see if messages were being sent under cover. He knew nothing about Ana except that she was recommended to him - he could never remember by whom - and was efficient at her job. That she was away erratically was not something for him to look into, because he sensed that whatever the cause it was important to her, and he knew that staff went through difficult phases in their private lives that required free time to work through.

When Ana came to him to tell of her experience with the police and her stalker, Felix paid close attention, and asked detailed questions. In fact he felt greater concern than his calm demeanour showed. After she left he sat, thinking. He sensed the stalker was a milicien and a danger to himself and his people, any of whom might succumb during interrogation. He was alarmed enough to arrange to meet a certain friend after work. Felix knew that killing a person would not be easy for him. He had no experience. He could easily botch it. And he did not own a pistol, or know where to get one. However, he thought as he drove, if necessary he would try to overcome those obstacles, but first he would approach somebody more experienced, hoping that together they might find a way to deal with the milicien, and sooner rather than later. The friend he was to meet, Louis Caperan, was an inactive army captain who had lost a leg in action along a northern river in 1940. At the time of the French surrender he had been in a military hospital near Lyon, and remained there for a further year after which, a little to his surprise, he was discharged home, instead of to imprisonment in Germany. He had continued to receive his pay and occasional medical treatment from the army, who rarely found anything for him to do. His spirits were low through being useless at a time of crisis for his country and its destiny when Felix brought his concern about the stalker. He knew at once he would help, and had only to work out how.

Jean-Pierre Demangeon had attended school with Ana. He barely remembered her, except that she seemed German or Jewish or both, and that she had not been very friendly when he had made overtures to her. He had not thought of her at all in the several intervening years until he was standing waiting at a bus stop. He saw her as she got off the bus, and was sure it was she despite her appearance had changed, and also that she had recognised him at the instant their eyes met, and he had been preparing to speak with her. But she hurried away without even a nod. As he was a recently accepted milicien and expected to use initiative in identifying suspects, and as it was official Vichy policy to hunt down Jews, he decided to keep an eye on her. He supposed she either lived or worked in the locality. By watching the buses and following her he identified the general area of her workplace, but was never able to track her precisely to it or from her home or workplace. Yet he became certain she was Jewish, and maybe also under cover, so he reported his findings to the central police station, letting it be known he was a milicien, and so always keen to help. He identified Ana to them. He would also keep in touch to learn what success the police had in the case. To himself he thought that if something really important should turn up, such as a nest of subversion in one or more factories, his stocks in the force would go up. In this he was driven by hope for the success he craved, but had so far proved most elusive during his 25 years of life. His efforts had led to Ana being arrested.

Felix created a new work station for a trusted employee overlooking the street, and she was to look out for a young male of certain appearance and likely style of movement. She was to report any sighting quietly and immediately to Felix, then return at once to her ordinary work station and forget the matter.

Jean-Pierre was methodically surveying the long and busy street, taking occasional notes, thinking there could be more fish to catch here, and anyway this was work that was out of the danger zone of hunting down maquisards, which he knew some of his colleagues did. On the present run he was nearing the end of the street on the opposite side to the Felix Briand factory when a car came around the corner and drove down the street past him. He did not see it turn and come back up the street slowly, on his side of the road, so he was a little surprised to see it come by and slow to a stop. The driver was looking around, as for an address. A cheerful looking man with a large moustache and a blue cap, he beckoned Jean-Pierre as if to ask him for help. He went, eager to oblige. As he came to the open window the driver leaned toward him as if to ask him to look at a street map lying on the dashboard. As he leaned in the driver reached over, very firmly pushed his head down with his left hand, grasped the pistol hidden behind him in his right hand, and fired a shot into the top of Jean-Pierre's head, making a whole in his beret through which a mixture of blood and other vital components immediately commenced oozing. The driver pushed the body back through the window, then got out and quickly ran his hands through the its pockets, removing some papers, including a notebook. He got back into the car and slowly drove off. As he did so a man came running down the street toward the scene. The driver called out to him: "There's been a terrible accident. I'm going for an ambulance and the police. Look after him, won't you?" As others gathered, the man was able to tell them that an ambulance and police were coming, and by the time he realised they weren't, a stolen car had been left in a street three blocks away. From it M Caperan, a clean shaven man in a grey hat, carrying a small case, had limped toward a bus stop. While waiting he glanced at the papers he had taken from his victim, and was satisfied he had got the right man, or at least an equivalent. He would now return the borrowed pistol and silencer to their owners. He was chuffed to feel useful again.

29

On a Sunday morning in early October 1943 Conchita telephoned Marta with a brief coded message: *"Hola. C'est moi. Trois. Tres."* It meant to Marta that the Santa Maria would arrive in Sète in a day or so. Next morning she left an envelope addressed to M Labouche at the friendly local sub-post-office. Its message would tell Manny, when he called for the mythical M Labouche's mail, of the boat's movements, which would imply those of the crew besides.

Conchita had taken charge of disposal of the catch, being better at French, although face-to-face communications on the waterfront included as much body language as speech. And Diego thought a woman would be generally less suspect. Most of the catch went to the official agents in whom it was vested by law, and who paid the skippers, less a percentage for tax. This was part of the official food control program, essential when much primary production was continuously diverted to Germany to serve its war interests. Nonetheless a few pieces of fish were always overlooked by the officials, so that all the boats had some catch they could sell for themselves on the black market, or to restaurants and hotels. This practice was countenanced on the basis that the officials also received their percentage of the proceeds from black market sales, and of course a few fish for themselves. They were thus conspirators, all of whom relied on the hold each had over the other for protection. The scheming created an air of secrecy over the waterfront, which also incidentally provided a shield for the crew of the *Santa Maria*. After the main disposal was ended that day, Conchita wrapped up the remnant edible fish in three parcels, one for Manny, one for Marta, and one for a restaurant; which would get two parcels if Manny wasn't home.

But he was there. He came to the boat in the evening. They all went to Marta's, and once together, Manny gave them his news.

First, the tragic affair of Ab and Klara, and the apparent danger of train travel. He told them how the Germans were vigorously and relentlessly hunting down the Jews in the former Italian zone, aided by miliciens, French police, and French collabos who were being paid rewards for locating Jews, and who, along with neighbours, plundered the premises and belongings of the Jews once they were whisked away. If his parents could be got out safely, the next questions would be how to get to Spain, and later, to Palestine. Taking it step by step, could Diego and Conchita take them from the coast near Nice? And if so, where to? Barcelona? There the consul might help, especially if Neil put in a good word for them. This voyage was to be a private job, to be paid for by the passengers.

The party heard him in silence. They were sad to hear of his uncle and aunt, and try as they might to think of something helpful, they were in fact quite helpless in this area. They did not need to say they would like to help his parents, nor that Diego and Conchita were ever mindful of the risk of imprisonment for themselves, though they felt a fading risk, at least in France. Their primary concern was to develop a feasible plan.

Diego said: "We must expect heavy beach and sea patrols around Nice. We'd have to come at a right angle. It could work, with luck, but what if we were intercepted? We'd have to explain our presence. Saying we were fishing, or coming in for repairs, wouldn't be convincing. That is a no-fishing and no-go area, and everyone knows it. I bet we would be taken in for questioning, then if they had any doubts about us we would soon be in prison. But even if we did the pickup, we would run risks from patrol boats and submarines. That's how sensitive the water is there. Someone could use us for gunnery practice and then we'd be just another boat lost at sea with all hands. Whatever the plan is it needs to have a fair chance of success. I don't like that coast. Another thing, it's much longer if we start from there, and your parents, not being used to the sea, would be doing it hard, even the shortest way."

Conchita, listening intently, nodded agreement. Manny took notice. The plan was impractical, so he dropped it. He said: "Then we must get them here by train. If they go the long way via Digne, then with the good papers and their good French they could make it. Now assume they do. What next?"

165

Diego had a word with Conchita, then replied: "We'd sail straight from here straight across the gulf to Móntago, and we'd be in international waters most of the time, for what that's worth. Your parents would be hidden if necessary. We would be a Spanish fishing boat heading for port. The Germans have no fight with Spain. We don't expect Spanish patrols to be a problem, as we've never seen any. I think they'll have a good chance at Barcelona. I've heard Spain doesn't send Jews back to France or Germany these days, not once they're actually inside Spain. I think they put them either in prison, or under a sort of house arrest, and look for ways to send them on to other countries. Sounds funny doesn't it? Maybe it's because Franco changed his idea about who'll win the war."

"So", said Conchita, "Manny's parents could have a chance even without the help of the consulate? "

"I hope so", replied Diego. "But of course we'd ask for help there. In any case, there seems no need to put them in gaol if they can support themselves, and are in transit. I suppose they'd have to keep in touch with the police, but people like them aren't a threat. The best thing would be to land them up the coast from Barcelona, where it's quieter, and take them down by train."

Conchita spoke: "I know my way around. If we landed them I could take them on. I'm beginning to think that the chances of Franco's police picking us up are a little less now. Maybe there's no record of either of us in the Spanish police files. But even so, it's not like we were generals. So I wouldn't mind taking your parents along, Manny."

"Thanks Conchita," said Manny. "That's really good news. But it'd be nice to know what the consulate might do before we start. I think I should ask Neil if he can put in a good word for my parents. But getting messages into and out of there would take time, and I don't know that my parents can afford to hang around here ...."

"Hang on," Conchita interrupted. "We could take Neil's message to the consulate. After that I could put your parents up at a hotel while something was worked out. Or they could stay at Móntago while I went on down. It's only a few hours."

"Or I could take them fishing and they could live on the boat while we waited," added Diego.

"Well," said Manny, "those options are great, but it's all a bit too much for me to digest just now.   Why don't we have another drink, and talk again tomorrow." They all agreed. It was getting late. It was bed time. But the morning brought nothing new. There was no change in anybody's position. It all depended on contacting Neil, and getting Manny's parents safely to Sète.

When Ana arrived the following afternoon Manny explained the position. She said: "Then the boat from here it'll be. We need to contact Neil soon. We can both look for him. In the meantime I must get Mum and Dad out. I'll bring them through Digne again, and we'll all be very, very, careful. I hope the other things happen quickly because I don't want them stuck in a safe house for too long."

Manny responded: "Yes, I know. But I know another place if we need it. You get them down here, and we'll find out what Neil thinks."

Then Ana went on to the safe house to rest before returning to her parents to break the news about Ab and Klara, and convince them to leave their rural home. She knew that none of it would be easy. There would be shock and grief, and the fear that by moving they would be tempting the same fate. It might seem easier to leave them there, yet all the pointers suggested that would be wrong. Therefore she must put the case for moving as firmly as possible. That was the best way of saving her parents. She could not bear the thought of losing them besides Ab and Klara.

The next morning Ana was walking toward the train station along a busy main street when she saw ahead two German soldiers, recognising their uniforms as Abwehr police, as she had learned during SOE training. It was important to know that the several different uniforms denoted various levels of viciousness; with the Gestapo the most dangerous for SOE personnel. The men appeared to be young foot soldiers, and so less frightening: at least before getting their prisoner into the station. She was surprised, as she had rarely seen German police in the area. She would cross the street so as to avoid contact, and then she noticed a woman between the two men; not handcuffed, but clearly under their control. She gave a little shudder, then looked again. Something about her attracted extra interest. She was seeing things. The female head she had caught a glimpse off was so like Monica, her FANY mentor when she had been screened for

SOE admission. But the head and its body were between, and walking with the men. She looked again, and noted they held her arms, not roughly, but firmly. She was not resisting. Anna moved behind the party to get a better view, by which she confirmed her first fear. She made a quick decision. She had no doubt about Monica's fate if she didn't act fast and brazenly. Her brain worked like lightning about how to handle the coming drama, and her first physical step was to move her revolver, which she carried more often since Henri Rée, from her shoulder bag into her overcoat pocket. She then quickly selected a card from several she carried, and placed it in another pocket. Coming up behind the walking party, she took command of herself to meet the ordeal ahead, knowing that otherwise the game would be lost before it started, and she, besides Monica, could be on the way to a deadly meeting with Gestapo interrogators. Total composure, and an air of authority, was called for; nothing else would do. Coming up behind the walking group she called out "Achtung!" in the most peremptory tone she could muster. The party stopped, and the soldiers looked around, and did not realise at first that the speaker had been the small young woman behind them. She saluted them with the cry, in German, "Heil Hitler!', to which they were bound to respond in kind, and did. She said: "I'm an Abwehr agent attached to special projects. Here is my card." She handed over the impressive document bearing her photograph and signed and stamped authoritatively. They perused it and checked the photograph and whispered together, and reluctantly decided she was legitimate, and the spokesman asked "What next?"

"You've interrupted an important undercover action in which your prisoner, who is my informant, is pointing out places and people of interest for my unit to investigate. You weren't to know, but I want her back or I'll be in big trouble, and if I am you will be too. Why did you take her in?'

"We were standing at a checkpoint where she was lined up with other people, and a policeman said to us she'd been overheard speaking English, so we thought we'd make ourselves useful and take her in for questioning. We knew nothing of your operation."

"Did you search her?"

"No, we weren't all that suspicious, and that would happen when we got back to the station anyway."

"You should always search, or else one day you mightn't get back." Turning to Monica she said, in French: "Hand me your bag." Monica raised her eyebrows. Ana added: "I'll be careful." She opened the bag, and quickly flashed it before the men before handing it back to Monica, saying to the men, in German: "So it's OK, so that's good. That's only for your information, as I know she's clean, because I searched her properly earlier." And to Monica, in French: "I'm aiming to retrieve you. Here comes the tricky bit. Get ready to run if it collapses. Don't wait for me."

Ana guessed the soldiers accepted the card, and were not perturbed by its being new to them, as there were many official German cards, and nobody knew them all. In fact this card had been created by SOE forgers. In accepting her authority, the captors also accepted Monica was her property, so she must act it out. She said: "I must take my informant back to my HQ in Montpellier, as we have lost speed and contacts now, and my commandant will want to start again. Can you take me there?"

"Us? We don't have any authority for that, and have no vehicle. In fact, our unit is moving out in an hour or so. You'll have to get there under your own steam."

"Oh! So that's how it must be. I'll cope. I'll give you my reference in case your commandant wants to look further into this matter." She produced a small notepad of official Abwehr paper and wrote her name and rank and the address of its HQ as 19 rue de Madeleine, Montpellier, and handed it over. The men took it, read it, and talked among themselves, showing doubt about the need for it. Ana overheard them, and kept up the momentum, saying: "How you handle this at your end is your affair. It may help you to know my people won't be making any complaints about you, because they have more important matters in hand. So it's goodbye." She snapped to attention, saluting and crying "Heil Hitler!", before turning away, taking Monica's arm, in proprietorial style. She said to Monica as they went: "Don't hurry. Don't look back. We'll turn left at the corner, then we can see what they're doing." When they looked back at the corner the soldiers had disappeared, so at least they weren't chasing them, which greatly relieved the women.

Monica said: "I can take us to a shop close by that's my safe house. Stay a little bit behind me and I'll lead the way." Ana was drained of initiative by now, so followed without question. They went down a lane to the rear entrance of a baker's shop, and they went in, and it was obvious to Ana that Monica was at home here, because she took them straight into a tiny secluded place, part tearoom, part storeroom, part lavatory. A young woman wearing a white apron and a baker's hat came in, and greeted Monica warmly. She introduced her as her friend Mirielle, to whom she said: "You won't believe this but we've just been harassed by some *boches*, and thanks to her" pointing to Ana, "we've survived to tell you. We're drained out, so we'd love a cup of something."

"Oh! My goodness! Sounds amazing. I'll fix you up, but I'll just get some proper chairs for you first." She got the chairs, then left them.

Alone, and though still stunned by their experience, Monica said: "I know you, don't I? And Ana replied: "Of course, and how could I forget you?"

"Still I must identify you. Where did we meet and who did I work for and where?"

Ana replied: "Good thinking. We met at an office in London. You worked for FANY, an officer in fact, at a compound in a London suburb, but I don't know its name. You were my minder while I was being looked over."

Monica replied: "Of course. That was last year. You've been here ever since, I suppose. I've only come in a few weeks ago. I'm still learning, aren't I?"

"So am I. That was a fluke, y'know. It only worked because they're new and raw."

"What do you think they'll do?"

"We can only guess. If they're moving out they might forget to make a report, because it would show they'd handed over a suspect without due cause, and to women mind you, which would be crystal clear if inquiry were made about an Abwehr HQ in Montpellier."

"You made that up?"

"Yes, but they won't know until or unless they follow through. No matter what, we have breathing space. But before we go on, I'm a mountain of curiousity about you, and I must know if you belong to SOE, as you know I do."

"I do. You were part of my inspiration to apply, thank you. I'm a telegraphist, as you might guess, but I'm here on a courier run. This safe house is run by Mireille and her father, and tomorrow one of them will go out into the country with deliveries, with me as an assistant baker in a white cap and apron, and deliver me to where I want to go. And no, I don't usually open my mouth as wide as I must have done to be taken in back there. What a fool! But what about you? Do you have a way out?"

Ana thought a moment, before saying: "I want an up train. I'll get near the station to see if there's anything suspicious. I'll look at the police station to see if it's clear of *boches.* First though, I'll unload my fancy goods like cards and the revolver in my brother's flat, so as to be clean if I get searched on the way. I'd go on home then. That's Lyon. On the other hand, if things look sticky I have a couple of places here to rest in."

"Or you come here and get delivered out of town by Alexandre or Mireille. So you'll get by, I bet."

Mireille came in with the refreshments and aspirin and the two women sighed with relief as they received them. Mireille was agog to hear the story, and as soon as she was composed Monica told her, recounting it in accurate detail while Mireille's eyes widened and her mouth opened. Monica turned to Ana, leaned over and kissed her, and said: "Thanks awfully, what a lovely reunion! But what are you doing with the gun?" Ana was moving it from her coat to her bag, and explained: "I'm putting the safety catch back on and putting it away. I had it at the ready back there."

"You mean you would have shot them?"

"What else, if it had to be them or us?"

Mireille cried: "Oh my God! Welcome to Amazon world!"

Monica exclaimed: "I was really frightened my gun would pop out when you opened my bag, and you even showed it to them!"

"It was alright. I felt it under the lining and knew they wouldn't see it if I showed the bag quickly, but don't ask what might have happened if they'd looked for themselves!"

"Let's not even think about it."

Monica told Mireille what she had in mind for herself, and of Ana's plans, so she knew the whole story and the plans, and said she would tell her father when he came in. Mireille added: "He'll want you to tell the story again yourself, you know."

Refreshed, Ana wanted to be on her way, and asked Mireille if she could leave with her the incriminating things she had thought to leave in Manny's flat, but to do so would take up precious time. Mireille readily agreed, and asked her to drop in at any time, and regard this as a friendly place. There was not time then, but one day Ana would learn more about father and daughter's maquisard support work.

30

Ab and Klara knew they were to be deported. Some people affected by such knowledge might become separated from the principles by which good lives should be governed, but not them, who always tried hard to be consistently courteous and helpful to those around them. In Drancy their outlook was sustained by the merciful activities of the few visiting social workers whose aim was to succour the children awaiting deportation. Alone, separated from their parents, some were just toddlers, whose days were filled with crying, aimlessly playing, looking for something to eat like stray animals at waste dumps, and following anybody who might seem like their mother. All, of any age, were bewildered, disturbed, and prone to illness through hunger and poor diet. Ab and Klara were given permission to help those workers, who were nearly all women, and whom they called the Drancy angels, like their counterparts at Rivesaltes. They had few helpers from the prisoners, as many of those had lost the gift of love, and existed in private cocoons. There was no end to the needs and demands of the children, which took all the time and effort that Ab and Klara could find, each day for weeks on end. The only breaks came during the frequent roll calls of adults, and when they were returned to their segregated dormitories and locked up for the night. But each morning both would awaken with hearts aching for the children, and hurry to them. So their days were filled with love, and effort, if little hope.

Aware that that in rare instances release from Drancy was

granted, Ab and Klara had applied on the basis that his poor health was caused by frontline service in the German army during the Great War, and her French citizenship, but were refused. They were not surprised, as they had seen that the few successful cases conformed to no obvious pattern, indicating they could have been flukes, or the result of hidden influence. Klara, as a French Jew, might have succeeded on a solo application, which she declined to make out of solidarity with her husband. The only benefit from the failed application was that the quality of Ab's medical treatment improved a little.

When departure day came they were walked, along with hundreds of others, the two kilometres from the prison to the railway siding of Le Bourget-Drancy, where a French steam train waited. Each was allowed to carry only a few possessions, which left the owners puzzled about the train journey. A count would have shown the train had 16 freight cars, plus a guard's van at the end, and a standard passenger car for train sentries in the middle, and a locomotive, hissing and puffing its readiness to move. Few passengers noticed that the car to which Ab and Klara were directed had external markings that showed it belonged to the SNCF, France's national railway company, its destination was Oswiecim, via Strasbourg, its maximum load was 20 tonnes, it was to carry 65 passengers, and was car 7. The climb up from the ground into the car was too much for many passengers, and they had to be pulled and pushed up by the stronger ones. The guards did not help at all, and there were no steps. The car had heavy wooden sides and floor, and a curved iron roof. The floor was largely covered by straw. A toilet bucket stood in one corner, and a bucket of water in another. The walls had no windows, and each side wall had a large sliding door in its middle, which when closed completed a solid wall. The end walls ran right to the roof. The side walls did not, and the space between their tops and the roof was heavily laced with barbed wire. The only light in was daylight. In pre-deportation days freight cars were at times used by the SNCF for cattle transportation, and even for troop transportation for short distances in emergencies. The train managers found them in order for Jews, for long distances, without any reference to emergencies.

Although those embarking had heard they were to be resettled in the east, this being the essentially vague message given out in prison, they did not know how they would be taken there, past the obvious point that the present train was the start. As nobody had ever been inside a freight car, other than those who had come to Drancy that way, they had no understanding of how one could be used for passengers on a journey of any length, despite the suspicions of some, based on talk about the east. So few were greatly perturbed to arrive at their designated cars, with their doors open expectantly, and the engine sighing as if to show it was ready to go. It was as well the passengers did not know; it was to be their hell on wheels for the next few days.

During boarding Ab and Klara had heard frequent cries of horror and dismay at the lack of comfort, and congestion, inside. Personal space was a prime cause of squabbling, so arguments and pushing resulted. Nobody knew enough to prefer a location, except that those who identified the toilet bucket chose distant spots, so that the last few to board, including Ab and Klara, found themselves nearer to it than they would have liked. The car leader, a Jew randomly nominated from the passengers by the camp officials with a view to him keeping reasonable order among his fellow passengers, tried to curb grabs of excessive space, but the basic problem of the strong taking precedence over the weak remained, and everybody understood he had no real authority. Ab and Klara knew from earlier observations of prisoners' conduct that great, prolonged and unjust denial of a person's humanity tended to erode their best attributes, not least being consideration for the needs of neighbours. And they resolved to try not to succumb here on the train, just as they had tried in Drancy.

The side walls were much higher than even the tallest passenger. The sliding door in the far wall was already closed when they entered. Nothing but the merest view outside would be available at the doors, and then only by one or two determined people at a time. The previous usage of car 7 was unknown, and its indefinable and unpleasant odour gave no clue. Once its quota was aboard nobody was allowed out. It did not take long for all cars to be filled, whereupon the guards went along and slid the heavy doors into their iron frames consecutively. Each closing thud, followed by the click of a heavy padlock, sounded chillingly final. But the train did not then move off, but was delayed for about two hours, and had the passengers known, that would be their most comfortable time for a few days.

While waiting Ab appraised some of the features surrounding

him. He mused: 'About half the space of a small single bed per passenger. People move around, and as there's nothing to hang onto, they'll fall. The toilet bucket will quickly fill up, and the water can emptied. So if this journey takes very long, and the buckets aren't renewed, our car will become a sewer. Getting to the toilet will be too much for many people; Oh! the smell! Oh! God! What have we all come to? And I wonder what will happen when somebody stands up and moves. Will his or her space be stolen? And people get sick from train motion, even in the good ones. Take the Vosges hills for example. All those bends. People aren't supposed to smoke, but some will, to counteract the stench: and who will stop them? But it will be a bad thing if the air circulation and supply are inadequate; as I expect. So I suppose we will all be gasping at times, and me as bad as any. If we're kept here long enough some might go mad, and others die. Maybe though this will be a short trip, and we'll be out of here before any of those things happen.' But he did not believe in the short trip, for they had been told a long journey was ahead.

He changed the direction of his thoughts: 'Who could escape from a car like this? Only young, strong, and determined men, of whom there are so few here, could even try it. I hope their absence means they're in the maquis, and not that they've been deported. So all we can do is escape in mind and spirit, and we must try. We can start with prayer.' Turning to Klara he said: "Let's pray for strength." They did.

Already the dire conditions were understood by the passengers. The fear that the journey in this car would be a long one had taken hold. Much wailing ensued, some prayerful, simply some despairing. Others, Ab supposed, had taken to a sort of dream world, trying to revive happiness from the past. But the most complete form of escape would be suicide. That would be deciding the time of one's death, instead of leaving it to God. Surely He would excuse such a person because of the circumstances, knowing they were headed for an early death anyway. And so on, for Ab had nothing else to do as he lay there waiting for the train to start its journey which his instincts said would kill him. Not that he would even breathe those notions to Klara, in case it might undermine the strength that made her so constantly brave and constructive, and concerned for the welfare of others. He could not imagine her changing, but then one never knew how stress and pressure of events might affect people. He looked across to her as she lay on his outstretched arm with her eyes closed. Her weight was hurting but he would not let on.

Klara's thoughts drifted to something more pleasant than her surroundings. She concentrated on Ana. She would feel badly about losing them at Montpellier, they being her charges on the escape trip, but it was not her fault. The risk had been there always. If only they could let her know she should not worry. She thought: 'How I love that girl. What a pleasure it has been to be her aunt. It's a pity Ab and I were too old to have children, but those of Naomi have made up for it. She's all beauty and high qualities and talents. She was the one who picked up her mother's philosophy about effort. How did it go? Today and effort were the key words. Plan the day ahead with worthwhile things. Put effort into them. At the end of the day measure success by your effort. Don't measure success by results, as much as effort. With practice every today becomes a successful day. There's no room or need for self pity along the way. Ana operates like that, and Naomi and I also. Just thinking about it reminds me that I've lost touch with it lately. But Oh! – and I must stop this weeping – it's been so hard.' She continued: 'I wonder what Ana is doing know. She's always so busy. We know she's doing something important and probably dangerous, but she never says. She's changed though. She used to smile more but those lovely eyes are more serious, more watchful than when she was younger. I guess that comes with her work. Doing her bit. Ab would like to be doing it too, but he's too sick. He never recovered properly from the gassing. He always jokes that he can't blame the enemy because he doesn't know whose gas it was. Both sides used it, their lines were close together, and sometimes the wind blew in the wrong direction. Look at him lying there, sick, when he should be in hospital with doctors and medication. And now they're taking away the little bit of life he had left. Oh God! Where are you?'

At last the sounds of departure came. The locomotive made restive, almost impatient sounds as it built up the head of steam it needed to get rolling with its heavy convoy of people and cars. Then a whistle from the station master, two sharp answering whistles from the engine, a lurch forward for each car as its weight was taken, and a gentle, slow motion as the train started to roll. A few half-hearted cheers came from within the cars, but only in relief after the boring wait; for there was no reason for anybody to be glad about this departure. Whistling warnings ahead, the train slowly and smoothly rolled away from Drancy. After half an hour or so its speed was fast enough for the passengers to know it was in the country. And they had this confirmed through two lads who entertained themselves and kept the passengers informed by taking up awkward elevated positions to look over the tops of the walls: one lad on each side.

A painfully high level of noise was soon heard. Most passengers knew that the floors of passenger cars were insulated against track noise, and more so in first class than in third. Now they realised the floors of freight cars were not insulated at all, so that the noise of wheels on rails came through strongly. It meant that people could not speak to each other without shouting into the other person's ear, for which few had the energy. Besides, some people had plugged their ears, and preferred to keep it so.

It soon became clear, from the angry competition for space, that many people who might normally be polite were now rude, after the dehumanising experience of Drancy, and the entrainment. The victims had regressed into more primitive habits, where protection of one's own territory, if only a little space on the dirty floor of a freight car, was highly important. In addition, there were some who were debased before entering Drancy, and simply got worse through the bitter experience of captivity. Passengers therefore had to be on guard, and even physically protect their meagre belongings and food and water. At the start of the journey, before the passengers boarded, each had been given a small packet of bread and cheese without advice as to how long it might last; or on any other relevant matter, which for some passengers included medical services. Some though had been farsighted enough to bring some water and scraps of food as supplements, and they would be proved to have been prudent.

While the train was stationary nobody had used the toilet. Ab wondered why. Perhaps it was disbelief in it being the real and total receptacle for their body wastes, and an expectation of something better being provided soon. And of course it was a very public and embarrassing way of attending to nature calls. However, it could not last. Pressures were building up and must be dealt with. An elderly man had been the first to move towards the toilet can after the train had been travelling for a few minutes. A tailor, a long-time resident of Paris, a very clean and tidy man, he had recently undergone surgery on his prostate gland, which left him with a frequent urge to pee, but often it was a false alarm, and he could not tell. The doctor had told him this was a part of recuperation, and that in time he should regain control over his bladder. But now, standing there at the can, after wobbling through the crowd, nothing came. He did not know if it was through embarrassment, or lack of fluid. He stood there concentrating and hoping for a result. The longer he stood there the more embarrassed he became, and the more his hopelessness took hold. He broke down, and struggled, sobbing, back to his place and lay down. There he drifted off into a doze and was awakened by the realisation that he was wetting himself. But he did not bother getting up. And he never rose from that position until, stinking and still distraught, he was discharged from the train at its destination.

The passengers in car 7 did not know it, but when deportations commenced in 1941 a freight car such as theirs would have carried fewer passengers. But not the train overall, the aim being exactly 1000 passengers per train: every train. And at times desperate measures were taken to fill the quota, such as raiding aged persons' nursing homes, and kindergartens. To the train managers Jews were units of cargo, and 1000 units per train was a manageable number for the workers at the destination to process. Less, and the system operated under its capacity; more, it would be overloaded. And, of course, to achieve order in the arrival at a common destination of trains from starting points scattered throughout Europe, overall coordination of movements was essential, which was managed through a centralized German office, supplemented by State railways, such as the SNCF of France. As the war went on several factors led to increased passenger numbers per car. Railway facilities were damaged by sabotage, and by the Allied air offensive. There was a shortage of manpower. To keep up deportation schedules unrealistically set by Germans aiming for killing efficiency without regard to supply realities, the loading of the cars had to increase, and fewer rail traffic movements undertaken. So the ratio of passengers per car grew, while the numbers per train stayed, so as not to gum up the works at the destinations. But timetable disruptions became more frequent, and the planning office could not control the causes. Hence slower travel, in overload-

178

ed cars, and more discomfort for the poor passengers. Not that the operators, the government rail authorities of Germany and France, cared about them.

The passengers were unaware in advance of the real reason for their journey and of their grim fate on arrival. Some knew in their hearts that it was a train of death, but most nurtured any slight hope that arose, and so clung to a wispy form of life as the train went slowly eastward.

31

Although it was dark Ab and Klara had clear mental pictures of the Rhine River Valley ahead. The lengthy stop shortly before had raised hopes of journey's end, but it was only to allow the train crews to be changed from French to German, the news of which was depressing. Soon they sensed - they could not see - that the train had crossed the great river they knew so well after many crossings from home into France, and pictured it running northerly through the broad valley floor that extended on both its sides, covered with orchards and fields, French on the left bank, German on the right. On the left bank the floor ran into the steep slopes of the Vosges; and on the right bank into the dark, timbered hills of the Black Forest: sister sierras. They wondered about the direction the train would take after the crossing. If southerly the train might pass through Offenburg, the thought of which cut into their hearts. But there was only Switzerland that way, so it seemed unlikely. More probable, both thought, north to Karlsruhe, but where after that was beyond them. Klara wanted to discuss these prospects with Ab but the hurtful, if faint prospect of this particular train going through Offenburg put her off, and it was so very noisy anyway. She thought: 'If it hurts me so much, then he could have a heart attack.' So she went against her natural feelings and didn't even try to discuss it. As the train was soon moving steadily with minimal twisting or change of pace, she took it to be the flat valley floor, and so they were moving in a straight line north, and not toward Offenburg, and this was confirmed by the light of the first traces of dawn colouring the sky. Later, as the morning light increased, she felt the train slowing as if it were going through a built-up area, and shortly after, it seemed from the light, the train had turned east, away from the river valley. Where would east be? If it were far away they could be facing a really bad time, for misery was upon them already. How, she asked herself, could people endure much more of these conditions? Klara recalled that the French and German police at Drancy had said they were all being sent east for resettlement. 'You'll help found a new settlement of Jews in the east, where there'll be plenty of work.' She wondered to herself: 'But could I believe that? Who among the passengers in this carriage would be workers, and what work could they do, even the young and fit ones, if they were starved and sick? It doesn't make sense. And if a new and useful life is proposed, why treat us so cruelly now? It's unreal. We're travelling east clearly enough, so it must be Germany or Poland that we're going to, as Russia isn't controlled by Germany. And if Germany is losing the war as people say, why do they bother with us? Why are old and sick people and little children important? We can't hurt anybody. The Nazis are mad, or terrible liars. Perhaps they'll all wake up one day and see that, but at the rate things are going it'll be too late for us.' And those were the questions being silently asked by the other passengers also: all unanswered.

Now, well into Germany, Klara reflected on the increase in antisemitism that had come with the Nazis taking power in 1933. It was not a complete surprise: they had made no bones about their intentions. But still, nobody could have foreseen the grim reality of Nazi hatred of Jews, and its spin-off, the attitudes of ordinary Germans, otherwise long at peace with their Jewish neighbours. That reality was ostracism, and economic deprivation, the humbling of Jews from every angle. She took it that economic hardship of Jews had the side – or even the main – effect of transferring Jewish wealth to the State, in bits little and big, and regardless of the financial and other circumstances of victims, causing multiple family tragedies and bankruptcies. She recalled some history from her student days, and could only wonder at the value of asset loss by European Jews during the preceding ten years, to the advantage of both the predator States and their Gentile citizens. The German rip-off was on the very highest scale, reminiscent of France and its Huguenots in the 18th century, and France and its émigrés fleeing the French Revolution, and Spain and its Jews and Moriscos during earlier times. And with its current aryanisation activity France was plundering people once more.

32

Oscar Katz and his wife and their four young children fled to France from Austrian persecution of Jews in 1939. They rented a small farm house west of Perpignan, in an area that would be within the unoccupied zone after France lost the war. This was a better location for foreign Jews than the northern, or occupied zone. But the difference would dissolve upon the extension of Occupation in November 1942.

He worked as a welder in a factory, for wages that reflected the small bargaining power of a foreign Jew. Yet freedom from the Nazi persecution known in other parts was satisfactory compensation for his ungenerous wages. The family was happy and healthy. They got on well with neighbours, and at school. Otto got a whiff of future trouble when Germany took over the unoccupied zone, but exactly what it meant was beyond his comprehension. A better idea sadly came soon, for in early 1943, after the roundups of foreign Jews had commenced in earnest in the former unoccupied zone, he and his family were arrested and taken into the prison camp of Rivesaltes, whose inmates by then were mainly Jews. For reasons that defied both logic and humanity, for a time the Germans had a policy, adopted copycat by the French as was their tendency in matters of Jewish internment, of separating not only men and women, including husbands and wives, but also, as will be seen, children from parents. This policy, the details of which varied from time to time and prison to prison, meant that Otto Katz was deported from Rivesaltes without his family. They never heard from him again. His wife asked every official she could for news but without any success. Then in planning the deportation of females from the internment prisons and camps, children were separated from the mothers with a view to deporting them separately later. During a period of administrative uncertainty about the children, the few social workers who nobly attempted to reduce a little the great misery suffered by the internees, with particular concern for the children orphaned by the separate transportation of their parents, convinced the camp administrator to allow some children out to into foster care in homes in the district, which would relieve the administrative burden, without impeding their deportation, if and when that was decided upon. The children were all under 16 years. That scheme brought 15 year old Nathan Katz to the home of Guy Nicol and his family in their village in the hills to the near west, where M Nicol was the principal of the primary school.

Nathan had been with the Nicol family for a few months when the camp administrator, acting on orders from the French police in their rôle as agents for the joint German-French deportation program, was required to prepare the women for deportation. A new policy required the children to be deported with their mothers, so those in foster care were to be brought back. The social workers learned of the plan, and decided against cooperating in it. They, and not the administrator, held complete records of all the placements, although each mother knew about her own child or children. In view of the attitude of the social workers the administrator sent his staff to the mothers to suggest to them that if they would like to see their children again, they should disclose their whereabouts. With the deceit that was characteristic of officials in relation to roundups, the mothers were not told: 'This is our way of getting in your children so they may be deported.' Some mothers were so eager to see their children they complied at once. While others were standing in line for discussion with the staff, the social workers moved among them quickly, quietly suggesting there was no need for them to see the children at present, as they would be safer where they were. Many saw the risk and prevaricated when questioned by the staff. The social workers then set out to warn the children, whose mothers had agreed, to hide. As the children were in widely separated locations in the local district, fast work would be needed.

The first Mme Nicol knew of the plan was a teenage boy jumping off his bike and racing up her front path, and breathlessly telling her that his mother had a request by telephone from a friend in Rivesaltes, to alert several foster families around the village to the danger. His job was to contact three families which meant a lot of riding. His message was for Nathan to leave the Nicol home and go into hiding if he wished to avoid deportation. The police could come for him as early as tomorrow. They should keep the warning a secret. He then raced off. Wanting to discuss the message with her husband Mme Nicol sent one of her children for him and another for Nathan, so by mid afternoon they were together. The Nicols decided, sadly, they had to tell him to leave their house and take to the hills. He asked what was happening at Rivesaltes. The Nicols told him all they knew. Nathan asked Mme Nicol: "Is my decision to be either go with my mother, or let her go without me?"

Mme Nicol winced at the direct simplicity of the question. "Yes, I'm afraid so," she replied. "But there's no certainty about children being kept with their mothers even if they go back, as the Germans are known for separating family members, just as they took your father alone. Besides, you can't protect your mother against deportation. We don't know what happens after that, because nobody has ever come back to say, and you can't believe the police. We don't want to keep you away from your mother, but also we don't want to see both of you deported."

M Nicol added: "You can decide to go back to the camp and be powerless, or you can look for a place where you can do something useful. What do I mean by that? I mean that if you decide to take to the hills you can expect support from good people. And there's not much time, because if you're not going back we have work to do. It's hard to have to grow up fast, but some people have to, and you're one of them. And so you must decide."

Nathan thought a minute. He said: "OK, I stay. I'll hide. What can I do then? Can I get a job on a farm, or say join the maquis, without them telling on me? Will the police be looking for me everywhere?"

Guy said: "You must take it one step at a time. Those questions are good ones, but we don't have the answers, and you must wait for them. But you choose well. We'll help you all we can. The maquisards won't be your enemy, nor will many farmers. But the main thing now is for us to get you ready to go as soon as it's dark. I know a good place to hide. I'll take you there, and return tomorrow afternoon. We'll work things out day by day, and I'll keep in touch, but expect to be alone at times. Don't ask me more questions than I can answer just now. I'll help you keep up your schoolwork. And you can practice keeping out of sight."

Nathan asked: "Who treats Jews worst, the French or the Germans? I don't mean you and Mme Nicol."

Guy thought for a few moments before replying. Then he said: "That's a big question. Probably the Germans. Although both countries are very antisemitic, I think Jews could generally expect more help from French people than from German."

Mme Nicol added: "I agree. Nathan, I can't tell you everything because there's no time, but please believe there are many good people in France who detest what the Germans are doing to the Jews and are ashamed of the French people who help them. But remember that some people accept propaganda not always because they believe it, but because they're too busy or and too frightened to think for themselves, to be humane." She paused, having almost said 'Christian', then continued: "What's happening in your life isn't new, but is part of being Jewish. It hurts us to see all this, but weeping won't help. Instead we must be strong, and look for hopeful signs. Then pray each day for the Allies to crush Germany, and the Vichy people, and for the courage to do all we can to help." She noticed Nathan's eyes moistening, and hoped he wouldn't lose control, or even change his mind. He had a chance by hiding, but none otherwise. She was relieved when he stayed calm. She reached out and took him in her arms, whispering in his ear: "Don't give in my dear."

For a moment he struggled to find words. Then: "Thank you both very much. I'll think about everything you've said. How will my mother know what I'm doing?"

Guy replied: "We'll get a message to her. We promise."

"You'll tell her I'm safe and well please."

"Yes, of course, and she will be glad."

"And that I love her?"

"Certainly."

"And tell my sister and little brothers I love them too?" And he added: "How will I find out about them?"

"We'll keep up an interest in them all and let you know when we have news."

They got busy with packing camping gear plus a haversack of essential gear, such as a hatchet, a large knife, a roll of two blankets and some food, matches, and waterproof sheeting. Being busy eased the pain of the pending parting, but nothing could dissolve it. He had been at peace in the village and with the Nicol family, who had accepted him as one of their own.

At dusk the party set out on their bicycles. Nathan on his, Guy on his with his son Maxime as a passenger to bring back Nathan's bike. In the foothills of the small mountain range they left the bikes in the scrub and proceeded upward on foot. Guy led them to a high and remote cave in the forest. Nearby were the stone ruins of a shepherd's hut he thought could be made useful, but Nathan should keep his fires inside, so that smoke would be diffused. They stayed with the lad until very late. Guy was pleased when Nathan declined an offer of one of them to stay the night. 'That's a very good start', he thought. At last, after seeing Nathan into bed, there was nothing to do but embrace and leave. Guy wondered if he would cry himself to sleep. He would try not to do so himself.

When the van with two policemen called at the Nicols' house next day, looking for Nathan, Mme Nicol said she was glad they had come because he had not come home to dine or to sleep last night, and she was getting worried about him, and indeed was thinking of reporting it to the police, but now they were here she asked them what to do. She said she had asked a couple of his friends but they didn't know anything. Her husband was making inquiries around the school today. Perhaps if they went there they would get some news, but she would have expected a call from her husband if Nathan had been found already. "Actually", she explained to her husband later, "their reaction was very interesting. They became concerned country policemen faced with the problem of a missing child. They took particulars, made suggestions, and would speak with their inspector about a search party. They didn't see the irony of talking about finding a missing child to bring him home, when they were here to take him away. But I think the penny had dropped by the time they left to see you."

At the school the policemen had a more or less predictable conversation with Guy. Puzzled, they left and moved to the next place where they were to pick up an adolescent boy, and where they had more luck. Sadly, they arrested him, and took back to Rivesaltes one frightened, thin, handcuffed 12-year old Jewish boy. The others on their list were not located, for a variety of reasons, so that by the time they had finished their rounds the policemen concluded that evasive action had been taken, which did not worry them, as that was not their fault, and anyway their hearts were not in this particular job. After delivering the prisoner to the camp and accounting for their searches, they returned to their station in Perpignan where they reported to their inspector on the day's events and asked for further instructions. He laughed at the small return for their effort. They all knew the targets had been tipped off, and would not be found unless betrayed.

Nathan wept, but only a little. He was afraid, but now he knew that was natural he could accept it, along with learning to feed himself, and keeping watch. He had some scouting and camping experience and had been taught by his father to be dexterous with his hands, so he could adapt to camping alone in the wild well enough. His 'wild' was a forest on a stony hill with scattered open spaces between rocky outcrops and rock piles. From above the cave he could see a village in the valley below, and a stream flowing by. He explored, practising moving swiftly from one sheltered spot to another and keeping alert at all times. He gathered firewood and read, but it was very lonely, coming as he had straight from the affectionate companionship of the Nicol family. How lucky he had been to find them! He must be careful to remember the good in his life when he started to feel sorry for himself, which happened mostly during the long hours of silent night, when his feeling of loss of two families threatened to overwhelm him. But he was strengthened by the knowledge of their love, and the need to be worthy of them.

On the third day he was near the ruins when he sensed, for no reason he could find, he was being watched. He moved quietly into the cover of a corner and looked out. He felt insecure. There was a sudden movement near a broken wall, and a man appeared. He was armed. He just stood, unmoving, looking at Nathan. The boy felt for the handle of his knife, and stared back. The man then said, in German: "Nathan Katz, don't take fright, as I've come to be your friend. I'm a Jew like you. OK?"

Nathan kept his eye on the man, and asked: "If you're a friend then show me. It might be a trick. I'm not going back."

"How can I show you? To do that you have to accept me,

and come with me. I want to help you, and I want your help too. My friends and I are fighters against the Germans. You can join us if you like, but you must realise it's hard and dangerous. Don't come if you're easily frightened. We're outlaws - bandits the police call us. Others call us maquisards." He paused, then continued: "What more do you want to know?"

Nathan thought, and slowly said: "I've nothing better to do. I don't mind if things are hard. I'm not frightened. But how do I know your friends won't be cruel to me?"

Manny winced as the boy spoke. He knew what he meant. The Nicols had told him about Oscar Katz and his family. Guy was a friend of the resistance group that Manny instructed in weaponry and explosives.

"My people aren't cruel to anybody but Germans and their friends. I promise to be your friend all the time you want me. Now will you come? If so put out your hand and walk over here."

Nathan thought a second, then did as he was told, and the two solemnly shook hands.

33

Ben and Naomi had begun to look a little, just a little, like peasants. It wasn't only their clothes, though they were suitable. It was also that the hard outdoor life was showing on their faces and limbs. They had worked hard for their farmer neighbours, who treated them with respect and civility, always a pleasant experience for Jews in France. In that location, and in that way of life, they were almost able to put out of their minds the fearsome regime in control not far away, but were abruptly reminded of it when Ana arrived. They knew as soon as they saw her that something awful had happened, and on hearing the news they plunged into a bout of wailing and praying such that Ana had never seen.

When, later, Ana tried to get her parents to concentrate on their own escape plan, they were disinterested. Her mother asked: "Why can we succeed if they failed? And say if they escaped, or were released, and came home, and we had left. How would they find us?"

Of course Ana did not know, and in fact had not contemplated that happening, for her despair was deeper than she had let on. She moved to cover the crack: "It's simple. I'll tell the mayor and Jean-Paul to expect word from one of us as to where they are to go, or who to contact, and for them to wait here until word comes through."

Her father asked: "Does that mean you don't know as of this minute, but you will find out?"

"Exactly. And I may have to change whatever I say at first, depending on events down the coast. I have to consult other people, on whom I depend, such as Manny."

Mention of their son's name, and participation, heartened her parents, and helped relieve them of the feeling they might be deserting their missing kin. They began to feel that their going would not necessarily harm the others, and Ana did nothing to change this new understanding of the affair. That Ab and Klara would escape and make their way back to the hut, was a pleasant chance to be accepted. She remained convinced her parents should leave, but would not fight with them over it. All she could do was point out, quietly and clearly, the risks of remaining.

As they regained some composure, and noticed that Ana was not arguing with them about their staying on, they started to review their attitude. During the afternoon of the third day Ben called for discussion. They discussed everything they could think of about the matter, interspersed with grief, but at all times Ana remained calm, leaving it to them to decide for themselves. The next morning they told her they were ready to leave as soon as she said.

M Jean-Paul Pinchemel and his wife were not surprised when told the news later that morning, because it was common knowledge that the position of Jews had changed lately, and they sensed the Mayers to be Jews, although it was never actually admitted by them. The farmer also had supposed that the absence of Ab and Klara was connected in some way with the new pressures. This was confirmed when, during the sombre farewells that took place on the day following, they told him they feared something awful had happened to the others.

While her parents were preparing themselves, Ana had negotiated with M Pinchemel the sale of the articles that must be left behind, and for him to convey the travellers to the railway station to begin their train journey. On the way Ana said to him: "Please tell the mayor we are all extremely grateful for his kindness, and our only reason for not approaching him directly is respect for his office."

Jean-Paul laughed as he said: "I think you mean you don't want him to know anything he shouldn't know as mayor. Sure, I'll tell him, but I can assure you he's pretty safe."

Ana added, in the presence of her parents: "I'll be writing to you both, you'll see."

"Now that's a nice thought. But you don't have to, you know."

Naomi intervened: "But she must. She expects to have some news for you."

Jean-Paul, a little puzzled, merely said that everything was OK.

So the party found themselves on the station platform of Puget-Theniers in the early afternoon of the next day, as they had come, but now with fewer chattels. In the train Ben and Naomi gave up prayers of thanks for the peace that had been theirs over the past year. Their sojourn in the hills would always be recalled with a mixture of happiness and grief. And as she shepherded her parents out of the hills, via the inland route, then along the coast to Sète, Ana incessantly prayed in silence for a safe arrival, and her prayers were answered.

Once in the safe house it was time for discussion about how to leave France. Manny said: "I've seen Neil. My ideas are different now. He said I wasn't to go away, as he has things for me to do here. And as we have the option of going by sea, he didn't offer to send you by land with somebody else, and I don't know of anybody. Getting you on the help list at the consulate is fundamental though. We need somebody there to swing a deal for you with the Spaniards. It would mean you being accepted as temporary residents under the recommendation of the consulate. Now say the residency were to be one year. A lot can happen in a year. And if you had met the other conditions of your stay, maybe you could extend. Neil has contacts in Barcelona who might help. Once the preliminaries are worked through you'll find a place to live, and find a destination. Let's just take it all one step at a time."

Ben could see the planning included much hope and faith, but saw no point in saying so, as the children were doing their best to help. He said: "Thanks. We feel so helpless, and are entirely in your hands. We trust you to do your best for us, and however it goes, we'll be content." He and Naomi had hoped that by some miracle Manny would have news for them of Ab and Klara. They also knew if there were they would have been told at once, so refrained from mentioning their hopes, as the young people had enough on their minds already.

Naomi spoke: "So we go by boat. Who takes us from the boat to the consulate?'

"Conchita. She's been there before."

"What's the cost of living there? And what would we live on?"

Manny replied: "Spain is a very poor place where everything costs less than here. As to what you would live on, I thought you had some money, but if you're short Ana and I will find some to send. Do you have enough for a while?"

Ben was impatient at this talk. Naomi knew very well they had enough money for it not to need discussion, so he supposed it was just her way of obtaining additional comfort. But he said nothing. Ana did though. She embraced her mother saying: "Dearest, have no fear. We won't ever see you short." Both sobbed a little, but both also knew this was an occasion calling for resolution and brave faces, so that all parties would be strengthened by the others. Ana added, "And who knows but you might find some work too when you settle in, but we won't bank on that. And I'd expect there's a synagogue and a few Jews in Barcelona, and you'll surely find them."

Naomi said: "Of course. We'll find out soon enough. But what about writing. We'll have so much to tell you, but where will we send our letters?"

Ana replied: "This is what we do. I have a code sheet here and when you write put your words in the code. Don't include formal parts, like names and signatures; nothing but the plain message. There's an address on the sheet to use at first, and if I change it later don't worry. When you have both put all that detail in your memories please destroy the sheet. You can take it with you. When we write we'll use the same code, but don't expect long letters from us for a while. Send us your postal address as soon as you can. We've talked about this but Manny and I don't see we can risk using the telephone, for it's very complicated as it is, and we guess that overseas calls come under extra scrutiny. We'll check all this again as we go."

Ben nodded, saying: "We understand. Safety first and last. It's the way to do it. We don't know how the Spaniards treat correspondence, especially from outside, so we'd better be cautious."

Ana said: "That's right. But try to find a third party, such as a rabbi, or another Jew, someone we can contact in an emergency, someone who will know where we can find you if we lose contact."

Naomi said, drying tears as she spoke: "Yes. We'll look for someone and let you know. Maybe the consulate, if there's nothing else."

Ana added: "Yes. Also keep in mind that one of us will visit when we can. I don't know how, and I'm not saying it would be easy, but remember we have contacts through Diego to start with. Actually we haven't discussed any of this with him yet, but we will, and maybe some other ideas will turn up on the voyage."

Ben and Naomi were comforted by the possibilities that had been aired, although they knew they all included guess work. Ben said: "Thanks. You're good children. Now Manny, I don't know if Ana has told you, but she said she's holding Ab and Klara's money. I'd like you and Ana to work out something safe for it, with both of you knowing everything. Will you do that?"

"Sure. She told me. I think it's simple enough. Both of us have non-Jewish identities. We could put it in a safe deposit box at a bank here in our joint names. How does that sound?"

"It will be if you keep those names. If you ever want to change them, such as back to Mayer, make sure you get the box out first, then deposit it again. OK, Ana?"

"Yes."

Naomi said: 'We're going to Barcelona by fishing boat. What an adventure! We're ready. We must find out how to change francs to pesetas, but that can wait until we get there."

As most of their business had been covered, Ana thought she should be confidential with her parents. She knew they were content knowing she was working against the Germans and never asked her for details, yet distance of a sort had come between them and she regretted that. Still, tempting as talk seemed, she must stay mute. But she thought, on this momentous occasion, she should add a light touch and take her parents into her confidence by recounting the episode there in Sète with Monica and the policemen, and proceeded to do so, with Manny listening, for he had not known either. They all thought it funny, if scary, and certainly enterprising, and Ana was greatly pleased that her parents had been distracted from their constant concern. Manny jokingly said: "So that's how you carry on behind our backs! I wonder what else you've been up to." But that meant he really wanted to know, and so she felt it was time to tell him about Henri, because he had never said he knew. But not in front of their parents. She couldn't have them in despair about their daughter wandering about shooting people, so she simply laughed at his question.

The voyage would be the first for both Ben and Naomi, though they had sailed on the Rhine River with friends a few years earlier. They knew that a small vessel at sea was potentially dangerous for those aboard in wartime, and always uncomfortable, but those things didn't concern them in the light of what had happened to Ab and Klara. They could not be as much concerned about themselves as otherwise they might. They knew that those who loved and cared for them were doing all they could. They waited in the safe house until called to go aboard, at night, so as not to attract attention on the wharf. They tearfully farewelled Ana, then were escorted by Manny to the street next to the wharf, where Conchita took them over.

34

For the *Santa Maria* enemy warships were like dogs to a rabbit. It was better not to meet them. The closer to shore the smaller the exposure, at least in Diego's experience in Spanish waters. And in general small fishing boats were ignored. On the voyage with Ben and Naomi the *Santa Maria* went straight out to sea, to cross the Golfe du Lion, as hugging the French coast would take too much time, and could even carry other dangers. Airplane attack from any source was unlikely. There were too many fishing boats to justify wasting valuable ammunition or bombs on small and probably innocent targets. They would make landfall close to Barcelona, so as to minimise time on land for Conchita: she and Diego having agreed upon a plan for delivery of their passengers. Moreover, if there were to be any difficulty with the fugitives' papers it would be better in Barcelona where help from the consulate might be called upon.

From Sète to Barcelona was close to 300 kilometres, or 162 nautical miles. The voyage might be completed well within two days using only the engine in normal weather, but as fuel coal was scarce they used steam sparingly. Sailing all the way was practical, for the sail was large, and of course the variability of winds and waves made all estimates vague. Catching fish while sailing would show the boat to be working, and less likely to attract an inquiry from an official vessel than if it were only in passage.

They were well into the voyage and moving freely under a gentle breeze in calm water when Conchita sighted the grey vessel on the horizon. It was well ahead of them, and passed across their line of travel, and seemed to be continuing on its easterly course, until it turned to port and circled back, soon showing itself to be a German patrol boat, an E-boat, new to the western Mediterranean, although Italian and British torpedo patrol boats had long participated in the local sea warfare. Diego took it to be related to current German concerns about its hold on the general area, which was said to be threatened on both sea and land, just as he, Diego, felt threatened as it slowly neared his boat before heaving to a few metres from the port side of the *Santa Maria*. Earlier, as soon as the patrol boat turned off its course, alarm hit those on board the fishing boat, whereupon their well-rehearsed plans went into action. First, Ben and Naomi went to their secret bunkers. Diego ran up the Spanish flag and inserted the Spanish board in the slot for the fishing boat registration number.

The Germans were watchful, and the guns they trained on the fishing boat left its crew in no doubt about the level of respect expected from them. The E-boat crew could not speak Spanish, and the crew of the *Santa Maria* showed that was all they knew. The Germans concentrated on scrutinising the fishing boat, including posting a lookout high on their own communication mast. Sensing doubt in their minds Diego kept pointing to the hold while crying Barcelona! Barcelona! to show they were homeward bound, heavy with catch, but was dismayed to see preparations for boarding.

On the patrol boat Ditmer, the skipper, had been in serious discussion with his first officer, Wolfgang. They had agreed there was something not quite right about this Spanish fishing vessel, which they could only find test by boarding her. If nothing turned up then there was no harm done, because inspecting vessels of all sorts in the war zone was a well known practice. All the same, they were uneasy about accosting a Spanish vessel, considering the close ties between Germany and Spain which dated back to the civil war. Though Spain was not a member of the Axis, and indeed was formally neutral, its preference for Axis interests had been shown often. So Ditmer was going to be careful. He must consider inspecting it, because it was a long way out to sea for one of its size, and especially after hearing a discussion between members of his crew. Wolfgang had said: "Helmut, you were a fisher before the war?"

"Yes, sir, in the Baltic. Our family had a boat something about the size of that one. There was my father, his brother and ....." pointing as he spoke.

"Never mind the family Helmut. You've had a good look at it. The captain is trying to decide if we should board her for inspection. What do you think?"

"Sir, it's a long way out for a boat that size. They're showing us they have catch, yet it rides high in the water. If it were my boat, with a good catch, it would sit lower. But then boats are different of course."

"Of course. Of course. Thank you Helmut. Dismissed."

But another point came to Ditmer's mind as he studied the deck of the other boat through his telescope. It was the presence of Diego, clothed only in shorts with a large knife in a belt scabbard. Ditmer had the feeling he was looking at a very strong man, whose countenance indicated a readiness for aggression. He cursed himself for picking this boat to check, when really there had been no need. He told Wolfgang to look for himself. He did, and said: "Is that a man or a gorilla? He sure looks a tough nut." And that sealed the matter for Ditmer. If Wolfgang had said something different, he could have changed his mind, and continued on toward home, but now a challenge was in the air, and as skipper he must meet it. He knew he had no reputation of being a hero, but that was vastly different from one who might shirk danger, and to turn about now, after Wolfgang had seen and appraised the man on the fishing boat, would make him vulnerable. It wasn't that Wolfgang was disloyal, but when lower deck ratings got drunk together one of their favourite topics of fun and conversation was their skippers, and Wolfgang was a man for a few drinks off duty. So they would board the *Santa Maria*, and probably find nothing, in which case they would apologise and leave. He would be on guard though, and cover the man, and assigned Wolfgang the like role for the woman, and both and would be ready to fire at the slightest whiff of danger. If something of concern came, he would have few feasible options, and instinct told him sinking the Santa Maria and its crew would likely be chosen. But first he would board and inspect.

On the fishing boat the mood was grim. By tapping on the bulkheads hiding the escapees Conchita had conveyed to them the imminent boarding. The escapees lay uncomfortably in the dark, aware that if one or both the Spaniards shouted Bang! all four aboard were about to be arrested. The hidden ones would simply have to trust the judgment of the Spaniards in this regard. On that all had agreed, as they had on the follow up plan, and which they had carefully rehearsed.

Although he was unsighted, Ben supposed from the sounds of the two vessels rubbing together, and the shouted commands of the Germans, they had boarded, and would turn the boat inside out. He could not tell that despite their noise the Germans were not unfriendly as they boarded. Nor that their skipper's attitude had changed to suspicion when Helmut delved into the fish hold to find that neither the catch nor the hold itself was as he had expected. Nor that in consequence a search in earnest was planned, and that Ditmer had ordered the two deck crew to stand closer together, for easier cover, and raise their arms high. He had seen the hate in their eyes, and the great arms and torso of the man, and wished he had never seen the *Santa Maria*. In complying both crew shouted Bang! Bang!, by which the Germans were astonished, and alarmed. And they heard Ben's answering shout in German, and another for emphasis, which indicated to the boarding party something bad was about to happen. It was: Ben tapped the metal striker he and Diego had rigged up, and it detonated the charge embedded in the ball of plastic explosive stored alongside him. Diego launched himself at Ditmer, drawing his knife with the speed of light as he did so, and plunging it deep into the German's body on the way. Yet the sailor, already fully alert, still managed to fire off two rounds from his automatic pistol, which both hit Diego in the chest, for the gun was so close they could not miss. Both men fell, mortally wounded, beating the death was about to come to them anyway through the deadly explosion that immediately followed the detonation. The shockwaves swept through and over both vessels, dissolving all who stood in its way, shattering the wooden boat, and rending a great hole in the port side of the warship, extending above and below its water line. Bits of both vessels, and their personnel went in all directions. The sea poured through the hole in the warship, right through the vessel, the seadoors of which had not been secured against such an emergency, and now nobody was there for the task. Within the hour after the explosion the calm surface of the sea was littered with reminders of the two vessels, but both of which had gone under.

Only part of the plastic explosive stored aboard in Gibraltar had been taken for sabotage by the Silence group prior to the commencement of the voyage, and the presence of the remainder right next to Ben had led to the plan that had produced the blast.

Conchita had surfaced with bursting lungs, after diving deeply and with no time to breathe fully beforehand. She had reached the point where the physical need to relieve the lung pressure almost outweighed the knowledge that to do so meant death, because her lungs would be filled with water at once. She hung on though, aided by the prayers flashing through her head. The shouting had presaged very great danger. She had seen that the sailor covering her had removed his attention from her toward Diego, the one most to be feared, and clearly a present threat to the warship's captain. So she had the merest chance of escaping his attention, and his gun, as Diego commenced his attack on the skipper. She knew the explosion was imminent, and that being in the water was her one chance of survival. In the same fraction of time as Diego's hurling himself forward, she was throwing herself into the sea, instinctively diving in the way she had learned as a child growing up by the Genil River at home in hot southern Spain. Poor pueblo children like herself had a long swimming season there each year, because it never ran completely dry, and rarely too fast and, importantly, it was free. Her body and brain had not forgotten. She was almost submerged when the shock waves came, but apart from being buffeted by turbulent air and sea, she was unhurt. She did not know if Wolfgang had fired at her, and it didn't matter, as she had not been hit. On surfacing, she took a few seconds to recover her breath, and was then astonished to see the damage. Treading water, and ready to dive again if anything threatening appeared, she watched the boats settle and sink, with the realisation that she was the sole survivor, slowly taking hold.

Surrounded by floating things, including body parts, and hats, she looked around for support, and saw two useful objects, one a life belt from the E-boat, the other the broken piece of raft that had sat in the dinghy on the top of the tiny cabin of the *Santa Maria*. She swam to them, and tied them together into a small raft. The lifebelt trailed a long rope, the end of which she tied to her ankle. She then taught herself to sit and lie on the most solid piece of the raft without capsizing it. Now there was nothing to do but to wait: and while waiting think about the disaster. But it was not thinking in a true sense. The enormity of the event simply seized control of her mind, which became full of images in random sequence. She sobbed until it hurt. She became exhausted, closed her eyes, and lay down, half in and half out of the water, and slept.

During the night she woke up to find her mind clearer, which brought on the realisation of the loss of Diego. Aching consumed her. She had not known how dependent on him, and how much she had come to love him, until now, when he was gone. Despair, more tears, more sleep; death or life – it was immaterial now. In the morning she was awake, her grief and despair undiminished, and wondering how she could see the day out. Already thirsty, even more than hungry, and wet, she had shivered through the night, and expected to suffer from the sun during the coming day. Her only clothes were the shirt and trousers she had on when the explosion came. She knew people could not survive long in those conditions, but was not particularly concerned about her fate. Life now had nothing good for her anyway. As the sun slowly climb in the morning sky she looked around at the horizon and was surprised to see how limited it was at sea level.

'What a tiny dot I am,' she thought. 'How little chance of a boat coming in view, let alone seeing me. My chances of living are really low.'

Barcelona had long been home port to many fishing boats; estuarine, coastal, and deep sea, or longliners, which were always sturdier and larger boats, with four and even more crew, and fished for large fish such as tuna and swordfish, far out to sea. One was *La Juana*, a four man 15 metre vessel, headed home after five days and nights fishing big fish, with which its freezers were now full. It would make landfall early the next morning, and had no need to hurry, and to do so would waste scarce fuel. The first mate, Manuel Casella, was helmsman and lookout over the glassy sea in the early afternoon when he saw something that made him blink; a floating object away from the starboard bow. Half putting it down to an optical illusion, he decided to investigate, as it was not far off their course. He would not disturb the skipper's siesta unless he had to.

When she saw the vessel approach, Conchita was dumbfounded, as she had given up hope of being found after two days and nights adrift. This was the first vessel she had seen. But was it a friend? She felt easier when she saw it was a Spanish fishing boat, a longliner as its gear showed. The crew saw a young woman, sitting sphinx-like on a makeshift raft, dejected of countenance, wearing trousers and a head cover, shoeless, with a large knife in her belt. She waited as the boat came closer, all the crew watching, astonished. Belatedly, Conchita realised she was bare chested, and took her shirt from her head and put it on, to cries of dismay from the fishers. She had been convinced no vessels would come by before she died. Rough water would come and sweep her off the raft, or thirst would drive her crazy. Even now she put off believing otherwise until rescue came.

She was quickly dragged aboard, and collapsed on the deck. The skipper, Jorge Salinas, gave her water, carried her into his tiny cabin, and laid her on his bunk. He told her to take off her wet clothes and put on some dry ones he would bring, with apologies for their roughness. He gave her a blanket and suggested she sleep. He looked in on her occasionally until, many hours after the rescue, she was awake. With what he regarded as great restraint, considering he, like all his crew, was bursting with curiousity, he said they could talk when she felt strong enough. He gave her some bread and sugar and coffee. He hoped she would not tackle him about the raft, which he had let drift away during the rescue, as it seemed a useless item, even allowing for how it had saved her life. Now he was thinking he should have kept it, at least until he had asked her. He would soon find out.

Conchita had not thought much about her story while adrift, but when awake she realised its importance, and must be told in the best light. If she told it truly from the beginning the skipper might hand her over to the harbour master in Barcelona, who could treat it as a police matter, and that would be uncomfortable for her. And maybe nobody would believe her anyway. If that were so, she might meet some torturers, Spanish, German, or both, for the police of both countries had reputations in this regard. But of course she could never tell the true story, as this would show secret Allied activity, to say nothing of the risks to Neil, Manny, Ana and their colleagues. And what reprisals might the Germans apply for the loss of an E-boat and its crew? But before she could make up a story she needed to know about the raft. It had been sitting upon the incriminating lifebelt of the patrol boat. So when Jorge started to talk she interrupted: "I'm a bit wobbly just yet, but is the raft safe?"

"Well, look, I must apologise. It drifted away while I was looking after you and nobody thought to go after it. It didn't look much, but we should have asked you. Did it really matter to you?"

"Oh!" She showed disappointment at the news. Then said: "Oh, don't worry, it can't be helped. The main thing is that you saved me. I had given up and was ready to die, you know. The skipper of the boat that saved my life can do no wrong. The raft served its purpose, and is no loss." With that she closed her yes and started dozing again, which was really only a way of finding time to think. Jorge left, relieved she was not upset about losing the raft. To her it was excellent news, as the lifebuoy and its origin would have been identifiable by a knowing person. Without any links to it she could now put a story together. She told it to Jorge when he returned.

"My man and I had a fishing boat. The fishers at our home port – La Escala, do you know it? - don't like women on the boats so it's been hard for us to work as a crew. Then he didn't want to spend too much time on land in case the fascists grabbed him for having been a red soldier. He was only a conscript, you know. I used to tell him not to worry, but he was really against going to prison, and so we fished up to France, with Sète, then Valras-Plage, as our home ports. Then we got the odd job smuggling people in and out of France, mainly out. Contacts brought them to us, and we'd take them to wherever we were told. Our boat was too small for really long trips, or for more than two passengers. A few days ago we were taking a man and a woman to Barcelona. They wanted to migrate. It was hard for some people to get visas y'know, and some people in France are frightened about showing themselves in case they are sent to prison. So we were doing this job, sailing during the day and sometimes steaming, just slowly y'know because fuel's so hard to get. Well, we were hove to at night, and all asleep except me. I was washing a pot over the side: the lady had been sick y'know. It was really dark. Then I heard engines and as the noise got louder I knew a big ship was close. Neither of us showed lights. At first I just listened and looked, until the noise got really close, then I yelled to wake the others, but the ship was closer than I'd thought, actually on top of us, then it hit, and just kept on going. I guess it didn't even notice us, and I didn't see enough to know what it was, but it was big. Then I was in the water. I suppose I jumped, but don't remember. Anyway I swam around, calling out, but there was nothing. It gradually got through to me that our boat had sunk. I caught a piece of cushion which helped me keep afloat for a while, then as it was sinking I caught the broken raft. We had kept it on top of the wheelhouse. It was made to float off if we ever went down, and I never thought I'd see the day when it worked. We had a dinghy there too, but it was tied down, so must have gone under. Then in the morning there was nothing but me on the raft. It was like as if I had been dropped there, on an empty sea. It was weird, like a bad dream. I kept looking around for the others, as I couldn't believe they had gone, but y'know, there it was. It was so weird - the whole thing - I wasn't scared much for a while, then I was, then I stopped that, and didn't care what happened. I was sure I was going to die, but you came. It was like another dream. I still can't believe it. Yet I know I'm here, like you. Thanks. And specially the lookout. But for him I was dead."

200

35

Having left the river valley, the train tracked north easterly through Karlsruhe, and at Nurnberg stopped at a suburban siding. The passengers didn't know that the main line ahead was bomb damaged, and a secondary line was being sought. During the long delay several passengers, desperate for a look at the outside world, pulled themselves up to look over the top of the car wall. A few spectators had come along, as close as the guards would permit, to gawk at the strange sight: people staring out from behind barbed wire, calling piteous pleas for water. It was equally strange for those inside seeing some of those on the platform cursing and deriding them, even though the passengers were clearly distressed. The Jews inside, some of whom were Germans, were disappointed by the rejection by their countrymen. It was one thing for the State to treat them inhumanely, and another for civilians, fellow Germans, to do so. Nor were there protests, no calls for restraint, from guards, or civilians, including parents of mocking children. On the contrary, the guards threatened the passengers on account of the noise of their wailing and cries for help, and deterred the few onlookers who set out to bring water from doing so. As they drooped back into their places on the floor, 'Why,' some asked themselves, 'Why do people act like that towards strangers neither harming nor threatening them? We see them as human beings, but not they us. Even allowing for Hitler's hate, and centuries of antisemitism, it's strange behaviour. Maybe it's unique, just those people.' But few believed that, without knowing just how many more there might be.

As the names of railway stations they passed through were called by the lookout lads, Ab recognised some of his father had known in his migration westward from Odessa to Offenburg more than half a century earlier. Dresden was an important one. Josef had worked there for a year and more. His landlady couldn't spell his surname, and so he became Josef Mayer. Then the train stopped at a siding and Gustav, from his perch, saw the great city far ahead. But there was smoke, and fire too. Then the sounds of guns and bombs filtered through to car 7. It was an air raid. The passengers were pleased about an aggressive act against the Germans who, in Jewish experience, had long been constantly ruthless oppressors. The passengers were not to know it, but the bombers in this daylight raid were protected by new, long-range fighters to which the weakened German Luftwaffe, short of fuel, planes and experienced pilots, had no effective counter, with consequent enormous bomb damage and deaths. Nor were they to know the raids were intended to demoralise the German population, and put pressure on their military rulers to end the war by capitulation, rather than a negotiated peace that could leave Nazism alive in Germany. Nor that like tactics would be applied again later to bring Japan to its knees. But they knew the sooner their miserable journey ended the better, so hoped the planes would bomb the lines ahead. But instead the train was soon able to go past Dresden, then south east to Breslau, where it arrived in mid-afternoon on the third day. By now everybody had accepted their destination was indeed eastern Europe. Thinking that his father had come this way took Ab back to the pogrom in Odessa from which he had fled for freedom, and the irony of the son now being in car 7 brought tears to his eyes.

He had been smiling less anyway. Change had disturbed his medication regime and his stability. Karla, knowing of his discomfort, did what she could to help him. She was also ever ready to uplift the spirits of the other passengers. She wondered where all the people had come from, what they had done in their lives. How interesting it could be to talk with them. As she looked around she thought: 'That pale, thin young man was a lawyer who, denied the right to practice at home in Romania, antisemitic, and controlled by fascists, fled to France where the French excluded him from work, so he had to rely on Jewish charities for sustenance. It was almost a relief when he was arrested by the French police and given shelter and food of sorts. But he learned of his error on being transferred to Drancy, whose reputation he knew in advance. He's now wondering where he went wrong. Why he didn't escape into Spain, or Switzerland, or even take to the hills with the maquis, is a puzzle. But that's what we all do. We're always saying 'if only' and 'why didn't I?', which shows we don't learn enough quickly, and then one day it's too late. If only I could help him now.'

'The man with a beard next to him looks like a labourer. May-

202

be Polish. I wonder where his wife is, for he looks a married one. And children? Perhaps he'll tell me more if I can get next to him. People like to talk about their families, which shows how much they love them. But it'll be hard to get close, as he's four people away.'

'And that chubby lady in the stylish clothes and furs, the one whose face is red and creased and wet from all her weeping. An opera singer, I heard. What a shock for her to be taken from her cultured surroundings and finish up here. Nothing in her past life could have prepared her for this. But then that applies to all of us. Of course you must weep, my dear.' Klara could not get near her, but looked her way long enough to make eye contact and smile encouragingly, and was gratified by an attempt at a smile from the other. 'And yet God never promised any of us Jews peace and privileges in a world that has, on the contrary, often provided pain and persecution. So it's our turn, we Jews here in this car, to suffer as many others have before us. But I still hope and pray things will get better for all of us.'

When day came there was nothing to mark its presence, apart from the light. Klara thought: 'At home there are so many things to do on waking up and getting going for the day. Here there is nothing. We must just lie here. We can eat a little food, but whether we do that now or later or never doesn't matter. We have no household chores before us, no business to transact, no change of clothes. Then there is the dreadful, constant noise. And the foul odour. The thirst and pain all around. There is nothing sweet or happy about anything. All is misery and pain and illness. Who could have created these conditions? Not God; it is not His work. Not an all powerful and loving God at least. Oh dear! What am I saying? I don't mean to doubt God, and yet ...... Perhaps there is a Devil after all, one who is more powerful than we thought. I mean who else could think up places like this train, and Drancy. Yes, I know it's mainly the Germans, and among them mainly the Nazis, so what drives the Nazis? It could be the Devil. Perhaps he influences the French too. But I won't decide finally until I've talked it over with a rabbi.'

A commotion came from the middle of the car. A young man and his wife had been lying immobile in an embrace since boarding in Drancy. People had recognised they were shutting out the dreadful world about them. Now those next to them were shocked to find both dead. They had cut their wrists during the night and had slowly bled to death, still embracing. Somebody said he was a chemist, and she a pianist, both refugees from Austria, whence they fled to France in 1939 when the Nazis in Austria had revoked the citizenship of all Jews. People were calling out conflicting advice about the correct mourning procedure to follow, but for many passengers normal Jewish rituals on death were inapplicable, and it was left to individuals to pray as they might for the deceased couple. So they covered the bodies with their blankets, and wondered how long it would be until they stank. This event shocked and numbed the passengers, just when they thought their spirits could sink no lower. The fact was the train conditions were conducive to death rather than life, to weakness, not the strength needed for work, to illness, not to health. Resettlement, work in labour camps; those notions were increasingly fanciful.

36

Neil's strategic plan, settled with SOE London, was to attack vital infrastructure when the Allied invasion commenced, forcing the enemy to move along roads would make them concentrated targets for mobile Resistance attacks. Selecting the hit points, storing the materials to be used, mapping the features, negotiating with locals for storage sites, liasing with other resisters groups to minimise duplication, took the Silence team many months, while building up cells and executing sabotage which was needed to show Germans and French alike resistance was at hand, and also to provide cell members with experience in operations. When Manny's main contribution to planning, and training local fighters, was over - and it was over the earlier because of some of the experienced Spanish brigaders having joined Silence cells - it seemed to him and to Neil and to HQ that he should form his own group, one of aggressive maquisards, in the hills and bush where they hid better, for the time had come to start picking off miliciens and German troops, and collabos, and Vichy police also, were they to get in the line of fire. Neil and Ana were both proud to see Manny starting up his group, entirely confident of his competence and leadership.

Jacques in Valras-Plage, as a sub-agent for Silence, worked with Diego, and other skippers, especially as a leader of beach reception committees, and manager of caches of war gear. It was to him that Conchita turned for guidance after landing back in France, as she wanted to be by the sea, and so she returned to SOE duty, gravitating to Manny's Madeleine group as it started up. Its purpose was preparing maquisards in the hills and forests between Montpellier and Toulouse, part of a general area of potentially high strategic importance. Germany had guarded France's south and north sea coasts not knowing where or when invasion would come, so when it came violently at Normandy in the north, extra German troops and armour were needed there. Then the cover of hill and forest that had protected maquis bands in training would cover them in surprise attacks on Germans trekking north.

The Madeleine group comprised men from diverse backgrounds, and some were now full time outlaws, as the authorities called them, while others, such as Guy Nicol, were in regular employment and lived at home. The part-timers were also the urban eyes and ears of the bands, and helped the leaders decide where to find money, clothing, materials and food, for the sustenance of those in the hills. They had in common the conviction that the Germans must be conquered one day, and that guerilla warfare would have a place in support of the regular forces when, eventually, France was invaded by the Allies. They were relatively young. They were supported by women who took weapons and messages between bands, fed them, spied on the enemy, sheltered the hunted, distributed patriotic pamphlets, and nursed the ill and wounded. There was plenty of room and need for experienced persons, and Manny welcomed Conchita warmly.

There was no single pattern about the emergence of resisters' bands. The desire to avenge the defeat of 1940 and evict the Germans was one mainspring. Some citizens, despite the difficulties and dangers in doing so, set out very early on the long road. Others, impressed by the earnestness of the Vichy regime under the nominal leadership of Marshall Pétain, and unimpressed by Britain for a variety of reasons, took longer in doing so. Nearly all who came required arms training and discipline, particularly as the officers of the defeated French defence forces generally looked down, in a military sense, on those they saw as amateurs in warfare, and so few joined the resistance bands, living instead in the hope of returning to the regular army when its reformation took place upon the Allied invasion. SOE agents were mentors, suppliers, and instructors in guerilla warfare trainers for the bands, which included several elements. Not only native French, but also Spanish republican refugees, Jews hiding from roundups, escaped POWs, communists and, in 1943 especially, young men dodging compulsory labour in Germany. All were persecuted and hunted by the authorities, but preferred very hard living in rugged bush to prison. Some came as experienced fighters from the civil war in Spain, or the brief war in France prior to defeat in 1940, and others with no experience in arms, including youths such as Nathan. All were enemies of fascism, and Germans in France.

The forms of secret resistance were many. Intellectuals wrote and distributed propaganda. Railwaymen sabotaged rail equipment. Postal and telephone workers provided services helpful to resisters, such as free and discreet telephone lines, and mail deliveries to invisible people. Churches and schools provided shelter. The staff of government and local government offices supplied blank ration and identity cards to resisters all over the country to help keep them alive and fed. Medical operations were performed in barns, and patients were smuggled into and out of friendly hospitals. As time passed the numbers of active resisters increased, some of whom became maquisards. Their bands normally started off with only a few members. Gradually they were trained, and their very presence attracted new members. To function effectively, in sabotage and harassment of German troops and military movements, the bands required organisation, and discipline and training for members. Leaders emerged naturally from within, or were nominated by SOE. It was of little use to the total war effort for the bands to engage in set battles against the very efficient and better armed Germans, until several factors came together, such as military type organisation, adequate weapons and training, and an imminent invasion to support. Until then they were better at hit-and-run actions, and sabotage. Then when the time came for major effort they were ready, without ever being on the same level of firepower as a regular army. It was hard for them to understand that weaponry and munitions were in heavy demand for the regular forces at all times, and especially as D-Day approached, and so often in short supply for the maquisards. And Allied HQ discouraged bands from prematurely engaging the Germans in open combat, which the leaders in London saw as highly dangerous for them, and better left to the regular forces.

Manny lived with his fighters in the bush. He learned of Guy Nicols' experience with Nathan, and worried that unless something positive was done to give the lad purpose he might drift, and nobody could foresee where he might end up. They all felt the lad was too young to be a regular maquisard, and subject to the stern discipline that kept the band in order; yet what were they to do with him? Manny decided he was the right person to mind a lonely Jewish boy. He put himself in Nathan's shoes, and from that position decided he would appreciate being answerable to and protected by someone like himself. The decision made, he had obtained Guy's assent, and went looking for Nathan, and took him under his wing.

Money was always needed, not least as minimal income for the fighters, and SOE was a major source of funds. It came too from selective stealing, with banks and public institutions the main targets. Such strikes were not always hazardous, as many of the apparent victims were friendly to the thieves from the maquis, or else knew that crossing them could be dangerous, as the bands never played down their ruthless images. Other favourite targets for robberies were black market operators, regarded as parasites who, quite frequently, were also collabos. Such were reluctant to report thefts in case the police brought charges against them on account of their illegal trafficking in food and restricted goods, and out of a sensible fear of retribution from the maquisards.

Most of the munitions for the bands Manny worked with came from the SOE, dropped by plane under arrangements made through Neil, or a group organiser in a neighbouring district, because the operations of SOE groups such as Silence often straddled large districts, and particularly so in the forest and bush of the south and south west. Raids on police stations and German outposts also added to the supply of weapons, along with supplies landed by boat on a Mediterranean beach, in which the *Santa Maria* had been a link several times, prior to its ill-fated voyage with Manny and Ana's parents.

It was part of the discipline and, for that matter, the patriotism, that the food and material comforts of the men in the bands were not to make them better off than that of the suffering and half starved ordinary citizens. Peasants got food from their farms. Black marketers made lots of money and so could buy food of the best quality. Rich and important people had ways of being well fed. But the other French men and women did not, and the members of the bands, often led by communists or other Leftists, were like them. But they had to eat, and as fighters sustain their strength. Their food sources included gifts, purchases, discretionary stealing, and for some, hunting and fishing.

Until battles approached bands were kept small enough to be highly mobile, for the French and German police, and the miliciens, were constantly on the look-out for them, and ready to attack them with the support of the German military. As German dominance slipped in 1943 and 1944, its need to suppress resistance ahead of the certain future invasion increased the tempo of its punitive operations. The ruthlessness of both sides grew in intensity in those times, with one atrocity being avenged by another. It was very serious warfare. In a strict legal sense the maquis were essentially lawless, while the police function was, as always, to keep order according to law; but then the German presence was also clearly lawless, and even the institution called the Vichy government was of doubtful validity. Concessions to higher morality or the rule of law were necessarily limited. The bands being clandestine, their members concealed their true identities with aliases. But the time duly came for them to fight their way out of hiding into the sight of a grateful France.

The normal apprehension of anyone in a battle zone applied to maquisards, but with a general culture of contempt for cowards, the fear of being branded as a weakling was greater, a result of which, as Manny found, was a high level of self confidence and coolness in times of danger. He saw those qualities as good as in most of the frontline units he had served with in Spain. The greatest fear of the maquisards was capture by the authorities, for they were treated brutally, and great numbers of captives were killed right away, or else subjected to the horror of German concentration camps where the prisoners were, quite literally, worked to death. Therefore vigilance was everybody's constant companion. Each watched his brothers and sisters in the band and, where they could, associates outside also, as a check on security. Breaches were not tolerated by the bosses.

Nobody was in a band for long without falling into line. And leaving the band with permission depended on extraordinary personal circumstances, as former members could pose security risks. Departing without permission would invite summary execution. It reminded Manny of like methods applied by the Russian communists when they assumed substantial control of the republican army toward the end of the civil war. He, and many others, always believed that if those standards had applied earlier the great potential of the republican army could have been brought victory for the Republic, instead of heartbreaking defeat.

Waiting was hard for maquisards living rough. Their lives were very restricted. It was easy enough, alone, to puff up their own potential in battle while downsizing that of the enemy. Men in the regular army could be kept busy in diverse ways, and had the advantage of disciplinary and leisure systems to eat into impatience. London told the maquis to wait until the time came, and it came on D-Day. Then the need for the SOE faded quickly. It became a stranger in France. The French wanted to show everybody, and not least themselves, they did not need help to liberate their homeland. They did, in fact.

37

By the morning of the third day the passengers knew the train was in Poland. So this would be the east they had heard of: farther on was Russia, where the Germans had no say. Ab reflected it was a pity his father had not chosen the United States to migrate to, as his sister Natasha had done, with her family, soon after Josef had settled in Offenburg. Not that Ab blamed him for anything, as Germany and Offenburg had both been good for them all for a very long time. And Klara put it well with her view, expressed from time to time: 'God never promised us our lives would be perfect and painless.' Josef was not to know. It was all fate.

Now Klara saw that Ab was losing strength. He lay with his eyes closed all the time, and even when he opened them they were unseeing. He became very thirsty and murmured 'water, water' occasionally. But there was none left, and there was no way of getting more. She tried to work up some spit in her mouth in the hope of transferring it to Ab, but her mouth was too dry. So she lay with him, holding him close. During the third afternoon his clasp tightened for a time, before relaxing. Klara took him to be asleep. She noticed he was cold and huddled closer to him and gave him some of her blanket. Then she saw he was extremely pale, and although his eyes were open, they had a sightless look about them, which was quite a new experience. Klara feared the worst. She clasped him and implored: "Don't go beloved. Don't leave me. Please hang on." She closed her eyes and prayed that he would open his eyes and talk to her. She kept her eyes closed and kept clasping him to give the prayer a chance to work. She felt he responded. She lay there cheek to cheek with him clasping his hand and hugging him. But his body grew colder and it stiffened. She did not notice. She did not want to.

Soon after a rumour that the train had passed through Cracow ran around car 7. Klara spoke into Ab's ear: "That was Cracow where your father was once. It won't be long now," and was glad that Ab did not ask how she knew that, or what she meant. By then he was really cold and lifeless, even on a warm day, with his ample clothing. Klara bent low and spoke to him. But still he did not respond. Suddenly she snapped. She wept. Then shrieked, alternatively tearing her hair and grasping Ab. Looking at Gustav, the lookout lad, perched high on the wall, she hallucinated, and said aloud: "What's Manny doing up there? He must come down before he falls." She called out to him to come down, but the sounds from her mouth were not words. Shortly afterwards she saw a young woman standing a little distance away. She thought: 'There's Ana. I'll attract her attention so she'll come by." But Klara's feeble attempt at a wave went unnoticed, and the woman lay down again.

When the train arrived in mid-afternoon on 17 July, all the living passengers were thirsty, hungry, in pain, stinking, spiritless and weak. As it slowed, stopped, and started slowly again, shouted orders from outside were heard. The lookouts, now more numerous, were calling out descriptions that included factories and huts, and the passengers started to feel their journey might be ending. As the train finally came to a stop pleasant band music could be heard. It grew louder, kindling a touch of hope for some passengers. How sweet the sounds! Had they been too sceptical? Welcoming passengers in such a nice way was not malevolent. And the lookouts saw and reported pretty flower gardens surrounding the platforms. A slight sense of civilisation came into the car. But then came, above the music, loud, guttural and authoritative shouting, and barking, and the noise of the heavy doors opening. A rush of fresh air and dazzling light invaded car 7. The platform sign proclaimed a strange name: Auschwitz. Near it was a small band of musicians, apparently Jews, neatly dressed in striped clothes. Beyond was a substantial plain, whose structures, it could now be seen, included two distant factories, both with smoking chimneys.

In a daze while adjusting to the light and changed environment, the passengers were abruptly brought back to the reality of being Jewish prisoners of Germans. For, suddenly, troops were at the open door of car 7 snapping out commands for everybody to get up and get out. At once! Hurry! To encourage prompt compliance three soldiers climbed in the car and laid about them with whips shouting 'Out! Out! Out! Leave your luggage! Out! Hurry! But it was just not possible for the passengers to be quick, as they were cold and weak, and had no warning to limber up for disembarking. The suddenness was a shock. Their slowness made the soldiers angry, and they used further force along with the shouting. As quickly as they could the passengers blinked their way out. Klara tried to pull Ab up, saying: "We must leave now, dear. Come along. I'll help you." But she could not lift him. A soldier came over to her shrieking; "Out! Out! Leave the stiff there! Hurry!" So she would have to come back for Ab. She would take their case though, to save him carrying it, and bent over for it. As she did so she was struck with a whip, and heard the barked order: "Leave it! Out! Out!" The blow hurt. She nursed her arm, looking reproachfully at the young guard. But he terrified her by bawling in her face: "Go! Go!", pointing outside. She said to herself: "I'll speak to his superior outside. I won't be bullied." But she was, for the guard struck her again on the leg which stung sharply and made her hop. She fell, hitting her face on the floor, now less cluttered as many passengers had left. She got up, bleeding from the forehead, in a daze. The guard pushed her violently. Her resistance crumbled. It was all too much. She moved out of the car, nursing her arm, weeping, to join the queue forming along the platform.

211

Several emaciated, solemn men, bright in striped suits and caps, appeared at the door. They were clearly convicts. They helped disabled passengers out, and also brought out the remaining luggage which they stacked, with that taken out by the passengers, in a row next to the car. They laid out the several corpses in another row, inside the car. On the platform the passengers were formed into a single, continuous line facing toward the end of the train away from the engine. The guards, some with attack dogs on leashes, kept the line orderly by shouted threats, pushing, prodding, and occasional blows. The passengers were terrified by the violence, grimmer than they had known in their long association with German and French brutality. Those separated from their families in the exodus were prevented from changing places in the line to regroup. Klara looked around for Ab as the line moved away from the door of car 7, but dare not break line. She asked a guard if he would find Ab and bring him to her. He said he would do so soon, for which she thanked him. The line was guided toward a desk at which sat uniformed clerks, who checked the passengers off against a train manifest, after which the line split into two, one to the right near some waiting motor lorries, the other to the left.

As a young woman left her car she noticed a little boy of three or so with fair curly hair, standing on his own, bewildered. There was no clue as to his owner, but clearly he needed care. The woman was torn between coping with her own misery, and helping the child. She looked around for the mother, but failing, and required to keep moving, she bent over and took the child's hand and moved him into the queue. As she did so a convict muttered in German: "If you take the child you will die. That's what happens to children and mothers." But the woman did not understand. She did not speak German. He did not speak again, but moved off. He was not supposed to speak at all. The young woman continued to hold the child's hand as they moved slowly with the queue. Klara though had understood the man. She summed up the situation. The woman was taking Manny and this would harm both of them. She did not really think the man meant to say 'die' as he had, but all the same Manny could be hurt. She must take him from the woman. She moved next to them in the line, and asked: "Parlez-vous Francaise, Mademoiselle?"

"Oui, Madame."

" L'enfant c'est moi. Je lui prends maintenant. Merci beaucoup."

There was no resistance as Klara firmly drew the child to herself, raising and kissing him. He smiled at her and clutched at her
face. She held him tightly, raining kisses on him until they came to the
checkpoint. There some family groups were separated. A healthy father to the left, his adolescent children or pregnant wife to the right,
toward the lorries. A young woman to the left, her frail mother or father to the right. A married couple according to their apparent states
of health. Where the parting was anguished, and resisted, the guards
intervened, forcefully, to complete it. But if a couple withstood the
blows and clung together, both were directed toward the lorries.
Soon the purpose of the separation, and formation of two lines, was
clear. Those relatively strong, young, and healthy formed the line to
the left. The others, either frail, old, disabled, or mothers with young
children, the right. None of the passengers knew the destinations
of either. As they left the checkpoint the young woman was sent to
the left and Klara, with the child, to the right. When the check was
completed the left line of passengers were marched off under guard.
Those in the right line were loaded into the lorries. They did so by
their own efforts, unassisted by the guards, unless shouting and hitting could be taken to be assistance. Klara put Manny up and helped
in the loading, keeping him as close as possible all the time. When it
was done she climbed in and hugged him again. The convoy moved
slowly toward the factory buildings. The line of marchers could be
seen going away, toward huts.

At the factory the lorry passengers were dismounted and re-
assembled into another line that was directed, still under guard, into
a hall. There the men were stood to one side, and the women and
children lined up to sit in chairs where barbers roughly cut their hair,
taking as much as possible with a few simple cuts. It was rough and
painful and humiliating. Then the prisoners were assembled into
lines, and each was required to undress completely, and put their
clothes and shoes together, ready for them after their shower, in anticipation of which each was given a small piece of soap and a towel.
The child did not understand Klara's nudity, and tugged at her skin,
saying: "All gone, all gone." Then he started to cry, clinging to Klara
who, with the little strength she had left, lifted him up, hugging and

kissing him all the while. Then he decided naked people were funny, and laughed - for the last time. Undressed, the passengers stood in line, cold, and listless, until the direction came that the showers were now hot, and the doors of the room ahead were opened. Some passengers were reluctant to enter, but there was no choice, and everybody was pushed in, with the aid of blows and whipping which stung thin flesh, drawing blood and leaving red marks. If Klara had not been too far gone, she may have wondered, as some did, how such a crush of people could take showers from the few shower heads in view, and which were oddly dry; with neither drips nor water stains. And why the doors into the shower room had been closed and bolted as they entered. And why the place did not have any water smell, but a strange, indefinable odour only. Nor were there any ventilation windows. As perception spread, so did alarm, and hysteria. The people sensed something evil was near. Wailing built up into a crescendo of cries, curses, prayers and terrified shrieking. The little boy became disturbed, and threw himself about. All Klara could do was hold him tight and repeat into his ear: "Manny darling, it's all right. Klara's here." Then, suddenly, she realised that hope was finished, and all that remained was for her to be brave for his sake. She was not one of the few who saw several small traps in the ceiling opening simultaneously, but all quickly became aware of brown tablets scattered through the room, emitting invisible fumes that filled the air, and suffocated them. The pitiful moaning and choking sounds of the dying passengers slowly merged into the silence of death.

38

For spies, and other clandestine workers, the better the cover the safer the person. SOE agents had real jobs, or other suitable cover, such as pretended disability. All members of secret services were hunted by the Gestapo as being dangerous to Germany, and as those of the SOE were also intent on actively and aggressively undermining the Occupation, they were a particular type of danger. Size turned out to be a factor in danger. The more trained people in a clandestine group the greater its potential power, but with more people came a higher risk of leakage, with likely fatal consequences. It was one thing to grow large bands of maquisards hidden in forests and hills, under discipline, whose members had limited contact with the public, but even there constant planning and movement of camps was required. It was a different matter in urban and closely settled areas where suspicion, if aroused, could be more readily followed up. Neil's style was to restrict the numbers of people in the Silence group, and drive home to each of them they were trustees of the lives of both themselves and their unknown colleagues and their families. He was uncertain of the ability of the average French man or woman to keep secrets at the high level required, so was particularly careful with them. In contrast, fugitive Spaniards and Jews came to SOE knowing that their freedom, and maybe their very lives, had already depended on secrecy. So far as possible Neil dealt only with cell leaders, with each of whom he developed a strong rapport, and tried to keep them from being curious about other members of the group. Real identities were hidden by aliases, for the families of all members had to be protected. By good management, and the necessary lick of luck, the Silence group stayed intact and active through its several years' life, and contributed, as was SOE's purpose, to the aggression of the Resistance both in anticipation of, and after, D-Day, 6 June 1944. It had suffered but few casualties from its several firefights along the way, specifically six deaths, and eight casualties; excluding minor ones such as Ana's sprained wrist, sustained in tripping while running from German sentries shooting at her and the others because they had just blown a lock gate on a Rhône River feeder canal. The group was closed down when the Allies and the Resistance liberated Lyon, its purpose accomplished.

Neil and Ana had been in love from the time of Neil's stay as a guest at 19 rue de la Madeleine on his return to France to start the Silence group. Neither had recognised it for what it was then, nor for another year or so. Their meetings had been few, and full of business, so love was not in the air for either of them. Yet the feeling, the affection, the wish to see the other again soon, recurred, and gradually were seen for what they were: symptoms of the noble state. Still, by the time Neil formally offered Ana an SOE position in September 1942, they both knew, and were happy in knowing. Yet the full flowering of their romance was constrained by unstated but real reservations on the part of Ana's parents about her marrying a Gentile, and Neil's decision to keep away from their home in case he were to be the unwitting cause of some sort of trouble for them with the authorities. Accordingly their meetings were usually brief, and infrequent, at least until Ana returned from her SOE training in England, and got her own flat, and work not centred on 19 rue de la Madelaine. That new work brought her more into contact with Neil, and after the older Mayers had fled to the hills they were so close that they discussed living together, but decided on security grounds not to. And that barrier fell too when the Allies and the Resistance took Lyon, and their SOE work was over, except for tidying up.

They met in a Lyon park in late September 1944. It was to be more relaxed than ever before. SOE's work in helping create the Resistance and fight with it was coming to an end in France, as the Free French forces, both regular and maquis, were growing in numbers and cohesion. General de Gaulle had proclaimed Paris liberated from the Germans on 26 August, and obliterated the Pétain regime simply by appointing new administrators under his command, pending a return to democracy. While heavy fighting continued in parts of the country, notably the Rhine River border regions, and in isolated pockets such as fortified ports on the Atlantic coast, the area of Silence group activity had been practically freed by early September. Not only were the Germans in flight or, euphemistically, strategic retreat, but they had as companions many miliciens and collabos, some out of fear, and others because of their loyalty to fascism. Neil explained to Ana that SOE's work in France would finish as areas were liberated, which meant that their work in Lyon was ended, and in fact France under General de Gaulle wanted SOE agents out, because his jingoism drove him to proclaim that France had liberated itself. He was not alone. With the Liberation the French collectively got a rush of bravery and self congratulation, necessary for a nation that had sunk so low in war, and in humaneness. But Neil had no orders, so he and Santo and the other fulltime agents stayed put, with nothing much to do, but enjoy the spectacle of cruel hunters being hunted, while remaining alert, as there were still some dangerous people about.

The young lovers were overjoyed at events, including their mutual survival. As their hugging and kissing slowed they got in some conversation. Neil said: "It seems to me the Allies could be on top in Germany within a year, even allowing for desperation defence. What do you think?"

Ana replied: "Well, it's not my field, but it sounds right, especially as Russia is so powerful. I think they're going to hurt the German people, as they hate each other so much. It's funny to be glad to be out of your home country, but I'm sure happy to be here with you and not there."

Neil laughed: "Not your field eh? I'd better look out when you say something is." His face turned serious. "I agree. Those poor civilians in Germany. You have to feel sorry for them even though they were so stupid."

"And cruel, remember."

"Of course. That keeps a balance." He paused, while collecting his thoughts, and continued: "I want to tell you about a job I'm thinking about. It's the United Nations War Crimes Commission. It was set up last year and will become progressively active. I don't know exactly what I would be doing, but they told me to learn some German, so there's a clue. It'd be very nice if something like that appealed to you too. I expect you'd be favourably considered, and I'd help you find the right people to talk to. If you're interested we could start looking into it."

She looked warmly at him, and smiled with clear joy, saying: "Thank you. Yes, indeed, thank you. But I don't know if I'm ready. There's unfinished business about my family, and I need to talk it through with Manny. I think he'd like to get into a shipyard when he finishes with the army, but where is he? You told me his cover name is Marc Matisse, and that he moved from the Resistance to the army when the change came, but what since then? If I knew I could go and see him and my mind would be clearer."

Neil replied: "Alright. That's how it will be. Locate Manny. We know the group he led in the Resistance, so we can find from them the army unit he went to, and follow it through. It might be slow going. Just imagine one of these days we might have our own car to get around in."

"Oh, don't. I couldn't give up trains and bikes. I'll be spoiled .... but maybe as a trial ...." She paused, with tears in her eyes: "It's awful to think there's only Manny and me left. All the hopes of the others gone west. But I'm beating the gun! Ab and Klara can still turn up as survivors. What am I saying?"

But she knew in her heart what she was saying. They had studied all the information they could about the trains and the death camps and the signs were bad. "At least, from what Conchita said, it was over quickly for my parents. Imagine though. All of them lost .... "

Neil was embracing her as she spoke. He found words hard. He said: "At least they knew their children did all they could to save them, and they died loving you for that. And I'll continue that love." Ana hugged him, and kept weeping.

After a while she sat up, and said: "I think about all the other lost people throughout Europe and feel I'd like to help there. And there's some property in Offenburg to look into, but only if Manny wants to. Going back wouldn't be pleasant. Then there's that part of me wanting to go and live in Palestine with the other Jews. So you see I'm all mixed up, and need time to think. But no matter what, I want to be with you."

Neil cried: "That's just marvellous! What about this for a plan? We'll contact Manny and get sorted out with him. I've been thinking about the refugees too and would be happy working there with you. I don't know what the qualifications might be, but finding out won't be hard. I've heard the UN has a refugee arm, or is getting one. And of course we must check our status with SOE before committing ourselves. We couldn't have them treating us as deserters."

"Have you ever heard of that?"

"No. I think if you didn't want to stay in, they'd let you go readily. What use could you be otherwise? But a few - very few I hope - turned y'know, and caused terrible trouble because the Gestapo then got the names of addresses of our people. Can you imagine?"

"It's hard to understand. That's what our friend Henri was after, wasn't it? Names and addresses. You warned us all back a bit that it only needed one agent to give over one name and the rest could fall like dominoes."

"Because of the torture. You can rarely find out how a person handled torture. They could be too ashamed to own up to breaking down, and could get away with it if there were no witnesses."

"Or the agent was dead. Once the Gestapo got information

through torture they might just kill him."

"I'm sure that happened. What were your plans if you were caught?"

"It was to be simple. I believed all you had warned us about and what they had told us during training, and I was determined to take the pill. I had trained myself not to have a private debate about it when captured - and praise God it never happened - but to be ready at once. Getting to that state of mind wasn't easy though. What about you?"

"Yes, just the same. I was ready. I had no confidence in my being brave under torture. There were always too many others in the chain to risk it."

"I've had enough of this gruesome talk. Though I feel so awful for those who were caught, and I can't help but wonder why they didn't take their pills."

"I've heard some never even accepted them when offered, so there must be many different explanations. Anyway we agree to concentrate on that plan and see what turns up?"

"Let's. Maybe one of your friends knows about Manny. I mean Marta, or Jacques."

"We might even visit them, I'll tell you why in a moment. But, yes, we'll keep on Manny's trail."

Said Ana: "I do want to see Conchita again. We didn't have much time when she landed. Manny was in a rush, so we just collected her from the beach, and later Jacques took her to his home. I came back to work. I never saw them again. Anyway she's a big loser through doing a job for my parents, and Manny and I must do the right thing by her: whatever that is. Do you have any ideas?"

Neil frowned, then asked: "Could you tell me more about what happened. I know the Santa Maria was blown up along with a German E-boat and that your parents and Diego were lost. Conchita was picked up and landed in Barcelona, then came back somehow, and you and Manny and Jacques met her on the beach and she finished up in Manny's Madeleine group. So she lost her man, and her living as boat crew. The boat wasn't hers, and as far as I know it was Diego's, with Manny having a half interest. As the boat was lost in an act of war I don't suppose an insurance claim could stand up, even if it had been insured, which I don't know. Now I'm just thinking aloud.

219

What you and Manny should do for Conchita, if anything, is a puzzle for you. Should SOE do something for her? I can see an argument that the boat was made into a floating bomb by SOE, and in setting it off an enemy warship was destroyed, which is a very good return for a lump of explosive. Yes, I can ask SOE for something for Conchita, but not until I know more, and then we must be ready for a refusal. She may feel she needs to square off with Diego's people, but that's not our worry. But do tell me what happened with her after the big bang."

Ana looked him in the eye and asked: "Were you ever with her?"

Neil was taken aback by the question, coming out of the blue as it were. He supposed it showed Ana wanted to know if Conchita was some sort of rival, for it was an intrusive question that he had never expected. But he was glad he could answer without either blinking or blushing.

He replied, while looking at Ana: "I must answer if you think it's any of your business. The answer is no. And in case you're still interested, no for Manny too. Conchita was only Diego's girl."

Ana realised she had been unduly inquisitive, and cried: "You must think me very rude. I don't know came over me to ask that. Please don't think I feel I have any right of interrogation of you, my beloved. Look, let me try to make up for it. You ask me anything you like. I'll sit here trembling and waiting."

Neil put on a serious, reflective expression. He took his time. He wanted to get Ana on edge. She exclaimed: "Oh, come on Mr Slowcoach, you're making me nervous."

But he kept her waiting, until it last his eyes widened, and he said: "I've got it. Are you ready?"

"You know I am. What is it?"

"I want to know when you will start teaching me German."

They both laughed. Ana said: "Would you like to hear Ana'a ripping yarn, as you English would call it, first?"

"Well. Yeah. Start from after she was rescued. I think I've got the earlier part."

"OK. Will I talk in German, or is it too soon?"

"A year too soon, depending on how clever my teacher is."

"So, the skipper talked about a duty to hand her over to the harbourmaster, which of course would become the port police, so she didn't want that. She pleaded with him to drop her off up the coast, but he wouldn't. So she told him that if the authorities decided to conduct an inquiry they would make him and his boat stay in port for a time, and who would pay for the crew while they did nothing? She knew the big fish were running, as he had a full catch on board, and that he was keen to get back out quickly. He got nervous, she could tell, because he starting talking about money, as if he would look after her for a bribe, but of course she had nothing. She told him if he lent her money to get dressed in Barcelona, she could then look decent enough to find a friend there to borrow enough to repay him, and also something extra for rescuing her. The trouble was that neither of them knew how much she could get, so she asked him to state his lowest price, and he said 5,000 pesetas. She said: 'That's a lot. More than I expected. But if that's your price I'll do my best.' She played it straight, though it was a ridiculous amount, and she had no earthly prospect of raising it. When she went ashore the skipper sent a lad with her to keep watch. She got the clothes, then told him to stay at a café while she went for the friend with the money. The boy wanted to come with her but she said her friend would be put off if she turned up with another man, and that would ruin everything. He didn't know how to handle that and she went alone, to the consulate, the friend. They knew her there, but found it hard to believe her story. She offered two clues. One was that they contact Gibraltar to check if they had heard of a missing E-boat. The other was to produce a piece of canvas with the boat's number on it. She guaranteed that would be the boat's number. While she was adrift she had cut out the piece for evidence, even though she was sure she was to die. She was greatly relieved to know the life belt had disappeared, because the skipper might have linked the E-boat to her, and handed her in on suspicion." Ana paused and whispered, as an aside: "Almost like girl murders German warship." She continued. "She came clean at the consulate about how the boats were sunk, but couldn't ask for an aerial inspection because the location was too uncertain, so she fed them all the clues she could. The clincher for her was an immediate telegraphed inquiry to Gibraltar, where they not only knew of the *Santa Maria*, the way she had said, but added that an RAF patrol plane had sighted wreckage and an oil slick in the area she had guessed about. So she was home. Then she had to get some money to give the boy to take to the skipper, and all she could get was enough to repay the loan, because the consulate said nobody charged for saving a life at sea, and the skipper mustn't get into bad habits. One of their men followed her back to the café where she gave the boy a sealed envelope to be given to the skipper, and in it was the loan money. She told the boy to thank the skipper again, and that was all the money she could raise for the time being, but if her fortunes changed she would see what she could do later. The lad didn't think much of all that, and demanded she come back with him, which made her mad, and she started shouting at him that he was trying to rob her, and she would call the police if he didn't buzz off, and the boy was now out of his depth and decided he would rather face his skipper than stay with that.

"The consular officer was watching and thought it all a great joke, but it fixed in his mind she was a genuine case, and that helped her along, because she needed a bed and some money while she sorted herself out.

"You know, that poor girl was in a dreadful position now. She had to tell Diego's parents. She knew the fishers would say it was her fault because women shouldn't crew fishing boats, and they had told her so. She expected the whole village to be against her, and she would rather not go there, yet she owed it to Diego to do so. If she did visit she couldn't stay, because she couldn't rely on anybody there to understand her position, or maybe even believe her. And she couldn't fight them, as they were Diegos's family and friends. Then there was the risk that somebody might betray her to the guardia civil, so she couldn't hang around for long. What a situation for her! She explained to the consulate people she and Diego had worked for SOE through you. She wanted to get back to that. They offered to find a way back for her, and a safe house there in the meantime. You know how that worked out. But she had to visit the village.

"Maybe you'd like to know what happened there?" Neil nodded, and she kept on: "She found Diego's parents at home. She came in mourning clothes which shocked them, of course. She just sat with them and calmly told them the whole story, or at least the safe parts. She told them about the E-boat because it was to their son's honour, and she knew they wouldn't be rushing off to tell a Nazi agent.

222

As Diego and my parents and the two boats were all gone it was a big enough story without trimmings. She didn't go into the question of Manny's part ownership, or his estate, because she didn't know about those matters, which maybe weren't her business either, for they hadn't married. She wanted to stay there and comfort his parents, and had they asked she might even have made Móntago her home, but that would have been subject to the fishers, and she doubted they would accept her. And also she felt that the longer she stayed the closer they would come to blaming her, the woman crew member, the jinx; maybe even turn on her. She wasn't strong enough for that. So when the taxi returned after two hours, she just up and left, saying she would get in touch when times were better. She was glad the parents invited her to stay for a while more, and have the priest say a Mass for Diego, which was a nice note on which to leave. As she said goodbye the father said to her: 'Our son lived for the sea, it owned him, and now has taken him. His spirit is at peace.' That shook her up, and she cried all the way back. You know the rest."

"Yes. I arranged for her to be landed, and you and the others met her. But I don't know since. We've a bit to fill in."

"Yes, it's past time, isn't it? We've sort of left her on her own. I hope Manny has done better than I have. We should go by Sète. I'd meet Marta at last. Don't tell me what she does. It's been a secret so long a little longer can't hurt."

"OK. Let's move on. There's another thing. Can we get married please? If we wait until everything's sorted out you might turn against me, and I couldn't stand that."

She looked at him, her lovely eyes lustrous. "Yes, we can, and I agree there's no reason to wait." They embraced again, and kissed long and passionately. Then Neil said:

"What about my mother? And father too. Even though we aren't very close we're still a family, and they're good people. We'll be able to meet again very soon, the way the war's going. I'd like you to see Paris, and getting there's not a problem now the zones are finished. Dad's always deep in his work, which he never talks about, while Mum is, or was, a strong Petainist, and so its been dangerous for me or Dad to be near. She'll have calmed down by now I hope, which would be better for everybody. She's been misguided, but not a collabo - I hope. Surely not. No, impossible. But I'll ask Dad before

223

we go."

"That's very interesting. I can hardly wait for the news. I hope she's clear. And, gee, don't I look forward to seeing Paris!"

Shortly, Neil said: "Here's that other future thing. I should visit our helpers to thank them, to pay them out, and update their personal details for London. It would be nice if you and Santo could come too. I guess there'd be some partying; I hope. We must also collect those caches of explosives we didn't need, or at least tell the army where they are. Your charts will make it easy for them. The places to visit include some in the country, so we'll need a car, or a driver. Certainly SOE has no vehicles. I can ask the Resistance chief here and the French army commander, and see what gives. They'll know if any of our roads are unsafe, but if they are it won't be for long. A new prefect, appointed by de Gaulle, is in charge of the department, while the head of the Resistance is also in charge, in a way. So there's competition for being the leader; the Resistance, the army, and the civil administration. Pity there hadn't been more leaders coming to the surface when the war started. What a difference between war and peace! Anyway, all the new leaders are significant now, so I'll tell the prefect what's happening, and rely on one of the others for transport. Why don't we go and ask now? Will you come too?"

"Sure. Let's go."

39

By the time the Free French under General de Gaulle returned triumphantly to France, most of the important resister groups had associated under the name of the Resistance which, although not as well disciplined and organised as a regular army division, still produced more coordinated and effective sabotage and attacks on the enemy than the bands were capable of separately. Now that the Allies had established a powerful presence there was no shortage of resisters, men and women. Little matter some were late on the scene. The combined effect of the Allied regular forces and the Resistance was to conquer and put the Germans and the miliciens to flight. The Germans could not now move reinforcements of men and munitions and weapons quickly to places where they were needed. Delays diminished their fighting ability, and delays were among the objects of the Resistance, and of the special commando-style hit teams infiltrated by the Allies behind the frontlines, and of bombing by sea and air. The regular forces of the Allies were then the better able to conquer the Germans in the battle fields. At times Resistance attacks on the Germans and their collaborators developed into frenzies of disorderly killing an end to which had to come. The maquisards had a strong revenge urge. There was also the potential threat to the renewed French State of a guerilla force not under regular military control; especially if led by the communists, who had political aspirations on top of their demonstrated fighting qualities. A paramilitary force like the Resistance was not to have a continuing place in a just and democratic society operating under the rule of law, with all armed forces responsible to elected government. So in August 1944 Manny's Madeleine band of fighters were given the choice of discharge, or enlistment in the regular army. This offer, made across the board, largely eliminated guerilla forces that might otherwise have transmuted into a revolutionary army in France. There was strong acceptance of the offer both generally, and by the Madeleine men. After all, the war was still raging. The several Spaniards and Jews in the band had special interests in continuing the fight; Jews for revenge, Spanish Republicans for continuance of the war against fascism in the hope of it spilling over to Spain, their suspended front. For all there was the prospect of better conditions of pay and food and dress than in the Resistance. Moreover, many young members knew no civilian life as adults, were untrained for civilian employment, and had no jobs to go to. So Manny, and Nathan also, after raising his age, became soldiers in an army infantry battalion under the control of the Free French. The Resistance was to be no more, its place in history secure.

Manny had been a lieutenant in the Resistance and carried that rank into the army, as did many others like him. His frontline experience, proven leadership attributes, and knowledge of weapons and explosives, meant that he was ready-made for the fighting French army.

By late 1944 the Germans had left France, or been captured,

apart from a few fighting futile final battles in accordance with Hitler's crazy commands, and their own genuine, and misguided, loyalties to him. So it was a needless slaughter, in which the German positions would certainly be taken, but rarely easily. Manny's battalion unit was sent to engage a remnant enemy force on the Atlantic coast north of La Rochelle. In the course of the skirmish his company was ordered to attack a fortified position which, with others like it, gave the Germans continued control of a small section of the coast. The Germans were dug in on the crest of a ridge looking down to a wooded valley. Manny's battalion having surrounded the ridge, he was to lead a company forward to infiltrate towards the peak so that when the battalion attacked it would have an advance party in place. The defenders, brave and fanatical, commanded the slopes with machine guns, small arms fire, grenades and mortars. Manny and six men volunteered to work their way around the hillside in the dark so as to be closer to the German command post for an attack in the early morning. Nathan had begged to be in the reconnaissance troop, and the captain had agreed, although Manny was not in favour. After nightfall the troop stealthily worked through the woods and up the hillside to the cover of some rocks where they would wait safely until it was light. But as dawn came closer Manny realised the plan had been anticipated by the Germans, and his troop was partly surrounded. He decided to try to break out while it was still dark, and also send for help. He crawled over to Nathan and whispered: "This is an order. The moment firing starts slide down the hill to the trees, then run back and tell the captain we need help quickly. Get ready, as it's about to start. Leave me your rifle and ammunition as you won't need them and I will. Understood?"

Whatever his misgivings were, Nathan could only answer "Yes", and get ready.

Then Manny spoke to his sergeant: "You must take the boys into the cover of the woods until the battalion arrives. The Germans seem to be over there", pointing. "They can't see us either, not yet anyway. Now this is the plan. We'll be sitting ducks if we don't use it. Go back the way we came up, but before you go everyone must fire at that position. Three rounds each, no more, then off you all go. I'll stay here and keep them guessing with more fire. Tell the men what we're doing, and make it snappy. Line them up to fire from a semi-circle. Tell them to imagine the targets. Fire and run. Be ready for more contact down the hill. Got it?"

The sergeant, a close friend of Manny, simply said: "Yes. Are you sure you want to stay here alone? Can't I stay with you?"

Manny replied: "Thanks, but didn't you hear the order? Go man, go!" "OK."

Two minutes later a burst of rifle and automatic gun fire spewed out from the rocks. The following shrieks and groans from the dark suggested there had been a couple of hits at least. The responding fire came promptly, and was almost as scattered as the first burst. Firing his submachine gun, his pistol, and Nathan's rifle in turn, Manny pretended the rocks area was manned by several men, so as to keep the Germans at bay for as long as possible. He calculated the ruse would last a little past daylight, which should be long enough for his troop to make it out, and with luck, also for Nathan's message to have results.

After the assault on the German position was successfully concluded, Manny's captain and a squad of his soldiers went to survey the area where the advance party had run into trouble. A stretcher bearer came to the captain, saying as he pointed to a rock formation: "There are dead men over there, sir. One of them is ours."

The party moved to it at once. On one side of a very big rock lay the bodies of three German soldiers, quite young, apparently Hitler Youth members pressed into emergency service. On the other side of the rock Manny lay dead. The captain reconstructed events. He had been badly wounded and dragged himself behind the rock. During a lull in the fighting an enemy patrol had paused on the other side of the rock, unaware of him. He had heard them, and found the strength, in a dying effort, to toss a grenade among them.

Word of the gruesome find spread quickly, and Nathan rushed to the scene. He knelt and gently took Manny's head in his hands, while stroking his forehead. He tried hard not to cry, thinking Manny would not have, but it was too much for him, and he sobbed while he cradled his hero's head. The Captain stood watch, unobtrusive, wiping away his own tears.

227

www.ingramcontent.com/pod-product-compliance
Lightning Source LLC
Chambersburg PA
CBHW051459170626
46811CB00002B/549